Suhayl Saadi is a widely published Glasgow-based novelist, poet and short story writer. In 1997, won third place in the Bridport Competition for his story 'Rabia', and in 1999 he won the second prize in one of the UK's largest literary short story competitions, SHORTS: The Macallan/*Scotland on Sunday* Competition, for his story 'Ninety-nine Kiss-o-grams'.

Recently his poetry and other work has appeared in the Pocketbooks collections *Wish I was Here*, *Atoms of Delight* and *Without Day*, and he has founded and continues to run the highly successful creative writing forum, Pollokshields Writers' Group in Glasgow, which is aimed at writers from minority ethnic backgrounds.

The Burning Mirror is Suhayl's first literary short story collection.

The Burning Mirror

Suhayl Saadi

Polygon

Published by Polygon
an imprint of
Birlinn Limited
West Newington House
10 Newington Road
Edinburgh
EH9 1QS

www.birlinn.co.uk

First published in 2000 by Polygon, Edinburgh
Reprinted 2003

ISBN 0 7486 6293 6 (paperback)

British Library Cataloguing-in-Publication Data
A catalogue record for this book is available
from the British Library

The publisher acknowledges subsidy from

THE SCOTTISH ARTS COUNCIL

towards the publication of this book

Printed and bound by
Creative Print and Design, Ebbw Vale, Wales

Contents

Acknowledgements	vii
Ninety-nine Kiss-o-grams	1
Solomon's Jar	9
The Queens of Govan	21
The White Eagles	37
Imbolc	61
Beltane	67
Samhain	81
Lughnasadh	87
Bandanna	109
The Dancers	121
The Naked Heart	131
The Ladder	143
The Seventh Chamber	155
Brick	165
Rabia	171
Qadi	179
Darkness	189
Mistigris	199
Dancing in Vienna	209
Killing God	221
Glossary	231

ACKNOWLEDGEMENTS

Thanks to . . .
my wife, Alina Ayub Mirza,
and
my daughter, Nadia Mirza-Saadi
and to my family

Thanks also to Miriam K. Ahmed, Shakeel Ahmed, Shami Ahmed, Muhammad Ali, Marion Arnott, Chris Ballance, Emily Blake, Martin Booth, Alison Bowden, Timothy Buckley, Larry Butler, Sophy Dale, Ricky Dilber, Chris Dolan, Nicholas Drake, Margaret Elphinstone, Gerrie Fellowes, Eck Finlay, Graeme Fulton, Margaret Fulton-Cook, Ernesto Guevara de la Serna, Patricia Grant, Shusha Guppy, George Harrison, Kathryn Heyman, Jack, Rana Kabbani, Kahii Nahii ka Aadmi, Hanif Kureishi, John Lennon, Doris Lessing, Sheila Lewis, Gerry Loose, Paul McCartney, Catherine McInerney, Estella Mackrill, Derek McLuckie, Kevin MacNeil, John McQuarrie, Dave Manderson, Alan Mathers, M. Ayub Mirza, Shireen Mirza, Stephen Mulrine, Donny O'Rourke, Agnes Owens, Edith Rahim, Sarmed Rubanik, Kamal Sangha, Raymond Soltysek, Kenneth Spiers, Richard Starkey, Shams-i-Tabriz, Ubeda de Valor, Khidr Verde, Ann Vinnicombe, James Williamson, Adam Zameenzad and all at Polygon.

Acknowledgements are due to the books and magazines in which some of these short stories were first published: *New Writing Scotland 16*, *New Writing Scotland 17*, *The Taxila Times*, *Nomad*, *Edinburgh Review*, *The Bridport Anthology* and *Macallan/Scotland on Sunday Shorts 2*.

Excerpt from 'Tattva' by kind permission of Kula Shaker © 1997, Hoodoo Music/Hit and Run Music Publishing Ltd/ EMI Music Publishing Ltd.

'Meri Awaz Suno' © 1997 Nameless Music LLC. All Rights Reserved. Lyrics written by Salman Ahmad, recorded by Junoon from the album *Azadi*, released by EMI Music International.

www.junoon.com

junoon@ cyber.net.pk

Excerpt from 'The days flash past', by Iain Crichton Smith (translated by Kevin MacNeil) is reproduced from *Love and Zen in the Outer Hebrides* by Kevin MacNeil, by kind permission of Canongate Books.

'Beyond the end . . .' is reproduced from *The Book of the Lamp* by Ciccone of Zemba (d.378) by kind permission of Aleph Books, Alfortville, France.

Strenuous, but unsuccessful, attempts were made to contact other agencies in order to obtain permission for reprinting certain song lyrics.

Seen hurrying along with a blazing brand and a bucket of water, and asked what she was doing, she said, 'I am going to quench the fires of Hell and burn Heaven, so that both these barriers to understanding shall vanish from the eyes of pilgrims, so that they may seek Truth without hope or fear.'

From the life of
Rabi 'a al-'Adawiyya (d. 185)

In the old days, the mirrors were forged from molten metal. If the beholder gazed hard enough, he might be consumed in the flames.

Azdi of Syracuse (446–527)

They polish their breasts with invocation and meditation,
That the mirror of the heart may receive images of virginal purity.

from *Mathnawi, Daftar I,*
Jalal al-Din Rumi (604–72)

. . . I remember each house
I find my footprints in the pathways
Its dreams and sins and virtues are in my eyes
In its desolate dwelling houses, in its ruined
  courtyards,
in its ponds and wells,
in its dreamless windows
in its zig-zag pathways;

In the particles of its soil,
I am discovering myself

from *Moenjodaro*, by
Farigh Bukhari (b. 1335), translated by
Yunus Ahmar (b. 1341)

Ah, world, did you indeed deceive us,
or was it us who misread you
all those days your face was lying
open, reflecting back on us?

from 'The days flash past', by
Iain Crichton Smith (1346–1419),
translated by Kevin MacNeil (b.1392)

The Burning Mirror

To my mother,
Shahzadi Shahgul Afza Sultana Tabassum Ahmed,
for giving me the flame

and to

my father, Salim Uddin Ahmed,
for showing me the mirror

Ninety-nine Kiss-o-grams

He must've been mad tae have come here at this time ae year. Either that, or desperate. Forty-five degrees in the shade, and climbin. And that wis just the official reading, the wan they put in newspapers and atlases and tourist brochures – not that ony tourists ever came here, mind you . . .

Sal looked up and closed his eyes. Tried to blank oot the sun. But it wisnae like back hame. In the banjar zameene around Lahore, the sun was like God; it wis cursed by everyone, fae jagirdaar tae bhikari, fae mohlvi tae kunjari. He scuffed his foot aroon and stirred up the dirt, made it swirl intae the air so that he began tae cough. Deep, wrenchin coughs that were mair like big bokes. I'll choke on ma ane land, he thought and then he almost laughed through the tears, but it wis too hot tae laugh. Behind him sat the stupit car he'd used tae get here; it wis meant tae be *only twelve miles, bhai, fifteen at the most,* but it had taken longer than the drive from Glasgee tae Edinburgh on a rainy day, road-works-an-aw. But then there wernae ony roadworks here. The roads never got repaired. Sometimes they nivir even got built. That wis the thing about Pakistan. You never knew anything, for certain. Temperature, direction, distance, the future . . . it wis aw up fur grabs. And money – well, money, that wis somehin else again. That wis why he wis oot here, Sal reminded himsel. Tae get money. And unlike maist ae whit went on here, it wisnae kala duhn he wis after. His dada had left aw his grandweans bits ae earth, thinkin that mibbee wan day, they would come back

1

tae Pakistan and build hooses, all in a row just like in the auld days. His dada had worked like a dog tae get enough money tae buy these plots just ootside ae Lahore. It wis the sixties, and everyhin had been lookin up and he'd been tell't that the city would expand along wi the population and that in twenty years, the same bits ae wasteland would be worth *ten times more, bhai, ten times more.* Sal looked at the straggly, brown grass so unlike the bright-green mud-grass of Glasgee, and wondered how anyone could have believed that this land would ever be anything other than dry shit. Far away, a row of scorched trees quivered against the horizon, while to the east, in the direction of the Indian border, Sal thought he spotted a white-turbanned kisaan ploughing, behind a pair of bulls, through the yellow soil. He inhaled, slowly. This wis his country, the land ae his fore-faithers and yet, the stink ae it sickened him tae his gut. That sweet smell ae rotting lemons, of uncollected rubbish, of unrepaired roads. Naa, he thought, and kicked the soil again, this isnae ma country. No ony mair. Mibbee, it nivir wis. He'd been tae Pakistan three or four times before, but nivir tae a shit-hole like this, and nivir in the depths ae summer, for God's sake!

The song he'd been playing, back in the car, seemed still to hover within the ripples of heat, the reel turning again and again as he walked slowly across the stretch of land. The groon wis hard, irregular, like wild-dog skulls, yet it crumbled into powder as his sandals touched the surface. Suddenly, a big, black bird swooped down and landed on a branch above his heid. He felt its eye slide along his spine. A perfect, black globe. Sal stopped walking, and tried tae stare back, but the light wis too strong, and his eyes began tae water. He wiped them wi the sleeve ae his kamise and removed a piece of paper from his shalvar pocket. Unfolded it. The sections came open uneasily and when they did, they left behind dirty-brown lines. Sal peered at the yellowed paper. The deeds. It had been written in Urdu script, and he couldnae read Urdu script. But right down at the dog-eared bottom, there were some letters in English which he'd tried tae make oot, all the way over, as he'd sat, bored and irritable, in the plane. They were probably meaningless, anyway. Most of the English here wis pretty meaningless. A kind ae jumbled-up mix ae auld colonial-speak and Amrikan Gangsta talk. His dada must have worn this piece ae paper like a lover as he'd sweatit thru the pissin rain an soor terraces ae Scola on his way tae makin it. Only he'd nivir really made it. No like the big Cash 'n' Carry Families, or the Restaurant Wallahs. Naw, his dada had ended up like a chhipkali in a bottle, always slidin up the glass walls and nivir really gettin onywhur. He felt like cryin as he remembered his dada's tired face, the cheeks sagging and full of lines, one crease for every year in exile. He focused down on the writing. *Half-an-acre*, it looked like, but you couldnae be sure. Some-whur between the burnin grass an the red sandstone, some-whur over those strange, blue seas, which they'd flash up alang wi the wee-whistle life jackets on the plane-flight, the exact measure of Sal's inheritance had got muddled, smudged, diluted. Sal jumped as the bird crowed through the heat. It had lost interest in him, and was gazing east, towards the land of Bhaarat. Now he'd come back to try and sell the land, to get what he could, and get oot again. But everything in Pakistan was cascading downwards like water from the Rawal Dam. The rupee had fallen from fifty-to-the-pound, to one hun-dred-and-thirteen (thirteen . . . for luck? Sal had wondered); the only things which held their value in this country were truth and the loudspeakers outside mosques. Truth was priceless, and it wis everywhere. Look under any bush (burnin or not) and, there, you might find another truth. Sal thought that mibbee this wis because it wis so close tae Hindustan, wi its million gods crawlin aroon all over the place, lookin fur worship. His dada had listened to wan version of the truth when he'd been telt tae buy these plots; the city was goin tae spread like the music ae The Beatles over everything and, soon, the wee plots (the cotees all in a row, with the fair-skinned wives and the kala servants and the almost inaudible pulse of the air-conditioning) would be worth twenty times, *twenty times, bhai,* what they had been bought fur. And right enough, the city had expanded, aye, and laacs-upon-laacs ae cotees had sprung up like teeth all over the place but the problem wis, it had expanded in the wrang direction. It had gan north-east, not south-east and so his dada's plots had remained a wee wasteland. They might even have been shaam laat e shair, common land of the city, and then they would not have been his dada's, after aw. Nuthin wis certain here. Nuthin. Mibbee you were alive, mibbee you were deid. Mibbee there wis a God, mibbee there were ten thoosand. Everyone had a different version of everything, and nuhin wis written doon. Or if it had been, then it would have got washed away in the waters of the Rawal Dam, the night they had burst through stane and concrete and flooded the valley of Punjab, killing thousands. Or mibbee that hasnae happened yet, Sal thought. It wis hard tae be sure. He'd not got very far, trying tae sell the plot; prices were dirt-low and almost no one wis buying land. Anyone who wis anyone wis tryin tae put money intae foreign banks, or tae get oot themselves. No one wanted land in a country that wis goin tae the dogs and the sand. He spat, and his spittle landed on a hump of yellow earth where it lay but did not dissolve. Sal bent down and stared into the dome of the blob. He'd often wondered what he would do with the money. It wisnae gonna be a fortune. It might buy the wheel-trims ae a Merc; or else, a wide-screen TV so that his behene could sit an watch stupit Bombay filmi films. Three hours ae *rim-jim* and *roo-roo* and violins that screeched around yer skull. Or mibbee he would invest it in the shop. Turn it fae a cornershop intae a boutique like the wan his bitch cousin hud on Cathcart Road. Get merrit, huv a family. Naw. He had

4

other dreams for his dada's land. In Sal's dream, the money, coverted like Sal, from rupees intae pounds, would go tae buy a kiss-o-gram. Or, to be mair precise, ninety-nine kiss-o-grams. All blond and bikini'd and stonin in a circle aroon him, and smilin at him wi thur thick, red lips . . . he saw himsel surroondit by them, their wee white breasts pushin intae his broon face, fillin his mooth, his body so that he couldnae breathe fur the whiteness. So that he could become invisible. But that wis jist a dream. In Scola, there wus nae room fur dreams; in Pakistan, dreams were all there wus. He scrunched up the deed and went to put it back in his pocket. Felt it slip from his hand. He bent down to pick it up but couldn't see where it had gone. There wis a clump ae grass, jis beneath his foot, but it wasnae in there. He swore aloud, but his voice was immediately swallowed up in the molten air, and, for the first time, Sal felt scared. He felt sweat spike along the line of his spine. His hair lay matted, dank over his scalp. He shouldnae huv driven oot here on his ane. The thought occurred to him that perhaps the deed might've slipped somehow (anything was possible) into the lining of his shalvar. He ran his hands over the smooth, white cotton, rapidly at first but then slowly, carefully as he held his breath and felt the heat enter him and swell in his chest. *Forty-six degrees, forty-seven* . . .

It wasn't there. It wasn't on the ground either and the earth all just looked the same. It wisnae like Scola, wi aw its shades like the different malts; naw, from the plane, Pakistan wis jis wan, scorched broon. Suddenly he longed for the cool spaces ae Scola, the feel ae the rain on his back. He rummaged aroon wi the tip ae his shoe, but all he got wis mair dust. There wouldn't be another copy – God knew when and where his dada had got it from and onyway nothing would ever huv been written down, and if it had been, then it would be a lie. Truth was held in the air like the waves of heat that burned his skin. He felt the glare of the bird on the back of his neck but fought the temptation to look back. He got down on his hands and knees and began to rummage his palms through the dry soil. The dust made him sneeze, and his eyes began to water, but he took no notice, and let the tears drip silently on to the earth. The soil tasted bitter, like ajwain. Sal had heard that farmers sometimes tasted the soil of their fields, to test its quality. Eejeuts. His breath burned the lining of his throat and he needed a drink. There was boiled water in the car, but Sal didnae dare leave the plot. His grand-father hud sweatit for this land and in the end, he hud died fur it and he wisnae goin tae jis let it slip away so that some fat zamindaar could come and swallow it up, for nothin. A year back, his papa hud ran aff wi a goree and the whole family had been disgraced (as a result of this, his maa had developed five thoosand illnesses, all of which seemed tae afflict her concur-rently, and his dada had gan tae his grave while watchin Madubala fling herself from the stone parapet in the video of the film, *Mahal*). Now Sal wis the man and, being the eldest, it wis up tae him tae save at least somehin ae the family's honour; he hud tae get a guid, or at the very least a reasonably pukka, price for this piece ae pure yellow shite and he couldnae go hame, empty-handed, he just couldnae . . .

There wis nae breeze, but Sal thought he felt wan. He paused for a moment. His face wis covered in dust, his clothes were no longer white, but had acquired the dun chamois in which most Pakistanis over here seemed to dress. His hair fell across his eyes, and he brushed it back wi his hond but it jis fell forwards again. His mother had told him (countless times) tae get it cut *and why don't you try to look like a respectable bundha?* So he'd got fed up and, wan day, he'd gan oot and got it cut. A Number Wan. After that, she'd thrown her honds up intae the air and screamed, *Hai-hai!* and had taken to her bed for two days. You couldnae please them, no matter what you did. He hated his faither fur what he had done, but he hated him mair because he'd landed Sal right in it. Now Sal

6

wis it. All eyes were on him, and he had tae succeed, or else he might as weil be deid. Mibbee he wuid be better aaf deid; at least then, he would be a hero, or a martyr or, at the very least, someone not tae be spoken ill of. An image of the goree, bein screwed by his faither flashed intae his mind. He pushed it away. In the past, they'd sometimes talked aboot the men who'd been seen hauding honds wi mini-skirtit gorees an walkin doon the street. And he'd despised those men and yet, at the same time, he'd wantit tae be wan ae them. Tae huv his ane long-legged, thin-waisted goree tae wave like a white flag at the world. And then his faither had gone an done that, and made it impossible fur Sal. Now, he would nivir be able tae surrender. Sal wus deid, right enough, deid an buried beneath the big, wet stanes ae Albert Drive. Beneath the big, white sky. He forced his mind back tae the deed, the plot, his honour. He had the insane thought of removing his shalvar and turning it inside-out to search for the piece ae paper. He looked around. There wis no one about. The peasant whom he had spotted earlier had vanished. He was far from any-where. It would take only a few seconds. And onyway, time here wis different. Everything around him had grown silent. Or mibbee it had always been like that, he wisnae sure. He got down on his hands and knees and began to search for the deed. He felt the cotton ae his claes stick tae his back like a lizard skin. After a while, he stopped and rolled over.

Everything looked different. The sky was everywhere, and its blueness had faded into a shimmering silver. The bird was no longer in the tree, but was scarpering along the ground. Every so often, its head would flick down and then up, and every time this happened, its beak would emerge empty, black. It seemed a lot smaller than before, its stupit wee deformed twig legs were like those of an auld wummin. It'll no find ony worms here, he thought. Sal began to feel uncomfortable. He felt as though he was sinking into the soil. His nails were all smashed and blood had begun to trickle from the end of his thumb. Slowly, he got up. The bird had disappeared. You couldnae even trust yer ane eyes. He removed his sandals and set them neatly aside. Spat again, to clear the dust from his mouth. He looked around, just tae check, and in one smooth movement, he slipped the elastic of his shalvar down and over his feet and stepped awkwardly out of it. He lifted it up, and shook the cloth so that a fine dust flew everywhere. Nothing. He turned it inside-out and shook it again but still, nothing. The dust smelt ae bhang. The whole country's gan tae pot, Sal thought, and then he laughed. He was about to put the shalvar back on, when the thought occurred to him that the paper might somehow have fallen, not into his shalvar but into his kamise. He threw the shalvar down on to the ground and slipped the long shirt up, over his head. The heat scalded his back, he could feel the cells begin to fry, one by one. His head felt like it was goin tae burst and his breath was coming in short rasps. *Forty-nine degrees, fifty* . . . He shook out the kamise but it, too, was empty. Exasperated, Sal tossed it aside and glared up at the sky which had become so bright, it held no colour at all. It was as though the sun had exploded and filled the entire sky with its burning substance. He tried to swear, but his mouth was parched, and no words came. He shook his fist at the sun, or God, or truth or whatever was up there. He fell to his knees and began frantically to search for the piece of paper which had hauled him across five thousand miles and three generations to the plot which he an his dada, both, had dreamt of and, as he churned up the earth, the dust swirled into the air so that there, in the land that was his by right of inheritance, he had, at last, become invisible.

And because of the clouds of ochre dust which surrounded him, Sal did not see the bird up in the tree as it flapped its wings, twice, and took off into the burning sky.

Solomon's Jar

E ight pm Friday. The Jinn had been in the jar for exactly
three millennia. It sounded simple when stated in his-
torical terms like this, and in one sense it was true. If the
second hands on a tiny, hidden clock were to have been
watched constantly for three thousand years, much as the
Museum Curator was watching his wall-clock at that very
moment, then the seconds would have rolled into minutes,
the minutes into hours and so on. Neat rolls of time, spiraling
up all the way to heaven. But the Jinn saw it differently, there
in the darkness of the vial.

*I have been put into this container by my Master, Son of David.
In jar time, there is no space and so I float along a fissure of
infinite possibilities. What appears to be smooth is, if viewed from
my position, a series of rugged mountain ranges that would take
centuries to crawl up. And so, the sides of the surahi, which once
were filled with the arak of princes, now form a world in
themselves. Every comma, every semicolon, is a jinn-in-the-works.
I have been in such a place before – seven times, in all – and this,
to me, is not punishment but is, rather, a normal part of my
manifold existence. In jar space, there is no time and so, while
millennia might have passed by on the outside, within the
darkness I still bear the sweat-marks of my Master's fingers
upon my head. In my ears, the echo of the laughter of his sixty-
fifth concubine. The slap of her skin tambourine. When next I*

shall mingle with the souls of men, I know not. But whether it be ten minutes, or ten thousand years, to me matters little, if at all.

The Curator shepherded the last of the cleaners through the already half-closed side-door, jangling his bunch of keys like a Victorian station-master. It was a familiar ritual, as much a part of the involuntary segments of his life as, say, brushing his teeth or eating bread in the morning. The Closing-up Rite had melded into the thrum of his daily inhalation and was on the way to becoming myth (though the Curator knew that this might well have taken another three thousand years). By which time, of course, the small-boned man, along with his obsolescent side-whiskers might have become part of the Great Sinai Desert or else a speck in the eye of the whore on Main Street, Sacramento, Calif.[1] The next part of the process would be for him to switch off all the lights, retire to his tiny room, and drink old coffee from a stained mug. The last note in the tapping Arabesque of his polished floor day. He closed the side-door, slid the bolts and then turned three keys in three locks, each one twice. He re-attached the keys to the large ring slung from his belt, removed a handkerchief from his pocket and wiped the top of his bald pate. He peered at the stain, trying to focus, but its edges were undefined and it extended through the white cloth in all directions at once. He found himself gazing into some non-existent distance. Not so much beyond the stain, as between it. He flipped the hankie over and saw that his sweat had seeped right through the material like some kind of insidious salt cloud. A noise sounded from behind him. He spun round, then rebuked himself for reacting. It wasn't as if he was unused to the creak and sputter which the old building generated as night crept

1. The name afforded to the western part of the land-mass known until the late twenty-first century as 'America'. The zone seceded from the main body of the state after the Wars of Intelligence, 2172–81 and 2186–90.

along its wood and glass and stone. There were so many halls, each arrayed with dozens of cases, every one of which contained multiple objects. He reminded himself that tonight of all nights, it was imperative that he keep a cool nerve. He held out both hands, carefully inspecting the fingertips for any sign of tremor. He blinked, slowly, and exhaled. Allowing his arms to swing in measured pendula, he walked over to the Temple Case.

The cabinet was the longest in the museum. Running almost half the length of the room, it contained relics thought to have been recovered from the Temples of Jerusalem, both Old and New. Many of the contents had only been discovered on recent archaeological digs, both beneath the Old City of Rome and in the soil of a dried-up oxbow lake by the Bosphorus. They accorded with the set of Temple artifacts listed in the (possibly apocryphal) Books of Solomon, which themselves had been rediscovered by one Ben-i-Amin Levi, an octogenarian Kabbalist, while he had been poring over one particularly faded set of punctuation marks in those Nag Hammadi Scrolls, which had been thought to have been burned by the wife of the peasant who had stumbled across them in a jar beneath the sands of Egypt, but which, in fact, had been sold by her to a Cairene manufacturer of backgammon sets.[2] Among the golden brooches and cryptic candelabras (each as accurately annotated as possible given the circumstances, and pinned to the green felt of the cabinet base) were several large porcelain jars. All the surahis, but one, were unstoppered. They were of different colours, and each had a shape and design unique to itself. Spiral serpents, reclining lions, abstract geometric patterns, a fish . . . The Curator looked at each of the jars, in turn as he had done every night and every morning for seven years, ever since they had

2. Codex XVIII, Para 27 ('Rings of Solomon') Zaragoza Municipal Library, Spain.

11

been brought to the museum. He couldn't bear the thought of any one of them being stolen. It would be worse than murder. It would be like pilfering a myth. Stealing a soul. When he had reassured himself that all the containers were present and unharmed, he came at last to the final, the stoppered jar. It had a sinuous, female shape and its long, slender neck rose high above the others. The ancient porcelain was decorated in blue fire designs. It was almost totally undamaged. He stood, motionless, beside the cabinet. At first, he had treated the jar as just one more relic. He had known, even then, that this was a lie. A necessary deception. He had behaved like a fusty academic with a beautiful woman. He had tried to ignore the surahi, yet his dreams had been filled with its dancing, curvaceous form. Sometimes, it would melt in reverse creation and assume manifold shapes, multiple existences. Until, at last, he could feel it taking the shape of the Curator. Becoming him. After a few months of this, he'd had the security sensors around the cabinet enhanced, so that even the most casual of glances, the tiniest of envies would tend to set off the alarm. Then he had it arranged so that when the bells did sound, they would cause a red light to flash, on and off, in his office.

Every morning, he would arrive before the post was delivered, and in the evening would exit the building only after the last of the cleaners had left. Eventually, even this had not been enough and he had begun, over the past few weeks, to sleep behind his office, in a room hardly bigger than one of the larger cabinets. He had made excuses to his wife, saying that an extremely important consignment had arrived at the museum and that someone would be needed to watch over it at night. 'Why you?' she had asked. 'Why do you have to do it? Why don't they get someone else for a change?' and he had replied, 'Who else would there be? I have no choice.' In some ways, he wasn't lying. And, in spite of the cramped conditions in his office, he had begun to feel a new kind of freedom there, one which he could never have had on the streets or in his home or in twenty years of marriage. It were as though time, that most precious of artifacts, had been suspended in the very substance of the glass cases, the creaking wood pillars, the musty, unchanging air. In the museum, at night, the Curator felt he could expand and fill himself. And yet, the facts remained solid, outside of him. His marriage, his job, his body . . . death. He shivered, though the night was warm, humid. He felt as though all his life, he'd been dodging between pillars of fear, hiding behind first one, then another, till his fear had trapped him in a temple of pillars. Perhaps that was why he had become a curator. It was a safe job. Hermetic, almost. He had slipped into it as he'd fallen into his marriage, through a combination of lack of confidence and his wife's need to dominate. He had never quite been able to handle women. To play them like other men played the clarinet. He gazed at the porcelain. It was familiar. Necessary. He knew every crack, every glaze-line. He lived along one of those random fissures. Nothing more. He felt an urge well up in his chest. An urge to be inside. To get within. The pressure forced itself out between his ribs and stretched across the empty hall. It seemed as though his life up to that moment had been merely a preparation for this night.

I am unaware of the difference between night and day. I am of fire, and so I create my own light in this place. What seems to be dark is thus illumined by the undefined swathes of me. I have no idea where the jar might be, nor does it really matter, since the reality of that within the jar bears no relation to the world outside, any more than does the entity within a man's head to the grass beneath his feet. In some ways, I dwell within men's heads while, in others, I am the fracture between their souls and their knowledge. I can be many things; an infinite number of things;

*and I can be all of these, at once. This is especially so in the jar,
since time and space here possess no properties, either within
themselves or between each other. If some ignorant peasant were
to break open the jar, then once again I would enter the world of
men as they see it and would be able to mingle with them. But
really, it makes little difference since I can create my own courts
within the darkness that is light. I can cause my own Paradise in
a jar.*

The Curator removed a small key from the ring and unlocked the
case. He reached out and touched the jar. It was fingertip cool.
The temperature within the cabinet was maintained at a steady
level, regardless of room temperature. But then, he mused, the
room temperature was also kept at a steady level, winter and
summer. His mind flipped through the convolutions of a
thousand realities, each one hovering in its own, unique weath-
er-pattern. He wondered whether, within the jar, there existed
still other, air-conditioned boxes, right down to an infinitesimal
room where a bald, moustached, middle-aged museum curator
was busy *wondering whether, within the jar* . . .

Using both hands, he lifted the surahi out and placed it on
the glass. Without relocking the cabinet, he carried the jar
from the gallery down the corridor, his shoes tap-tapping on
the newly-polished wood of the floor. He cradled it to his
chest. Like a baby, or a heart attack. Once in his office, he
carefully placed the object on the centre of his desk, and
switched the on kettle. Rituals within rituals. Safe, he thought,
as the water began to hiss. He sat down. The top of the jar was
at eye-level. The thick bung which blocked its slender neck
was composed of multiple layers of some greasy material
wrapped, one upon the next, in infinite jamming roundels.
The blue flames burned along the porcelain. Kiln-fresh. Repetitive pink motifs circled the belly of the jar. He saw his face,
his eyes, reflected in the cream-white background. Wondered

if something was looking out at him. He pulled himself away, went over to a shelf and took out a large book. Sipping black coffee, the Curator read from the old tome. Or rather, he traced his fingers along the esoteric shapes and numbers within its pages.

Ah! The Incantation Of Harut and Marut.[3] One of my favourites! The cantillations of the upside-down twin angels, the magical duet of darkness. I listen to the harmonics of chaos and realise that some thing is about to happen. But wait! The imminence of change causes its opposite to be manifest upon the walls of the jar. And so I begin to wonder how a concept which is timeless and without dimension could possibly be contained by the walls of a porcelain jug. The walls themselves are full of tiny holes, and yet I am unable to escape through these. It is the incantation of my Master which holds me within this jar. A lamp of scintillation filters down through the bung and fixes the entity which is me in this limbo state. I recognise the sounds, as each breath vibration slices through another strand of my Master's light. Yeah! I shall soon be free.

The Curator finished reading and reached out to remove the bung from the top of the jar. He paused, his hand in mid-air. The electric light was still on. He got up and plunged the room into darkness. Since he had already switched off all the other lights in the museum, the Curator found he was totally blind. He stood, stock-still in the pitch, the only sound that of his own breathing. Gradually, that too became merged with the night. From somewhere, doubts began to slide up the back of his neck. This whole thing, and his part in it, was crazy. The jar had lain in the cabinet for years, and he had walked

3. For a discussion of the dichotomy of the inverted angels of black magic, see Akhter Ahsen, (1994), *Illuminations on the Path of Solomon*, Lahore, Pakistan, Dastawez Mutbuat.

past it countless times, one in the crowd, merely. A spectator. The lie, again. He had wondered who had removed the bungs from the other jars, and what had become of them. And what had been released from the darkness of their interiors. It had begun to obsess him. His days had become filled with its strange shadow, its ancient light. His nights hovered around the jar's rim, tantalising him as he craned his neck to get a look inside. His mind ran on automatic. The decision had been made gradually, over the months, and any doubts were now like the breeze in a candle flame. The Curator began to make out vague shapes. He stumbled back to the desk and sat down. His breath echoed in the jar of his body, and the harmonics danced along the walls of the windowless room, chimed within the glass cases with their spirit objects, blew cacophonies along the fissures between the cracked paint and the sinews of the artist.

I pirouette on paradox. The impossible is my domain. Thy wish is my command, Master; Thou commandest that which I wish. Out of fire was I created, and change is my essence. I am a shape-shifter. For a thousand years and a day, I dwelt in a jar on the sand at the bottom of the Arabian Sea, having been imprisoned there by one of the sons of Noah just before the Flood. I was rescued by another, weaker jinn who had been sent out by my Master to search for me. In the exhalation of my Master's last breath, was I confined to this jug, and soon shall I be released again into the world of mass and time. My lifespan has been extended beyond that which a normal jinn could expect (for we have our own timescales, our own mortality). Within the jar, I am almost immortal. Here, I am closest to my Creator. But my eternity is finite, and soon I shall be freed into decay. He who will release me, shall be my Master. I shall render power unto my Master. I shall venture into the cracks of his soul, and there will I vanish. Through my non-existence, will he perceive of his own

16

existence. In this way, am I sometimes glass, sometimes mirror. He will come to realise that my commands – his wishes – cut both ways. A paradox. For just as Humanity was created from mud, to partake in the essence of God through leaf, stone and artifice, so were the jinnaat formed from flame and may rejoin the One through ambiguity. We are the mirrors of creation, blown in hot fractal madness. Our freedom sails in the wind.

The Curator placed his right hand over the neck of the jar, while, with the left, he pinned the vase to the table. The bung (he had never touched it before) felt oily, yielding, beneath his palm. He wondered what it was made of. An image of snakes slithered through his skin. He withdrew. Though they were not cold, he blew into his hands as though they were, and tried again. He gripped the bung, and pulled. It was stuck. His fingers kept slipping off. Removing a handkerchief from his pocket, he tugged and twisted simultaneously, switching hands after several attempts. As it slid away from the porcelain, it seemed to disintegrate and he let it fall. A loud pop sounded from outside of him. A blinding light filled his eyes and in the light he had a momentary vision of the infinite regression of time and space, before a whoosh of air gathered up the streets, the museum, the room, the cabinets, the jar. He felt the light enter him and fill him with its clarity. He felt himself break apart and come together again. All of his possible existences fragmented and then evanesced in the light. But, in between fragmentation and reunion, something had changed. Something in the core of his being. Then the light faded and died and the Curator sank into a state which might have been sleep, but which might also have been non-existence.

When he opened his eyes, everything was pink. The jar lay on its side on the table before him. A long, grin-shaped crack ran from bottom to top and blue porcelain flakes had scattered on to the wood. He reached out and touched the jar with the tips of his fingers. It rocked from side to side, and then became still. Sand on wood. It held no mystery. He felt his joints move stiffly as he walked towards the door. A mauve luminescence streamed in through the high windows. Dawn was breaking over the museum. He walked down the hall, passing by the grey shapes of cabinets, statues, jars, and, in one smooth movement, he threw open the outer doors. Stepped out. Closed his eyes. Inhaled. Let the breeze slip over his face. He opened his eyes and descended the steps. At the bottom, he paused for a moment and then turned to the right. Behind him, the doors lay wide open. The streets were deserted, except for the odd lone figure trudging back from some sweatshop nightshift or other. He entered an early-morning café and sat down. The only customer. Ordered an espresso from the blond waitress. Watched her as she disappeared into the kitchen at the back. Ran his finger along the wood of the table. Listened to the sound of the coffee machine. Smelled the aroma of morning cigarettes. Everything seemed so real.

She brought his coffee in a demitasse cup balanced on a brass tray, and again he watched her as she went over to the counter and sat on a stool. Crossed her legs. She took out a cigarette. He felt the movement of her muscles, the feel of her hair against the skin of her scalp. He saw through her eyes. Morning blue. In a harmony of mirrors, he saw himself. The same, and yet not the same. The coffee tasted pungent, in the pink dawn light. She was having difficulty lighting the cigarette. They were alone in the café. Just him and the waitress and the steaming, bubbling coffee machine. He put down his cup. Met her eye. Looked away. Then picked it up again but did not sip. Met her eye, got up, went towards her. Saw her, seeing him. Blue-on-pink. Held out his hand, the fingers steady, porcelain. Flicked the lighter. She craned her neck and her hair fell across her olive skin. Just so. She inhaled, twice. Sat back. Removed the cigarette. Looked him full in the eyes, and smiled. But already he was smiling back at her. From somewhere down the street, the strains of an old clarinet filtered through the morning. Single notes. One after the next. Pure, melismatic. His smile broadened. The Curator was free.

The Queens of Govan

The street wis wetter than ever, and that wis saying somethin. She walked, faster than before so that the rows of terraced houses became a blur of dirty white an then she broke intae a run, worried, short strides at first, but then, as her pace increased, her trainers began tae bounce over the water and she wis almost flyin through the darkness. The black of her jeans and leather jacket made her skin seem whiter. That an the make-up. It wis aw in the contrast. There wis nae danger ae her bumpin intae anyone. Like a bat, Ruby possessed a radar which steered her between lives. If she ran fast enough, she might escape. The shopfronts were shuttered against the rain and the weekend, but the street teemed wi people: busy men wi mobiles an braces and bare-armed, high-heeled women, tipsy on the June rain. An in the dark corners everywhere, the junkies wi hooded eyes an lang teeth an nae shaddaes. The noise ae cars as they swished through the wet. It wis like the Clyde had burst its banks an was washin doon the Copland Road, but the waters it brought would not be pure. It wis Saturday night in Govan, jis before ten, an soon, like paradise, the pubs would be spewin out their punters in varyin states ae intoxication an the men and women would teeter across pavements an wade through headlights an, quite possibly, would end up queuein fur a kebab carry-out, which Ruby would huv tae serve tae them. But she wis late an all because ae those bloody phone-calls. Qaisara would be . . .

21

difficult. When she wis upset, her boss would become sullen, moody like a teenager. And then, all night, Ruby would be swimmin through glue.

She felt the back ae the mobile, flap against her thigh as she ran, plastic on denim. It wis a nifty wee thing wi a case which flipped open like wan ae those communicators in *Star Trek*; the stuff her bhai watched, all the fuckin time. *Beam me up.* An she wished she could jis beam up intae the Qaisara Kebab House. She wis meant tae huv been there ten minutes earlier, but she'd got talkin tae wan ae her friends an time had jist seemed tae lengthen, the way it did on Saturday nights an sometimes on Sunday mornins, as weil; so long as her papa didnae huv a hangover. It wis that sense that anythin wis possible, that ye might yet be a film-star like Madhuri Dixit or that ye could be a TV presenter or a pop icon like that girl in *The Wind Machines.* She wis Asian an blond and Ruby reckoned she must be wearin a light honey wig, but it wis pretty convincin, all the same. Blondness wis an attitude. *The Wind Machines.* That famous shot ae Marilyn Monroe, stonin over the windy vent . . .

She felt the air balloon in her chest, the night air filled wi the diesel ae taxis an last buses an the bleary breath of men in whisky-bottle suits an it wis a darkness with which she wis familiar. Twenty-two years. Twenty-three, if ye counted the time before she wis born. But then, if ye counted that . . .

The TV wis always on in their house. Even when visitors came, the big box would still be blastin out adverts, or a love-song fae some sunny hillside in the valley of Kashmir, or mibbee Shah Rukh Khan would be leapin an grinnin his way through yet another field of rape seed on his way tae gettin the girl. When her papa came home in a waft ae booze an regret, her bhai an her would turn the thing up an would close the door, in the hope that mibbee he wouldnae come intae the livin-room an would go straight tae bed. Their maa would remove his clothes, one-by-one, an then would lie down on a separate mattress on the floor where she would remain awake for most of the night, listenin tae his whisky breathin an tae the sounds ae lone cars acceleratin away in the night. Sometimes, Ruby would dream of her maa 'n' her papa. Two filmi stars on a mountain-side, singin an dancin by a silver stream. Only the stream wis whisky an the geet wis a lament. Ruby 'n' her maa had conversations. They never talked. Sometimes, she wished her maa would confide in her, she wished they could be like sisters. But her maa wis too busy wi her papa to bother about anyone else. If Ruby ever did get married, it would be by default. But she didnae care. Who needed a man, anyway? Occasionally, he would come home sober, an then things would be different an they would all have tae pretend tae give him the same respect which they gave tae their uncles. It wis an act, the whole thing wis jist a fuckin Mashriki mask. Their life here. Love. Her chastity. Everything. Beneath it all, the dogs of the West had taken control. So the mullah had told them. Her 'n' her bhai. He had wanted them to join the Young Muslims an tae go about wi clean-cut attitudes an big chips on their shooders. Beards an hijaabs. But her bhai watched TV, instead, an she . . . she had got a job in the kebab house. The place wis in the heart ae Govan which wis gie unusual fur an Asian-run Carry-out. Maist ae those were in the slightly safer territory ae Kinnin Park, where broon faces outnumbered the pink and where the Changezi family held an easy sway wi machetes an hockey-sticks. The Qaisara Kebab House wis right next door tae the Govan Town Hall, a great red sandstone building which now functioned as *The Social*, but which stood opposite Plantation Quay, where, once, the slaves had washed up in great black waves on their way tae America. Qaisara had told her that, soon after she'd started workin there. Qaisara had told her many things. The woman wis filled wi wisdom and what ye saw in Qaisara wis only the tiniest bit of what wis there. She glanced at her watch, as she ran. Qaisara couldnae abide people bein late. She would be paagal in her own, strange way. Ruby didnae blame her. It wisnae easy, tae run a business. Things didnae jis fall intae place, like in a movie. Take One, Take Two . . . No, it wis different, in real life. Ye had tae bleed, fur a drap ae silver. Ye had tae die, over an over again. An Qaisara had had her fair share ae death.

The rain wis tankin it down, an Ruby felt the black bomber leather ae her jacket grow heavier as it soaked up the water. She didnae need anythin on her heid; her hair wis so thick and black. Nae blond wigs in Glasgae. Aw that stuff wis for them in London, where ye might pretend tae be anythin and no one would give a shit. Sometimes, she longed fur that kindae anonymity, fur the chance of jist droppin off the edge of the world and seeing where y'ended up. The problem wis, ye only had wan life. Ye could take the wrong turn, and ruin it an there would never be any goin back. Like her papa, an his drink. Fuck that. She glanced up at the sky but could make out only the broken silver of the rain. She slowed down, jist a fraction, and let the drops splash on to her face, felt the tiny pin-pricks against the skin. Ah know ah'm alive, she thought. Ah know ah'm alive.

A mass against her shooder sent her reelin. She almost fell intae the gutter. Jis managed tae get her balance, but felt her money slip outae her inside pocket. The clatter ae change.

'. . . fuck!'

She had forgotten tae close the zip.

'Eh! Want some ae this?'

He wis white, thirty and overweight. His face wis aw loose an pasty like a used punchbag.

She began tae pick up her money. He tottered, drunkenly, towards her. Her hand moved quickly across the asphalt. She

24

got it all back, except fur a ten-pence piece, which glinted in the middle ae a puddle. She decided it wisnae worth it, and sprang away fae him. His eyes were dirty blue. She spoke to his forehead.

'Fuck off.'

Behind him, in the shadows ae a shopfront, a couple ae guys were watchin. Waitin.

'Ah'd love tae. Whit ye runnin fae, darlin?'

His hand waved about like he wis a Hindi hero, about tae break intae song. But there were nae hillsides, hereabouts.

She stepped back, right intae a puddle in the gutter. Felt the black water splash up her jeans tae the place above her ankle. She swore under her breath.

'Get lost, arsehole.'

He mouthed a kiss. She could smell his breath. Deid whisky. Her papa. She wanted tae vomit.

'Aw, come on. Dinnae be like that. Ah'm a good yin wi the ladies, always huv been.'

He glanced round at the other men who had become his companions.

'. . . An the night, Ah fancy a wee bit ae spice.'

'A vindaloo!' wan ae them shouted, 'tae take away!'

Dirty Blue wis droolin. He reeled, an his hond reached out.

'Come here, ma wee Asian Babe . . .'

Ruby tried tae spit, but found that her mouth had dried up. She wisnae gan tae wait. She leapt outae the puddle and ran. The man called after her, somethin about her legs, but she didnae want tae listen. For an awful moment, she had the feelin that he wis followin her, slowly but inexorably like the monsters in those horror movies her bhai watched, when he wisnae watchin *Star Trek*. They never died, those monsters. They were indestructible. Like fear. Or hate. She ran all the way tae the end ae Copland Road and turned right and only then did she ease down again. Her whole body wis tremblin, an the rain drove intae her face. She cursed hersel fur leavin so late. That's what ye get, she thought. Talkin tae yer friends, dollin yersel up. Dark-blue lipstick an pale make-up, jis so you'd look a wee bit mair Mediterranean. Workin yer body, tryin tae wipe out the curves an tae appear, as straight an white as possible. Who're you tryin tae fool? That man knew what ye were. It shines through, especially when they're pissed. People could see more when they were drunk, or after they'd had sex. It dulled the senses but sharpened the wits. They could see through the masks. Ye couldnae hide in Govan. It wis aw pubs an carry-oots an alleyways where dogs an hookers plied their trade. Dark places, amidst the neon. It wis either wan, or the other. If ye tried tae live between the two, you would split apart like the moon. Or like Pakistan. Her breastbone hurt with each breath, an she felt the relief flood through her as, up ahead, she spotted the flashin blue sign of the Qaisara Kebab House.

She paused. Didnae want tae go intae the place, lookin desperate. Desperation wis weakness. An Ruby had never let weakness direct her actions. No like her papa. He'd once been a real painter-an-decorator, an Ruby remembered that in the early days, before the booze had completely taken over, he had painted her room all purple an orange. Well, it wis the seventies. But she only remembered it fae a photo. Her 'n' her papa, up against the wall. He wis tall and he had his hand on her left shoulder. But she couldnae remember his touch. The thing wis, because her papa had slowly sunk intae the long, green bottles ae the pub next door, their flat had remained in a state of suspended animation; the walls, the furniture, the smells even, had stayed stuck in 1975. The year she wis born. The year he turned tae drink. Fuck that. She walked intae the shop.

Sayin nothin, she went intae the back, took off her jacket and hung it up. She noticed that wan ae the cheap, brass hooks wis beginnin tae come aff the wall. She fingered the plaster underneath. It wis crumbling, grey. She pulled out what seemed to be a hair. Gazed at it. Dead horses. The back ae the shop smelt damp, as though the Clyde wis seepin through the bricks. She could hear music fae out in the shop. 'Anjaana', by Lata Mangeshkar. Malika-e-Tarunum. Lata had a child's voice, yet she could reach Ruby like no other singer. Ruby had never had a voice. An anyway, her maa'd said it wis only whoors and Hindus that sang an danced. But behind the masks, everyone wis a whoor. Everyone danced and screamed their way through life. She flicked the horse hair off her fingers, but it seemed tae stick tae the skin. *Shit*, she said, *shit*, and she rubbed it off along the seam ae her jeans. Washed her hands, an her face. Went through tae the front of the shop. Tried tae be busy. She almost wished fur customers. Qaisara wis slicin some meat. The gas behind the donner sputtered and coughed. That wis wan ae Ruby's jobs. Tae light the fire behind the donner. Qaisara didnae look at her as she spoke. O fuck, Ruby thought.

'You do the salads,' she said. 'The lamb can wait.'

Her voice wis bowstring taut, and Ruby did not ask whether or not she should also do the chicken.

The heat of the place soon dried her off. After a shift at the kebab house, her skin would be raised and puckered like that of a sailor, and, later, she would gaze at herself in the bathroom mirror for ages, and try tae soothe her face wi cold water and cucumbers. She didnae want tae end up like Qaisara. A face, swollen with the long nights of bein burned slowly over the open fires ae the cookers. She'd heard that once, Qaisara had been beautiful. Young, slim and beautiful. It wis hard tae see, now. She had a long face, the colour ae dark honey and her eyes were piercin black. The hair which, once, had been sable wis now streaked wi grey, although Ruby knew that she dyed it, fae time tae time. The skin wis beginnin tae sag aroon the eyes as though the fingers were already weighin on her lids. Qaisara wisnae fat but she wis bulky wi muscle. One night, she'd watched her boss throw out three young wankers who'd come in and given her mouth. Totally calm, she'd grabbed two ae them by the collars an rammed them up against the wall an the other one had jist taken fright an run. They were all cowards, those guys. Big mooths but, behind the mooths, nuhin. Jis air and a Rangers' scarf. Nuthin. Qaisara wis wearin a sunflower-yellow shalvar-kamise wi the sleeves rolled up. She watched Qaisara's airms as she worked, watched the way the wee muscles in her fingers moved as she sliced the meat, watched the manner in which she bore herself. There wis a grace about her boss which Ruby had never seen in anyone else. And she knew that that wis why she worked here, in spite ae the moods an the long hours an the crap money an the danger ae fuckin up her looks. An in the early hours ae the mornin, when she got outae the burnin shop, the air would be clean and dark, and she would breath it in and feel cleansed by it. God nivir slept, she thought, but, if he did, it would be then. In the depths ae the night, she would feel that she could do anythin.

Ruby thought ae the girls she'd known fae school. Some ae them had gone on tae do wonderful things. Social things, or medical. Some ae the girls had got married, the moment they'd stepped outae the school gates, often tae guys hauled up fae wan ae the gao around Faisalabad. One day, those guys would be pushin a plow an, the next, they would be lyin in bed on top ae a frightened eighteen-year-old wi five Higher Grade Certificates stacked up on her parents' shelves. And the funny thing wis, sometimes it worked. It wisnae any worse than the drunken romances which the gorees seemed tae fall intae, at the drop ae a rubber. Ruby wis kindae in-between. Or sometimes, she thought, ah'm nowhere. Like a lot ae her saheli, she'd lost her virginity a few years earlier, doon some dark alley

28

wan night wi a guy she could barely recall. All she remembered wis a scarlet baseball cap wi letters sewn intae the fabric. She could see them now, the way each thread curled and twisted and stabbed intae the cloth like tiny, pulsing arteries. But she wis used tae the double-life. At home, she wis totally, nauseatingly Mashriki, *Ah ho, God-be-with-you, behtiye khala ji*, while, outside, in the darkness of night or beneath the burnin sun of the parks, she would be rampant and would slip off towards dives which no one knew the names of. And Ruby'd had boyfriends, mainly white, but none had been serious, so tae speak. It wis jis supplyin a mutual need. A trade, ye might say. They needed her brown-ness as she needed their white. It wis fair, if not equal. But then, she thought as she laid out the last of the lettuce, nothin had ever been equal. She moved on tae the lamb.

Qaisara looked up. She wis a woman ae few words. That wis part ae her mystique. Everyone had their secret places. Take someone's secrets away and you would destroy them.

She glanced up at the wall clock. Nodded.

'Closin time, soon.'

Qaisara wis a Muhajir fae 'Forty-Sieven. 1947. Blood and Partition. Lost identities . . . death.

And later, she'd married Qaisar Sahb, who wis almost two decades her senior, for financial security and a modicum of respectability. Romance had never been an issue. Asians were very pragmatic about romance, love, an aw that. It wis fine, as long as it remained trapped in the box: in filums, songs an the bathroom mirror; but, if it should be allowed tae escape intae real life, if the ink of its delicate nastaliq symbolism should invade the gullies ae Karachi or Kinnin Park, then it could cause only strife and unhappiness. Because the expectations born in the dreams ae romance could never be fulfilled, this side ae Kiamath. Her maa had once told her that love wis only fur poets, madmen and gorees. An she should know. She'd had a love-marriage an look where it had got her. Guilt and alcoholism. She had the guilt; he had the sharaab. Or rather, the sharaab had him. Anyway, Qaisara's mia had driven the Corporation buses while she'd worked in *Mr Singh's Sweat-Shop*, where, one day, she'd taken a needle tae Singh's throat and demanded, and got, her Back Pay. She'd lost her job and had earned the title of *That Paagal Woman*, but she couldnae huv cared. Fear an respect, as she would say, were priceless commodities. With the money they'd earned, they'd set up the Qaisar Kebab House. Her mia wis an auld man by then and Qaisara had done maist ae the work. Which she wis used tae. And then, one day, he collapsed and died. Everyone thought that would be the end ae the Kebab Shop. They expected tae see the shutters adorned wi *For Sale* signs. Black-suited Cash 'n' Carry owners wi suitably mournful faces had drawn up in white Mercedes and made her offers which they thought she couldnae refuse. The family who ran protection in the whole ae Kinnin Park began tae wonder who would be movin in and when, since Qaisar Sahb had always paid on time and had always been most respectful like the true Muhajir he wis. But when, one sunny Sunday evenin, Qaisara had re-opened the shop, almost everyone had crowded in, tae see jist how she would manage. The thing wis, she made sure she wis in control. Like everyone, she paid protection, but only on condition that the runners, the baggers and aw the rest would buy their kebabs exclusively fae the Qaisara Kebab House, as she had renamed it. Then folk had expected her tae remarry, but, as the years had gone by, that expectation, too, had fallen by the wayside and now everyone jist let Qaisara be. She had nae sons, nae mia, an she ran her ane business. An Ruby respected that. Sometimes, she admired Qaisara mair than she did Madhuri Dixit. Qaisara wis real.

Anyway, tonight they were expectin the usual Saturday-night crowd, swollen by the end ae a footba match that wis bein beamed intae the pubs by satellite fae some far-off Latin American country, whose name she couldnae remember. Her bhai had been watchin fur it tae come on when she'd left the flat. Watchin an eatin like he always did. Munch, munch, munch. He wis already a barrel an would probably grow even fatter, by the time he wis married. He had taken after his papa. He had nae honour. Not like Qaisara. She turned towards Ruby. The rain had lightened up a little and the sound ae the city broke through the spaces.

'How's yer papa?' she asked.

Ruby shrugged. Didnae meet her eye.

'. . . Okay.' Her voice sounded small. Like she had fallen back, ten years.

'Tumari maa?'

She slapped some lamb skewers down in the display case. Then some more.

'Teek.'

'She's had a lot to cope with, your maa.'

Ruby spun round.

'D'ye want the sauce over there or will ah leave it where it is? And what about the keema? Will I put it on now or later?'

Quietly, Qaisara showed her where tae put the stuff, even though she knew that Ruby had done it a hundred times before. Ruby wis surprised. She'd expected her boss tae be in a bad mood. She'd wantit tae tell her about the drunk but she hadnae dared.

The first folk in fae the rain were some slap-happy football fans in tee-shirts. They were polite and playful wi Ruby but she avoided their eyes. Ye couldnae give guys an inch or they'd take a mile. After that, punters arrived in batches of half-a-dozen at a time. Wet faces, some smilin, others jis plain drunk. And one or two came in alone, wi a blue sadness in their eyes. Ruby knew the look but she wisnae givin anythin tae anyone.

31

The hands moved smoothly over the white clock-face while the insect light buzzed with tiny incinerations. It wis good, bein busy. They skewered pieces of lamb and chicken and laid the skewers on the grill and, while the chunks were cookin away, they went over to the donner spit and hived off sleeks of brown meat, which they laid on a bed of salad. An then the whole lot wis placed in the belly of a long slab of pitta bread and wrapped in paper, once, twice, and then was served. Donners on their own were the most common order. They filled bellies which rolled wi beer an lager. Filled and neu-tralised the rage which simmered beneath the skins ae Govan. The rage ae the dead ships an the closed factory gates an the games lost and won; an the rage of the marchers wi their blue-an-orange banners which had been hauled, blood-spattered, fae houses ae God. An sometimes Ruby had felt herself tae be a part of that inchoate fury but she had shied away from it because she knew that, like the great, black waters ae the Clyde River, it would sweep her away, not to the sea but to a darkness from whence there would be nae return.

When they were busy, Ruby an Qaisara would begin tae dance. The one, thin and dressed totally in black; the other, fleshy and swathed in yellow cotton. Both their faces were flushed, and they spoke not a word beyond what wis strictly necessary. *It's aw trade*, Qaisara had said, once, at the end ae a particularly gruelling shift, *It's aw trade*. Their bodies glis-tened with a fine sweat and their hands worked in a rhythm that slipped through Lata's quiet notes and, by one o'clock in the morning, they were moving a kind of fugue. 'Anjaana'. They were women and maist of the punters were men. It wis aw trade.

By one-thirty, the rain had stopped and the runnels of water wormed down the glass and began tae evaporate in the night breeze. Ruby wis slicin meat aff ae the donner stand when she

32

saw a group ae women stondin on the other side ae the street. They were huddled together and were all around fifty years old. Every so often, the huddle would sway in the wind and begin tae break apart, an Ruby supposed they must've been the worse fur drink. They were pointin up at the kebab-shop sign. She sliced off some mair ae the meat and collected it in a circular steel tray. Between the women, at the centre of their huddle, wis a bundle of cloth wi a pair ae legs. They came through the door in a mess ae giggles an cheer. A woman wi a face like a half-chewed turnip spoke. Her words slurred gently into one another like lovers.

'. . . Wan mixed, eh, wan mixed, what ye want, Jeanie? A mixed? What'd ye want?'

A chorus of Jeanies joined in an Qaisara waited patiently for the women to decide just what it was they desired. Ruby stood behind her. Drunk women were scary. It wis like she wis lookin at herself, thirty years down the road. If she kept well back, the smell of the meat would drown the stink ae sharaab. Then the bundle unfolded and a head popped out. At first, it meant nothin. Jis wan mair Saturday night drunk. His toothless smile. The soft focus. Once, she'd believed he wis God. But, later, she had known that it wis jist the softening effect of sharaab. Alcohol had always been his beginning and his end and Ruby wis jist an interloper. An imposter.

'. . . Papa,' she said.

She hated herself.

Her throat wis closin over and the heat wis unbearable. Her father wis bein half-carried by the women. He didnae recognise her. But then, it had been years since he had really looked at her. She could've been anyone. She could've been no one. The soundae Lata's voice rose and filled the shop. 'Anjaana'. She smelled burnin skin and dropped the donner tray. The clatter woke him up and, like a tortoise, he stretched his neck and peered over the glass counter. He wis gazin intae space.

Whisky an vomit. Somethin cracked, inside, and everythin began tae drift in slow motion. She didn't know where it came fae, she didn't know it wis comin. She wis aware ae Qaisara, movin towards her, an of the gapin mouths ae the tarts which seemed tae merge intae one, black hole ae a mouth. A scream came fae the mouth and filled her and then she, too, wis screamin. Ruby turned and gripped the donner spit and ripped it off its bolts. The lamb spilled everywhere. She raised it above her head and flung it intae the centre of the crowd. It hit the man in the middle ae his chest an his eyes rolled upward an he went reelin intae the women who fell about like chess pieces. With the rebound, she toppled back and her head hit the wall. She felt somethin cold slip down her spine. A dead snake. Burnin flesh. The Queen ae Song.

When she opened her eyes, everything wis Qaisara.

'. . . Rubina? Rubina?'

Her long face wis singed wi worry and her voice wis pressing, insistent, lovin.

'Are you alright?'

Ruby felt as though she wis far away. She looked around her. They were in the back room, among the coats and the horsehair plaster. She could hear the rushing of the Clyde as it poured westwards. She tried tae get up but Qaisara gently stopped her.

'It's okay, meri behtee, you just lie there and rest. It'll get better. Soon, it will get better. The ambulance is on its way.'

She saw Qaisara adjust the front ae her chest and, for a moment, she thought that one breast wis higher than the other. But then she blinked and it wis gone. She tried tae shake her heid tae say tae Qaisara, no, it nivir gets better. That's a lie. Nuthin ever gets better. But she wis too weak and, besides, her head felt as though it wis stuffed wi cotton wool jis like wan ae those toys that came swaddled in white. She touched her

34

forehead and realised that there were bandages on her hands. Pain filled her an she felt no pain. She let her neck go loose against the back ae the chair and her eyes drifted over tae where the hook wis slowly comin aff the wall. Gradually, as she stared, the hole became bigger until she could see right through tae the night beyond. She saw the deid horses, gallopin about in fields ae lang grass, she smelled the sweat on their skins. She saw hairs sproutin fae Qaisara's chin an, behind her, she heard the voice of the Malika-e-Tarunum loop and dive in the clean early mornin air. An she felt the cold waters ae the Clyde flow around her and take her down intae a darkness without end. An she saw hersel, thirty years on, her face puckered wi the long, burnin nights, her sleeves bundled up around the elbows an she wis movin behind the silver counter in a dance, which she had always known, would be hers.

The White Eagles

T he building was in the middle of nowhere. It was an almost square structure set on a flat, Balkan plain, so that the shadows of clouds moved over the terrain unimpeded until they reached the walls of the building when abruptly they broke up into shards, dark fingers, running over stone, tall weeds, the walls of a room painted yellow many years earlier. The cloud fingers slipped along cracks in the paint, opening up the gaps just a little more every time, so that, with each slippage, a new layer would be uncovered, an old skin peeled back to reveal the green beneath the yellow, the pink beneath both and the plaster beneath the pink. The hands ran through each room, skirted soft, relentless along the corridor and then they left the house and sank into one another as if nothing had happened, as though they had remained untouched by the broken stone, the shattered windows, the portraits skewed on the yellow. This happened many times during the day and the house had become a palace of sorts, a realm of light and shadow, where shape, alone, defined existence. At night, the house did not exist.

The land's lack of contour extended right to the horizon and so the shepherd was able to see the ruined building from miles away. At first, it appeared as a small dark spot, but as he drew closer it began to acquire shape, contour, reality. Then he was close enough to make out the gaps in the walls where once, at the beginning of spring, the windows would have swung open, allowing the house to breathe. He stopped by a rock and sat down. To his left, lay a small copse and close to the top of one of the trees, a large white bird preened its feathers. Every so often, its head would jerk upwards and its eyes become fixed on the house, on the shepherd, on something else . . .

He removed a stained leather pouch from the inside pocket of his jacket, laid it on the stone and thrust his index finger and thumb into it. Using his other hand, he drew out a pipe. He worked the tobacco into the belly of the pipe until it was ready to ignite. Letting the sunlight fall into his eyes, he crossed one leg over the other and began to smoke. The air was still and the smoke floated upwards in elegant white shafts which danced with the slivers of light.

Dragutin cleared his throat and carefully poured the clear sjivovic into small glasses. The others shifted a little on their wooden seats and tried to look down at the table. His face remained impassive, which made it even more difficult for his companions to remain serious. Sanja began to giggle and was nudged in the ribs by Radovan. Dragutin, however, performed his task meticulously, as though he were some kind of toastmaster. He leaned across the table and filled four glasses. A gentle, aniseed breeze flitted around the tablecloth while the spring sunshine shed an even light across the plain. Sanja sat facing Ramo, with Radovan and Dragutin at opposite ends. Radovan and Dragutin always ended up sitting opposite each other. They joked that it was because both men wore their hair at shoulder-length and Radovan's hair was as red as Dragutin's was black. Radovan's eyes were deep brown while Dragutin's held the same blue as those of Ramo. The three of them were like counterpoints. They formed a kind of harmony. At last, the glasses were full. Dragutin had managed not to spill a drop. He set the half-empty bottle down and moved to his seat. But he did not sit and, instead, he raised his glass, paused for a moment and, then, in a voice deep with pomposity, he proposed a toast.

'To Ramo. To Sanja. To Ramo and Sanja.'

Laughter erupted around the table, then dissolved as they downed the sjivovic.

'To us all!' Ramo shouted and they drank again.

Setting their glasses down, they began to eat. It was a meal of flat loaves and cheese and a few kebabs which lay on a plate, but there, as their young voices danced on air before the old house, it seemed like a feast. A few high, white clouds moved slowly through the deep, April blue. The shutters around the windows had been thrown open and the roof tiles burned red beneath the already-warm sun. A few early insects darted around the table, the flowers, the ears of the people.

Dragutin broke the silence of the meal.

'So, when's the wedding to be?'

Ramo shrugged.

'We haven't set a date yet. Autumn sometime, maybe. Autumn next year, after my course is finished.'

'You don't seem very sure,' Sanja commented, her mouth full of bread.

Ramo turned to her.

'I'm sure. It's just the date. It depends on my getting a job. And, then, when I can get time off.'

Sanja nodded and shrugged at the same time.

'Your job.'

'Well, I can't just toss everything up in the air.'

'No.'

Dragutin intervened.

'Hey! I didn't mean to start an argument, already. There'll be enough time for that.'

'It's not an argument. It's just a question of priorities,' Sanja said.

'She always has to have the last word.'

Dragutin held his hands up.

'Okay! Okay! It's my fault. I take the blame.'

Ramo and Sanja smiled, first at Dragutin with his long, black hair fanning out over his shoulders and then at each other. And then they both looked away. Sanja reached out and touched Ramo's hand. Her complexion was olive, her eyes, deep-brown marbles and she had a nose which an unkind person might have called parrot-like. But Ramo loved every part of her and it was her very avian qualities which endeared her to him. Sometimes, he felt as though, at any moment, they might both take to the air and soar high above the plain, the city, the dark river to the east. Perhaps it was something to do with them being opposites, at least in appearance. He was tall and had cropped, blond hair, while his eyes (the eyes into which she loved to gaze) were May blue. It was still April, but already she could feel his eyes begin to acquire the perfect colours which they would attain a month from now. She didn't know why, it must have been a certain quality of the light at that particular time of year or maybe it was just her imagination, but whenever she gazed into Ramo's eyes, especially during May, she would feel the light stream from them in torrents of pure blue and roll across her in soft waves.

Behind him, along the horizon, she could make out the gleaming minarets of Gornji Donje, the sedate, pink domes slumbering beneath the sky as they had slumbered for five hundred years. Interspersed among the minarets and steeples were the more modern buildings of the shoe factory, the tee-shirt factory and the local council buildings. The café in the square where they had first met. Minaret shadows, the smell of strong coffee, conversation. She worked in the café where Ramo and his friends would go during breaks from the holiday job he was doing in the shoe factory. The three of them would come in together and order bread and coffee. Ramo, Dragutin and Radovan. Three friends on the brink of life. Actually, she'd noticed Radovan first, with his shock of red hair and his overconfidence. The easy certainties of friendship. Dragutin had always struck her as being an intellectual, his every expression, movement, thought seeming tainted by his sense of irony. She'd always thought that Ramo had been the most attractive to her because of his plain humanity (that and his eyes). If the café was quiet, she might sit with them, just listening at first, but later joining in their conversations. And gradually, her life had become linked with theirs. And especially with Ramo's. He had come to know her family and they liked him, especially her uncle. Sanja lived with her mother, her two sisters, one older and one younger than her, and an uncle who lived in the basement. He spent his time, listening to music and attempting to play the violin. He had never made anything of his life and it was thought that he had been damaged at birth. When their mother's back was turned, Sanja's sisters would tease and taunt him and lead him along false trails and, sometimes, Sanja would join in and then, later, she would feel intensely guilty. But guilt was worse than useless, she thought. It was what you did that counted. Or, maybe, nothing counted. Ramo was different. He got on with the old man and would comfort him after they'd done with their teasing, and Sanja would hear them laughing and singing down in the basement. Ramo would bring her uncle cassettes to play on his music system and, occasionally, she had watched them dance together, old-style, wheeling, silent dances.

During the course of the two years in which they had known each other, Ramo had become almost as familiar to her as the city. It seemed almost beautiful there, from a distance. The town seemed to tremble slightly on the edge of the land, as though it was a mirage. As though at any moment, it might take off and fly into the emptiness like some great eagle, feather white in the afternoon sun. It was always

41

like that in spring, when the cool currents met the warm, sending the air up into ripples like those in the middle of a concerto, in the quiet bit. During the course of her life, she had seen nearly twenty springs, but now they seemed to have merged into one another so that she could no longer tell which had been which. Time had become compressed in her memory where everything was pink and white. Pink dolls, white dresses, pink domes, white minarets. It was locked away, safe.

Ramo was Muslim and she a Serb. But, in Bosnia, inter-marriage had never been an issue. For that matter, she thought, as she glanced around the table, Dragutin was a Croat and red-haired Radovan was Serbian. There were politicians who asserted that different ethnic groups should live in separate enclaves. The national socialists in Belgrade wanted a Greater Serbia, while the democratic fascism of Zagreb's ruling party yearned for a Croatia, purged of every-thing Byzantine and Islamic. One was backed by Russia, the other by Germany. It was really quite simple. It was not a matter of age-old hatreds, but of money and the control of money. Yet the politicians' voices were at once seductive and powerful and, even as they divided, they caused other unities to form. They were an alternative music, one without discord of thought. She'd known people, friends, who had gone off into the woods to join one or other of the paramilitary groups and who now liked nothing better than to strut around, dressed in American khaki and British boots. Bazooka-heads, she called them, though not to their faces. Everyone seemed to carry a sense of grievance, but no one seemed really to know where it had come from.

Beyond the town, far to the east, the Drina flowed by, deep, black, silent. As a child, she'd had nightmares about the great river. In her dream, it would pulse and swell and burst its banks, rolling towards her as it covered the land with its blackness. Just at the moment of suffocation, of death-within-the-dream, she would awaken, drenched in dark sweat. Sanja shivered there, in the spring sunshine. Pulled herself from nightmare. Radovan had gone inside the house and had switched on the radio, and the sounds of the ilahija filtered out into the yard. He appeared in the doorway, his eyes closed, his long, red hair swaying and his arms doing a half-dance in tune with the violin. His lips moved silently, mouthing the words of the sevdalinka.

> *When I went to Benbasa*
> *To Benbasa for water*
> *I took a small white lamb.*
> *A small white lamb with me.*
> *Because of the suffering and passion of love*
> *Because of sorrow and longing, I went and looked*
>   *everywhere*
> *To try to see my darling . . .*

She was startled out of her reverie by Dragutin's voice. He was relentless and, once he got talking, it would take a steam-roller or a tank to stop him.

'Well, whatever you decide,' he said, glancing meaningfully at both of them. 'Remember, I will have to travel all the way from Sarajevo.'

'Your course,' cut in Sanja, still slightly fazed.

Dragutin nodded.

'Comparative Religion. And Economics.'

He almost shrugged as he said it, but something stopped him. A shadow ran across his face, his chiselled nose, the ends of his black lanks. The shadow filled his eyes so that, for a moment, he seemed like a man drowning in darkness. No one made any response to what he had said. They continued eating, drinking, breathing in the clear spring air and there were no shadows on the land but a strange sense of dislocation had settled upon the table and on the house behind it. Dragutin looked up at the ancient building with its two-hundred-year-old walls and, as he looked, he searched desperately for some sense of permanence, some sign that might dispel his fears, as the smile of a parent or the shrug of an elder brother might. The sound of a violin was issuing from deep in the interior of the house. He half-attempted to recognise the tune. 'Sedam Puta Lola Se Oženio'. He made out the fiddle-playing of Alia Salkić. The music seemed to hover between two or, possibly, more melodies. The notes flitted across a number of progressions, triads, triplets . . . it seemed to sink into the day so that Dragutin was no longer certain whether a violin was actually being played or whether it was just the breeze against the old stone. He saw a cat sleek out from under the wood store. It moved slowly, like a leopard. First one paw, then the next. One, two, three, four. The sun blasted down on the earth of the yard, on the fur of the cat's back, on the air which had been so light, just a moment earlier. He felt a sense of oppression sink into his gut. It spread out and filled the courtyard, the house, the fields, the eyes of the cat. He closed his eyes. Didn't dare open them. Saw only red. Blood red.

The shepherd moved among the stones. Picked his way from one broken room to the next. The picture of the girl lay twisted on the yellow wall. The shepherd gazed at it. He found himself unable to look away; it was as though he was gazing into one of those religious shrines. She had the eyes of a saint. Not an angel, a saint. Earth brown and deep beyond even morning dreams. He let his head tilt to one side, allowed his lids to half-fall. The girl was all he could see. Everything, the patch of sky above the smashed roof, the dark, dead walls, the cracks in the plaster, all of it collapsed into one, clear image. The girl, eight years old, smiling, unaware of time. Totally wise. Playing on the lawn. Spring. Her freckled shoulders bathed in sunshine. Noon. No shadows. Perfect.

Sanja ran up to the bush which marked the boundary of her garden. Beyond this, she'd been told never to go. The dark spirits of the field were crouching behind the bush, just waiting for some foolish, ignorant girl to wander through. Then they'd take her and she'd never be seen again. So her grandma had told her, countless times. And now she was growing old enough to wonder, to question simple truths. But the fear was still there. She reached out her hand and touched the new leaves which had sprouted along the outstretched arms of the bush. They were green and felt soft like the feet of babies. Surely, such a young bush could harbour no evil. She looked up at the sky. Surely, God would protect her. The bush had been created by God and so had the evil creatures, so what did that mean? She wasn't sure, but it didn't matter because it was spring and she had her game and nothing else was of any account. She was about to turn back, but stopped. The bush seemed to beckon her on. The soft velour of its young leaves, the hard, twisted wood of its branches, the shadow template of itself which hovered along the garden boundary, all seemed to be challenging her to walk through the gate and see what lay beyond. A chill gust blew through the leaves. Through the white feathers of the eagle which sat in the trees beyond the gate. She shivered and let go of the bush. Stepped back, one pace. Two. The bush quivered and was still. She drew her arms around her body. The eagle watched her. She had the urge to turn around, to check the old house was still there. Didn't dare. Just in case. What if it wasn't? What then? Her past, gone, her present, non-existent. No. She mustn't look back. She must never, ever look back. She closed her eyes and walked through the gate.

*   *   *

45

The shepherd rubbed his eyes and moved away from the portrait. When he looked again, it seemed suddenly to have gone dull, to have become anonymous. Its images held no meaning; it would be easy to kill. There was a stain across the bottom of the frame. Red on gold. The colours of Christ in heaven. The shepherd drew his fingertip down over the dried stain and then examined the skin. The contours had not changed. Lines running into infinity. The collective curse of his ancestors, waves of idiocy, each blindly following the next into oblivion. He backed away from the dead painting. His leg caught on a fallen rafter and he tumbled backwards. A sudden pain at the back of his head. The light in the sky. The small sky, contracting in his skull. Yellow on blue. Fake.

They were walking along a ridge. A forested gorge opened up to their right, while, on the other side, the plain stretched to the sky. Ramo took her hand and they descended a narrow half-path which had been scuffed out by the feet of other, earlier lovers. The light down here was filtered, verdant. The scent of cherry blossom drifted into her, softening. She steadied herself against the tree-trunks. Her shoes were really not up to this. They would be ruined. But she didn't care. They reached the base of the gorge, which was flat like a miniature valley. The entire crevasse had been created by some enormous bomb during the Second World War. She couldn't remember which side had dropped it or whether it might not have been dropped at all, but, rather, might have flown in like a rocket. Did they have rockets in those days?, she wondered. They stopped at a shaded spot beneath a tall beech tree and laid out the blanket. Ramo lay down, hands behind his head, and gazed up at the sky, closed his eyes, opened them, saw her above him, smiled. Birdsong filled the air and yet still there seemed an infinity of space above them as they lay there on the chequered blanket which had been her mother's and drank in the blue. Far above, a flock of white birds tracked across the sky. For a moment, Ramo wondered if they might be white eagles, but then he dismissed the thought. The mountains where the white eagles lived lay too far to the east. She let out a sigh. He turned to her, put his arm around her.

'What is it?' he asked, quietly.

She glanced away.

'Nothing. It just seems so far away.'

'The time will pass. A year-and-a-half. It's not so long. Think what you were doing a year-and-a-half back. Where you were. Doesn't seem very long ago, does it?'

'I know. But this is different.'

'Of course, it is. Because we have something to look forward to. That's why. That's the only reason.'

He half-rolled over and kissed her on the lips. A gentle, spring kiss.

His lips tasted salty. Dry. She sat up and opened the bottle of water. Offered him a glass. Watched him drink.

The bushes rose above them, already heavily coated in new leaves. And the trees above the bushes.

'What are the women like in Sarajevo?'

He shrugged, didn't meet her gaze.

'Like women everywhere. More sophisticated, maybe. They sit at cafés and sip coffee and cognac while, behind them, the ezan echoes across the city from the dzamije Ghazi Husrev Beg. It's a city. You get all kinds of personalities. All kinds of people.'

He paused.

'. . . It's the same with the men,' he added, quickly.

She nodded slowly and looked up. The leaves on the bushes rustled gently, the air lifting an invisible skin from their surfaces.

She looked straight at him.

'You'll never leave me, will you?'

He sat up and hugged her to him. His deep-blue eyes.

'Don't be silly. I've been there three years already. I'm not suddenly going to go off with someone else.'

He said it casually, like he was talking about another person. A different couple.

'. . . Anyway, we're going to be married next year. I love you.'

He said it too quickly, *I love you*, just like that.

She felt a smile begin to form across her cheeks. He frowned at her, a mock frown. Because she was crying. Didn't know why. Just was. He wiped her tears with his index finger. Gently lifted them off her skin. Kissed them. She flung her arms around his shoulders and pulled him to her. Closed her eyes. Felt more tears run down. The taste of salt again, amidst the green.

The shepherd opened his eyes. Saw a slab of wood, varnished brown, stretching far above him. He could make out the narrow lines of the brush. Behind the lines . . .

He lifted up his head. His neck ached and a sharp pain fired through his temples. Using his arms, he levered himself up. The wooden slab became a door and the door was slightly ajar. Beyond the door lay darkness. He reached out and pushed. The door swung open as though it had been oiled just the day before. The shepherd peered through the gap. A staircase led downwards. He couldn't see the bottom. Pushing the door completely open, he wedged a broken piece of rafter beneath the handle. In spite of the missing roof, the light was dim, the air stale. The floor of the house had remained intact in places so that shafts of light poured like waterfalls through the dust. As his eyes grew accustomed to the murk, he began to move around in what once had been a basement or a cellar. Perhaps a wine cellar. Or the place where a lodger might stay. Or might have stayed. Anything was possible, since the house was no longer a place. Like all pasts it was infinitely malleable. It seemed to have been deserted for years. His sandals creaked on the bits of wood which had fallen into the cellar. Then something more substantial came under his foot. He bent down and picked it up. Held it before him. It was a violin. Cracked across the body, its varnish dull but the strings still intact. He ran his finger along the surface, felt the slip of contour upon contour. He tipped it upside-down to let the dust fall out. Flipped it back again. Put it under his chin. Plucked a string. A flat, dank sound. He moved his hand across all four strings. Tuned it by twisting the small wooden keys above the neck. The sounds were still half-formed. Not flat, but not quite right. He felt a desire to find the bow. He began to search among the fragments of furniture, some of which had fallen in from the floor above; others looked as though they might deliberately have been stored in the cellar (or maybe had belonged to the lodger). Clothes, ornaments, lightbulbs, sheets printed with musical scores; the detritus of a life, of many possible lives, held no interest for him. He needed only to find the horsehair and wood of the bow to make the violin play again. To complete the cycle of the concerto. Just as he had no sheep, the house held no music.

Ramo helped pile the last of the sandbags up against the walls of the house as darkness fell swiftly across the plain. With the darkness would come the flares and the deep pitch of mortars tearing the black air apart. He turned to Sanja. The perspiration dripped from his brow. His tee-shirt announced *Bjelo Dugme* in large, white letters, which stood out even more because the rest of the shirt, once scarlet, was now soaked in the darker red of sweat. The White Button Rock Concert. It seemed like another world.

Everyone had gone. Her family – her mother, her two sisters, a simple-minded uncle – had departed for the capital several weeks earlier. Sanja had been meant to lock up the house and follow them, but, for some reason, she had found herself unable to leave. And then Ramo had come back to get her, to take her, finally, to Sarajevo, where the orchestra played, daily, opposite the morgue. Ramo had told her that some of the musicians' hands had been bandaged and bloody and yet, as dusk had fallen and the bullets had outnumbered the birds, they had played their best ever and, in the fading light, an old woman had yelled out that she could see the souls of the dead rise and soar, high above the circle of mountains, and that the souls had outnumbered the bullets. But the conductor of the orchestra had calmed the old woman, saying that the reason the souls outnumbered the bullets was that one bullet destroyed two people: the one who was shot and the one who fired; the former in this life, the latter in the next. Ramo had said to her that he thought the conductor had lied to comfort the woman. The one who fired the gun did not suffer anything.

Even the cat had left. She'd seen it running. Had called after it, but it had not turned back. She had known it would not return. In the days before it left the house, it had already changed its allegiance. It had begun to go out scavenging for food from the villages which lay to the east and would only return deep in the night. And then one day it did not return. Sometimes, she wished she was a cat with black and white patches and green eyes. But then she didn't. His voice cut in on her. Tired, desperate.

'Why do you insist on staying here? Everyone has left. Everyone. Even the old, the ancient, the crones. Only you remain in this dark house.'

'You loved it, once.'

He threw his arms out, exasperated.

'It's not a question of love. It's a question of danger. You have to get away.'

50

'So why are you hanging around, if you're so worried?'

Ramo looked at the already-purple sky and let out a long sigh. The Ice-cream Man had been spotted in the area. The leader of the White Eagles Serbian paramilitary group, the bearded butcher, who once had smiled and sold ice cones to children, now was roaming like a beast over the plain.

'I should've stayed with Dragutin in Sarajevo. Could've helped run the schools. They are still running, even though half the teachers are dead. I heard the Kosovo morgue had no more room left and they'd begun to burn bodies outside the Lion Cemetery. They're closing in on the city itself. And when they do, that'll be the end. There'll be no more frontline, because the back line will have gone. This place will be overrun with the bastards.'

'Have you seen Radovan recently?' she asked.

He shook his head.

'We kind of lost touch. I heard he had gone east.'

'East.'

'Yeah. Across the river. To Belgrade.'

He paused, then went on.

'Actually, we had an argument.'

'About what?'

He shrugged and looked away.

'About nothing. And everything.'

He glared at her.

'I was worried about you. I came back for you, to take you out of here, to bring you to Sarajevo. You think the Chetniks will spare you because you are a Serb? They won't ask. And if you tell them, they won't believe you. They'll just shoot. Or worse.'

'I'm not a Serb.'

'You are a Serb. A Christian.'

'I'm a human being. This is my home. Bosnia-Herzegovina is my home.'

Ramo laughed cynically.

'What does that mean? Nothing. Absolutely nothing. Don't you understand? You are no longer an individual, with job, family, future. There is no such thing as a citizen. A comrade. Those great dreams have died here, on this earth, on this plain.' He kicked a lump of soil, which exploded into powder.

'When they find out – or are told – that you've been with a Muslim . . .'

'I'm your fiancée.'

'Oh, for God's sake!'

He paused, as if half-regretting what he had said. Then he resumed, in a gentler tone.

'You sound like Dragutin. That's the sort of thing he kept saying. It's why he stayed around. He believed in logic and in the scientific progression of economic forces. People act as they do because they're placed in situations in which they cannot act otherwise or, if they do act otherwise, then it's of no consequence to what happens. But according to them, he's just a Croat. And you're a Serb. It's the logic of the ice-cream salesman. White and black. Smiles and punishment. Pity and fear.'

She gazed at her feet and at the earth beneath. Behind her, the notes of a solitary violin. He laughed.

'The bombs are about to go off around us and we're talking philosophy. Look, you're correct and Dragutin's correct. You're both absolutely one hundred per cent correct. And I agree with you. But it doesn't matter. But it's too late for that. Things are out of control. People. No one will save you.'

'Yes . . . too late.'

Sanja was not looking at him. She was gazing beyond him, at something behind his figure, something already half-hidden in shadow. Ramo fought the urge to turn around. She was often like that, nowadays. It had got worse since her family had left. She'd insisted on staying. It was madness. They were right in the middle of the frontline. In no-man's land. Only a crazy person would have stayed here. Even the stray dogs had left. Even the rats. Her uncle was meant to have been the simple-minded one. And, yet, it was Sanja who was still here, in the old house, defenceless in the middle of the plain. And so was he. I'm as mad as she is, thought Ramo.

She glared at him. Her fists were clenched at her sides. There were tears in her eyes. Her voice was cracking apart.

'What the Hell is wrong with us? We used to be friends, we were part of each other's families. I'm not saying there weren't problems. Belgrade and Sarajevo. But it was just football. Nothing more.'

Ramo turned slowly away from her. He had let his hair grow so that his long, blond locks sleeked over his shoulders. His gaze fell far away, beyond the copse, the gorge, the valley and towards the east and the darkening sky which hung beyond the horizon. He spoke quietly.

'It's no longer a game.'

'But what's wrong with us? I mean, us. We never used to argue . . .'

'Yes, we did. It's just that those things weren't really important, when you look back.'

Her voice broke.

'I stayed, because I knew you would come. I wanted us to be together.'

Her shoulders shook. She was sobbing. He moved forwards, intending to touch her. But it seemed awkward, unnatural. He stopped. She turned and began to walk back towards the house. He held out his hand but she never saw it. The breeze caught his hair and swept the locks across his face, hiding the perfect, May blue of his eyes. Smoke rose from where the town had been. Fires from within the city cast a pink glow over the sky's edge, a pulsing light which swooped across the plain until the colour of the entire sky had changed and there was no longer any blue left. There was something in the wind. A scent without smell. She felt naked. For the first time, she wanted to be far away. To be thousands of miles away from this plain, this valley where everything had to be revealed and then run to its eternity. Where there were no walls, no dykes, only the sky with its elusive stars and the land steeped brown in old blood.

That night, as the guns pounded the villages which lay on the other side of the horizon, Sanja read out recipes from an Italian cookbook while the sound of the violin flowed upward in waves from the cellar.

The shepherd had not found the bow but, tucked away in the corner and, virtually undamaged, he did come across a music centre. He wiped the dust off with his index finger. It was black, plastic, new. Expecting nothing, he pushed the power button. Turned his back. A rash of high-frequency static burst across the room. He spun round. The cuboid machine sparkled with tiny lights, green and red, so that in the semi-darkness of the cellar, it resembled an airstrip. The walls of the room, invisible till now, began to glow with a strange, pullulating movement. The hacking sound of machine-gun fire came from far off, and the tear of a mortar entering the earth, from nearby. The sounds seemed to come from all directions at once, to be possessed of no focus. But they merged with the electric of the machine, jarring each pulse, staggering the troughs, so that they reached one frequency and then stayed there. Then the static faded slowly away and, from it, there emerged the sound of a lone violin. Making sure it, would take his weight, the shepherd sat on a low stool, hitched up his left knee and rested his bearded chin in the palm of his left hand. His eyes closed. The playing was slow, soporific, modal almost. A woman's voice accompanied the solo. 'Aljamiado'. A lament from the seventeenth century, perhaps by Hasan Qa'imi Baba, or else by Ala 'al-Din 'Ali b. 'Abdallah al-Busnawi Thabit of Uziče. The shepherd felt himself begin to sink below the level of the cellar, into the mud beneath and into the rock below that and then down, along streams of magma into the core itself, iron black like the mortar bombs which were descending around the house. The violin was joined by other instruments: sargija, accordion, drums. The tune ran along the circle of a mode, slicing out new melismas with each spin. Then it splayed out into harmony, chords, majors and minors. 'Alaj volim orati'. The shepherd was in the song.

> *My darling gives me tiny kisses*
> *the toothmarks will be recognised.*
> *My mother will recognise that I was caressed.*
> *My darling, you have one fault*
> *that you left, that you left*
> *a wound on my heart, a wound on my heart*

With each thud, the playing grew steadily faster until it was 6/8, 12/8, 24/8, allegro staccato, impossible runs of notes screaming upward from the cellar, massing in plumed waves to drive back the blind iron, to reverse the explosions, the death, to make hate implode until only love would remain.

Smoke filled the air, a burnt, pink mist which covered the entire plain. It was a mixture of dawn and the breath of mortars and yet it erupted from something far deeper. And now the plain, like the mountains before them, would become a realm of death and fallen minarets. And the people ... there would be no people. Just emptiness and distant flocks of birds. *Kajda.* A lone voice, high-wiring on a short-wave radio band perhaps, waxing, waning and then fading out altogether. Eventually, the smoke would lift and the flat bowl of the valley would be revealed. But the plain would have changed, then in the time of bombs and would no longer know of the house, the cat, Sanja, Ramo, Dragutin, the others. It would not be a valley of life, of disparate lives which once had swirled, without boundaries, beneath the sky.

> *The mountain nymph shouts from the top of Trebevic,*
> *'Is Sarajevo where it used to be?*
> *Is the inn near the Moric's house?*
> *Do the boys from Sarajevo drink wine?*
> *Is Mara, the barmaid, serving them?*
> *Is Mara wearing three flowers?'*
>
> *The first, a blue one, is the one that attracts the bey.*
> *The second, a yellow one, is the one that angers the*
>   *ladies.*
> *The third, a white one, is the one that the girls divide.*

The shepherd sat down on the floor of the cellar as bombs began to fall around the house and he let his head sink into his hands. The bow moved across the violin strings, faster and faster, merging with the beat of the mortars. The bow which he had not been able to find. The sound of his failure thudded inside his skull. He could feel the force of it tear the skin from his face.

Mechanically, relentlessly, he began to beat his forehead against the stone wall of the cellar. Faster, harder. Again, again, again, until he felt like vomiting. Until he felt as though he would throw the whole thing up. The sound of the violin, the cellar, the house, the cat, the mortars, the plain, the sky . . . everything.

A low whistle began to pierce through the fog, a distant wind, perhaps from the mountains. Then, like the sound of night-mare, it grew wider until the strange, unified note filled up the entire valley. The note became an earthquake and, some fifty metres in front of the house, a long line of tanks emerged from the fog. The convoy had a beginning, but seemed to have no end. They were brand-new, probably just out of the factory, and they moved along the ground like vertebrae. In one action, the whole train came to a stop. There was no movement. Everything remained constant in the mist. The old house with its shuttered windows and sandbags, its only strength lying in the memories it held silently within, a dangerous strength; across the flat yard, just a dog's crawl away, the dun-metal power of the tank. In time it, too, would accumulate memory, a terrible, screaming memory. Its pasts were yet to be generated; for now, it was a tabula rasa and so anything was possible. The death of a country, the death of a soul. But, always, it would be there at the end. The last archangel. The turret of the leading tank circled round, as though searching for prey. Then a helmet emerged, then a huge figure clad in full battle gear. He clambered down from the turret and leapt on to the ground. The top of his head was swathed in metal. The frame of the helmet was skirted with cropped red hair. In his right hand, a pistol. He was followed by more soldiers, all clad in the same uniforms. They carried heavier weapons: rifles, machine-guns, a British-made bazooka. He approached the house, and stopped at the door. From somewhere, possibly behind him, possibly in front, he thought he heard the sound of a violin. For a moment, he listened to the tune, trying to make it out. The recognition spread in waves across his face.

Sevdalinka, he whispered. *Sevdalinka*.

He paused for a moment in the doorway and glanced back at the armoured column. His soldiers stood a few metres behind him, guns in hand, ready. The mist rolled and swirled around the tanks, casting a morning pentimento over the metal. He wheeled back. The door was green. Old, wooden.

The music behind it, Sevdalinka. Memories. A dangerous power. With one long swing of his boot, he smashed it open. He ventured in, pistol first. He was followed by six or seven others, all of whom, like their commander, wore the symbol of the white eagle on their right upper arm.

The shepherd climbed up the steps leading from the cellar. He walked across the room with its walls painted yellow (the portrait of the girl was gone) and left the house. Outside, it had begun to snow. For a while, he followed the tracks which the tanks had made but already the deep ruts were beginning to be obliterated by the snow, which was now falling fast, thick like milk from the mountains, so that the shepherd was unable to see much beyond six steps in front of him. Every so often, a gust of wind would tease the snow into dancing pirouettes. The sound of the šota swirled around him, faint at first but then louder so that his feet began to slide and slip over the white. Faster and faster, the šota danced through the frozen water and the shepherd moved upon the snow lake which the valley had become. And through its insistent rhythm, came the voices of the women singing silence. The shepherd closed his eyes which had seen so much, forsaken as he had been for so long, and he wandered away from the awful, searing tank steps, away from the booming sound of the guns, the burning screams of the town, the cracking of white on the horizon, fingers being broken. He began to climb the only hill there was, its gradual incline like the slope into nightmare, up to where the old bomb had created another, an alternative valley in the midst of the first. There, perhaps, might he find his sheep. His lambs. White, innocent, bleeding. Perhaps, there at last would he be able to rest. To drink in the love which for so long he had given out. He was weary and needed to slumber. To lay his head in the lap of his mother and to rest. To sleep in melisma. The loud voices of the women swept him up the slope and down into the gorge, where there would be no snow, no wind and where the trees would always have leaves. He trod along a narrow, non-tempered track of pure tone, a path of light amidst the darkness which was falling in thick curtains of night and smoke over the valley. Over the market-place café, lying deserted in bullets, over the broken dzamiyas where the Mevlud would sound no more, into the ezan silenced in the explosion of deep night rockets. And there, in the cleavage of his mother, would the shepherd lay down his locks grown to his shoulders and there would he sleep. After the tanks, beyond the mist, he would fiddle away and scream the ganga of light, the harmonic dissonance of love.

Barely visible through the thick smoke, two figures ran silently towards the line of trees which skirted the edge of the gorge. They were holding hands. The figures moved rapidly between two trunks and then vanished.

Imbolc

J is beyond the leathad which fell behind our hoose, there wis a wee coille. It wis aw the kina trees that would shed their leaves in the autumn and, at that time, you could see richt through them and they seemed aw lighted up and open. But it wisnae autumn, it wis spring and the leaves were sproutin all over the place like the saft wee lambs up on the moor. I wisane supposed tae venture onywhur close tae the coille, for ma grannie said thur wur wild deer that roamed aboot in it and that they wud attack onyone who went near thur young, especially in spring. Some hings were oota boonds and no jis places. Fowk an tids were beyond the pale as weil. Like Big Bridie fae the craft across the wa'ar. Ah wisnae allowed tae talk aboot her, no even tae mention her name if Grannie wis payin heed. It wisnae jis ma grannie, aw the grannies, the auld wumin, they never talked aboot her save the odd comment like *An Diabhal toirt leis i!* or other such curses. Aye. Big Bridie wis the scorn o the glen. We lads wur aw feart ae her, ah don't know how. We never looked her in the ee when she passed us on the path. Naw, no wi her rid rid locks. We shook oor heids jis as oor grannies did. Naw, naw, *She'll go tae the divil, aye*, her n her callants, her big bothy boys aye n there wur feck o them tae. Big Bridie wuid jis toss back her rid heid and laugh that boomin laugh ae hers and the soon ae it wud echo through the glen and set aw the grannies fae wan end tae th'other tae shakin thur heids and tut-tuttin and missin the slip-stitches in thur knittin.

Weel, ah must've been aleeven or twalt at the time, ah canny remember rightly since as the oors kinda went aw funny aroon then. It wis a gae spring morn an ah wis playin wi ma baw ootside ma grannie's gate (she widnae let me play in the garden cause ah knacked her floors, which she wis gae pruidae, aye she used tae win local competitions, so she did, wi her floors the brichtest an her kails the biggest in the glen ah weil remember ma Grannie Urquart stonin haudin a kail in yan hond ae a great big tulip in th'other an that wis before yer fertilisers it wis aw crap then ah mean guid crap, the crap o the coos an the sheep and sometimes, aye sometimes thur's nae shame in admittin it, the kak e human bains as weil). Onyhow, ah wis kickin ma baw aboot in the lang, wild gress o the beinn when aw ae a sudden this notion comes intae ma heid tae venture doon intae the coille. Ah dinnae know how it came intae ma heid ah dinnae know but it did, mibbee it wis the guid fowk, mibbee, ah couldnae say no noo ah couldnae. So kickin ma wee baw a wee bit further every time jis a wee bit further, aw the while keepin a gae close ee on the kitchen ae the craft in case ma grannie might spie me an caw me back intae the hoose an it wud be nae supper and early tae bed. It's nae that ah wantit tae begowk ma guid grannie. It wis jis that ah wis a wee boy and ah wis up tae wee boy's swicks. So there ah wis, movin towards the coille, an neither mon nor beast nearby no even the shepies no even the troddles ae sheep no even the braith ae a sheep let alane that ae a carle. Weil, ah got tae the wood's edge and paused. Jis fur a moment, jis enough to feel timorsome. But ah wisnae gan tae go back noo, no noo ah wisnae so ah gathert up ma baw ma freen aw yella wi green stripes it wis an ah walked like a mon straucht intae the coille.

The trees wur gae heich, the cabers, the blae lift. An then thur wur some which wur jis scrunts like they'd jis stapped growin, they wur stunted, like grumphie aud carles. But the shanks wur no like that. They wur aw smilin a bit like ma gran.

Aud, but freendlie. Aye. An thur leaves wur sproutin oot in aw directions, saft, green fingers shakin honds wi me aye like wan wean tae another. Ah fain likt the touch o those young leaves all over ma shooders, ma back aye an ah took aff ma shaes an trod wi ma bar fit alang the saft grun. Aye, it wis saft wi aud leaves, last year's faw an the faw ae the year afore and the wan afore that. In fact the mair ah thocht on't, the mair ah realised that ah wis plowterin through history. Mibbee somewhur beneath ma fit thur lay Saint Brendan's Island as ah'd been tailt by ma grannie. That's whur aw the magic came fae. It didnae occur tae me that, come autumn, all those young leaves would be drappin aaf nineteen-tae-the-dozen. It didnae occur tae me then but it does noo, aye so it does. Ah couldnae see through tae th'other side so ah wuntit tae go through tae th'other side it's gae strynge how that happens tae a wean and it still happens tae the mon because we never really grow up no really no like those bastarts ye see in the stories ah mean the tippie stories whur they grow tae a resolution, naw that nivir happens in real life. Nivir.

Ah looked back tae see if ah could spot ma grannie's hoose ma hoose whur ah'd been born an raised an thur wis jis me'n ma grannie, ma granpa hovin been kilt in the War ah dinnae remember which war but it wis some big stour or other. Ma maw . . . och, nivir mind aboot that. Ah looked back an couldnae see ocht. A shither ran through ma body an ah felt like greetin but ah didnae cause ah knew it wuid do nae guid. It nivir did. Ah wis treadin through the coille aw careful like, wan foot after the other, balancin wi ma baw tucked alow ma car airm an ma richt aw balancin like in the circus since the grun wis aw bumpy what wi stanes an tufts ae grass an the like. Aye, an then ah saw a pad, a wee road, weil it wis mair like a track, a trinkit track, aw ruts an bits ae heather comin awa aw over wi iteodha an hawthorne aw towerin over reachin doon so low that, wean as ah wis, ah hud tae bow ma heid as ah walked. The passage wis narra an low jis like two honds perched in prayer like the minister in the kirk. But this wis nae kirk. Aw ae a sudden, ah came across a stane. A big, tall stane. Moss wis growin all over it which made it seem gae ault. Near wan side ae the stane wis a hole, jis big enough tae fit ma hond and nae mair. It ran richt through the stane, richt through. Ah stretched ma airms roon the clach chaol, àrd so that ma lisk wis pressin up agin the cool rock and ah wis jis able tae haud honds through the hole. It wis gae strange, but ah didnae want tae let go, ah felt as if it wis some other body's hond ah wis claspin on th'other side ae the stonin stane. Ah wis feart but ah wis also gae blithe an a terrible drùis seemed tae come fae the big, cauld stane and tae rise up through ma wee stanes and alang ma tadger, the insides ae ma thighs, ma belly, ma back, richt the way up tae ma heid which began poundin it wis like Cailleach a' Gheamhraidh bangin her hammer on the grun tae steek the earth fur the wold month aye, thump-thump-thump ma heid pounded wi the beat ae ma hairt the blood bellowin in ma lugs O Goad whit wis this the sow-thistles at the base ae the stane wur stingin ma bare legs but ah didnae care ah didnae care it made the torrent intae wan, flowin richt through ma body, fae ma tadger, which wis sprung like the cabers up above, aw the way doon tae ma taes an aw the way up tae ma tap. An in ma mind wis a picture, a movin picture ae Big Bridie, her ae the craft across the wa'ar, her wi the big breists tae big fur hur ane guid they said and her big milky thighs and she wis movin an smilin and ah wis movin an smilin there agin the stane wi ma ees shut tight an ma back straicht as a silver tree. O Goad O Goad O Goad an the rock wis rippin through ma breeks but ah didnae care naw ah didnae cause ah always ae fancied Big Bridie so did aw the boays thereaboots but ma grannie an they said she wis gan wi aw kinds ae billies ten or mair years awder an her aye in the fields and clais an by the baunk ae the burns a' beucaich aw fuck an ah wantit Big Bridie ah wantit her hot, braw thighs tae clasp aroon ma back ah wantit her tae ram me aye ah did jis like she rammed them big carles in thur creakin bothies aifter the coos hud been taken hame tae the coo-shed. An the stonin stane wis Bridie wi her rid hair jis like mine an she wis smilin at me, me, wee Scott who wis jis ootae his grannie's braw airms cause his maa'd gan aff wi some gallus Sasunnach so his grannie had telt him. An he couldnae even remember her face naw, no even whun he wis fawin asleep no even whun he wis hingin, no even whun he wis feelin like greetin but he didnae care cause it nivir did ony guid o fuck naw naw naw and the stane wis his maa and the stane wis Big Bridie an the stane wis his maa an the stane wis Big Bridie the dun coo wi her lang white wand touchin the hard earth touchin me makin ma body feel sae guid sae bloody guid an the siol flowin freely like the shairp whistle o the gawden and green plover, heavin an lyin, lyin an heavin in the deid calm o the coille wi the thistles an dockins aw aroon ma fit, the sow-thistle wi its thick white juice and ah wis Goad, Goad forgive me, ah wis Goad. An ah nivir noticed, as ah washed mysel in the wee alltan nearby that the whole coille wis growin aroon an awd broch, an awd faery broch aye an that wis why ma grannie hud said ah should nivir go there.

But she wis wrang, ma auld grannie, she wis wrang.

Beltane

The saun formed a miniature landscape between her calves, a malleable world which was utterly under her control. She brought her right leg up to form a humple which spilled over the skin of the other calf in a tickling avalanche of silver. Moving the left foot outwards so it touched the middle of Scott's calf, she lingered for a moment, before swinging it back in a smooth movement, bunching up the saun intae a miniature dune. There they were – Deirdre's legs, her legs – creating, preserving, destroying beneath the burning speur. And she was burning, her skin raised red by the dog-day sun. She knew she ought to rub on mair lotion, but she quite liked the feel of the heat on her skin, much as she liked the touch of Scott. But that wisnae under her control, not like the saun. Scott was something – someone – who had happened to her against her best intentions. Despite herself. It wisnae her fault. No entirely. Partly. Okay, partly. You couldnae absolve yersel of all your sins. Some, mibbee. Not adultery, though. Not that. It wis wan-o-the-ten. The great cardinals. The errant, roaming wolf, cho breagha, and her soul, the deer. Naw, that wisnae accurate. Anyway, who cares about it bein accurate? No one. Not wan bloody soul on this whole beach. In the whole world . . .

She rolled on to her side and gazed at Scott. Eyes-closed Scott. Red, Viking hair. Skin white, o-so-white that it'd birn and beal even wi the factor twenty-seven or whatever the hell it wis he had tae cover himsel wi. He would sizzle jist for her, out of ana-miann for her. For passion, he would do anything. Deirdre felt good, having that sort of control. Like she'd never had wi Struan. No. Shut that out. Scott, think only of Scott . . . his big, boomin laugh, the time they'd met in that shop. A shop meeting. A general store. Unromantic. But she'd almost dropped the eggs and he'd saved the eggs and they'd got talkin, the way one does (does one? she hadnae ever, ever before Scott, so he must've been special, cut-out for her, fated). So wis Struan, there in his chair. O damn! Back to the shop. The druggies had watched them, there, in the queue wi thur hunched-up shooders, thur shiverin poly bags, thur junkie eyes nivir makin contact wi any other eyes, any other souls. Thur poly bags fulla Goad knows whit and hers full of . . . things they got on holiday. Eggs, bread, the usual. Anyway, they'd got tae talkin, Scott 'n her, and on and on they'd talked richt intae the street and doon the street and on and on.

They saw each other iviry second day at the shop. Her 'n Scott. The jaggers had lost interest but she hadnae and wan thing'd led tae another. Coffee. Lunch. Dinner. Nardini's. Billies. Infidelity.

Every summer after that, doon in Ardkirk, her and Struan, husband and wife, all wan like that; only he couldnae be, could never be, not again. And Scott, there in the shaddaes, waitin fur her. Waitin. And she, askin. He wis tall, mibbee six inches taller than her and she wisnae short, no fur a wumin, that wis the first thing she'd noticed aboot Scott. The presence of him, smeddum behind her. Tall and angular. He wis on his ane. Had split wi his girlfriend, the year before. Didnae talk much aboot her. Didnae like it. She widnae force him, either. People had tae keep some secrets. To preserve the soul. Goad! So profound, fur the beach. Scott brought that out in her. Deirdre raised her hond tae her hair and tossed back the long locks, and she smiled. She didnae really know him. No really. No like . . . like she knew Struan. You couldnae expect it. Nine years wis nine years, after aw (she'd known him afore that, but that didnae coont. He wis a different man, then). And mair than that, she thought. When you had looked down, literally looked down, on someone fur that long and when they wur dependent on you like you were their bloody mother or goddess or somehin, ye got tae know them pretty well. Too well. And they got tae know you. Because then there are nae barriers. Nae pretences. Nae wee dignities. An if yer a callous bastart, it'll come oot. Deirdre wisnae like that. Mibbee it would've been better if she hud been. But she wisnae. So she loved Struan, but no as a man. But she didnae love him like a wean, either. He wis a kindae a hauf-man, a puppet, and a broken wan at that, and yet he wis a partae her, a part of Deirdre, as much as her left airm or her . . . naw, no her hert. Her hert wis her ane. She stroked her long legs with the palm of her hand. First wan, then the other. She'd always been proud of her legs. She could've been a model, someone had once commented. Not Struan. Not Scott. Jist someone. But it wis always her strings bein pulled. Aw the time, it wis her that wis the puppet. Not Struan. Not Scott. But she needed Struan as she needed the dumb, unconscious cells that made up her body. Sometimes she felt like she wis in a play. The beach wis the stage, the sea, the audience. Seethin and swayin. Constantly applauding, urging her on. And she, a shadow-puppet against the flaying sun. It wis always a different excuse, every time. Deirdre had almost begun to pride hersel on the alacrity with which she seemed tae be able tae come up wi yet another explanation. Plausible, always and low, low key. The ordinary reasons of an aefauld wife. Sometimes, she almost believed them hersel. Almost. She sighed, but the air wis hot; it trapped her breath inside her.

The truth: Struan wis a begowk'd cuckold and she, an

adulteress. Scott wis Okay. He wisnae commitin ony sin. No really. The sin wis hers. She smiled, there at his flickerin eyelids wi their well-nigh invisible lashes (the ones she loved tae slaik wi her big fat lips, the tip ae her tongue). She leaned towards his face, smellin his presence ever stronger as she approached and gently kissed his eyes, feeling the globes through the thin skin. He woke. Big blue eyes, the colour of seawater loch. She drowned braw iviry time she looked intae them . . .

He smiled back at her, in the easy, natural way of a lover. Their lips met in a delicate arc. The arc danced gently outwards, matching the contours of their bodies, the crescent of the beach, the flight of a gull, the bowl of the sky. They needed no explanations. Just the perfect curve of love. The harmony of silence. A child dashed past, spraying saun in their faces. Its mother, billowed after, ruaidhe, fat-legged, apologetic, through the beach.

'Kids!' Scott spluttered through the saun.

'Ah know. Glad a never had ony,' she concurred, then regretted it. No not havin kids. No that. But sayin it. Sayin it wisnae right. She could've had a kid. Before the accident, mibbee. But then it would've been even mair difficult. Hovin wan invalid tae run after – well, no exactly run but it wis jist as tirin – wis enough fur anyone. Too much. And after, after, Struan hudnae been . . . hadn't been able.

She reached across and picked out a small sandwich and then another. She handed the first to Scott, who immediately began munching, and kept the other for herself. Cheese and tomato. She'd always liked cheese. Ever since she wis a wee girl. Occasionally, like when Struan had fallen asleep on the other side of the bed and at last she wis in her ane time (which wis a place ootside ae time), she would begin tae ache deep in the hollow of her womb. An ache where a child oughtae be, her mother would've said. Her mother had come fae up north where they worshipped gods ae granite. Stone faces. Her

mother's face. Mother alive. Mother dead. She shut out the
image. Pushed it away, away till it wis nuhin, less than nuhin.
Pressed her feet down on tae the saun and began tae swallow.
Thick, difficult dollops. Stopped. Started. Stopped. Started.
Felt the taste of molten cheese slide from the cavern of her
mouth, down her throat. Where, hauf-an-hour before, Scott
had slid. And Scott's stream. But nae weans ever came that
way, her mother said. She swigged fae the boa'le. And again.
Washed doon the thoughts so they'd sit inside her, right deep
doon in her gut's gut, a place where she could be alone in the
unending blackness, awa fae the leamin laughter ae weans.
And husbands. And lovers. Sometimes water wis like wine.

Scott's voice in among the cheese.

'You want some mair?'

She shook her head.

'You've only had wan.'

He was on his fourth.

'I'm no hungry.'

He was looking at her, quizzically, she thought.

'No when it's hot, I don't feel like eatin.'

But he'd already lost interest and was scouring the beach,
his palm shading his eyes.

'No too busy, today. It's good that way. Mair space tae
breathe.'

'Aye.'

'When ah wis a boy, ah used tae come doon here – and
further alang the coast – we used tae bike it, the lot ae us, and
spend the day roamin aroon. It wis great. You couldnae do
that, now. Too dangerous. Fur kids, I mean. Too many
nutters about.'

She wished he would shut up about children. She pointed
across the waves.

'Look at those mountains. They're blue, just like the sea.'

'The Blue Bens.'

'Och. That's a terrible one!'

She grimaced and dug him in the ribs. He pretended to roll but overdid it and got saun all over his back where it stuck to the lotion like gold dust. She helped him brush it off and then rubbed some more cream on to the delicate skin where she liked to link her calves.

You know me, he'd said, as he'd scooped himself up, *You know me*.

Naw. She didnae. No really. But it didnae matter cause she wisnae livin wi him and onyway too much knowledge aboot a person brings contempt. Her mother, again.

She knew Struan's body. His crippled, useless body. Lifting him intae that steel, electric chair. Her guilt wheeled the chair away and dutifully helped lift Struan's body back out again. Her biceps were turning copper. She'd always had strong muscles. Just as well. Struan's airms were strong, but his legs . . .

There wis an album somewhere wi pictures ae him fae way back, before, when he'd been young and tall, though no as tall as Scott. Nine years, give or take a few months (and she had given them). But Deirdre held no pictures in her mind of the two of them together. He was gazing out to where the waves massed and became moving slopes. Am muir allaidh.

'Can ye see Ireland?' he intoned.

'Ireland?'

'Aye. On a clear day . . .'

'Aye, aye, ah'll believe anythin you say.'

'Can ye no see, wumin? That's a coastline.'

He pointed wi his supple, couthie airm and drew it along the golden hair of the horizon. For a moment, as she blinked, Deirdre thought she could see a long ship, a wooden, three-tiered bata wi nine times nine times nine sailors guarding a veiled ban-dia on her way tae the Isle of Mull and the well of eternal youth, na fuaran fo na cruachan . . .

72

Then it was gone. Along with Dalriada and Don, and the smile of a leaping dog.

'Naw. That's jist an island.'

'Which, then?' he taunted her.

She shrugged.

'How should ah know? Ah don't carry a fuckin atlas aroon wi me. Ye great oaf.'

A pause, stretching out along the watermark. The tide had turned and the sea was beginning to creep in.

'It could be Ireland.'

'It's no Ireland. Don't be silly. Ireland's thirty miles away – at least. Ye cannae see Ireland fae here. Ah know. We've been comin here fur seven years. It's jist a legend the Tourist Board makes up. It's aw wishful thinkin. Lies.'

She was aware of Scott glancing at her and then looking away again towards the waves. Her guilty eye. Regret swept over her. She felt her cheeks flush. Wasn't this a lie? And Struan? Untruths surrounded, enveloped her. She tried to breathe, but felt suffocated by her own creations. Her faults. Like cancer, the body destroys itself. The unconscious cells become overbearing, think they can be gods, each one a creator, a shouter of words. And Struan wis the dumb cell in her and she in Struan. And Scott? Scott wisnae in this body, that wis why he wis safe. They were safe. Safe as eggs. Because they didnae know each other. No really. No at all.

She got up. Scott's shoulders were getting burnt. He winced as she rubbed more lotion on to the already blistering skin.

'You should put on a tee-shirt.'

'Och. I'll be alright.'

She stopped rubbing.

'Let's walk,' she said.

They strolled along by the water's edge, where the saun wis hard, barely yielding, washed cold by the incoming tide.

Deirdre flattened her soles as she trod, so that she might feel the sappie grains push up against the backs of her toes and into the hollow of the arches making the skin tingle and birstle. It wis delicious, almost painful. It made her feel closer tae the earth. She kind ae balanced her heid that wis spinnin roon in the palm ae the speuran. Like she wis oot here wi a man who wisnae her man, well he wis but he wisnae, and it made her feel like she wis up in the clouds, naw, nae clouds jist the skire blae adhar and the squawkin seagulls and there her hubby sittin hame in a fuckin wheelchair it wisnae right naw it wisnae but she didnae care she didnae care Deirdre she wis an adulteress jist like Desdemona and she didnae give a whit cause her hond wis in his hond his big muscle fingered hond and her heid wis agin his shooder cause that's as far up as it reached, her heid wi its big braw broon shock ae hair hangin lang doon tae her shooders tae his elbow fur Goad's sake and his rid hair O Goad she loved him so much so bloody much and she loved Struan tae, but in a different way. Scott wis pointin at her feet.

'Look at the fushes. I didnae think they came in sae claise tae the shore. Look at them, they're aw swimmin roon yer tootsies. Mibbee they're piranhas.'

Deirdre leapt sideways, stumbled and landed on her bum richt in the water. Scott wis laughin, killin hisel laughin the big rid bastart so he wis. And she wis tryin tae get up, tae raise hersel on her palms, the palms that jis an hour before had stroked the lang lines ae his back, his glorious lion's spine, and, now, spittin oot salt wa'ar and feelin the cool between her buttocks, she wanted tae do it again, tae fuck then and there in the wet saun wi the soles ae her feet an the palms ae her honds all over his skin and the tide comin in aroon their gleamin copperin bodies. He helped her up and she punched him gently in the stomach. A lover's jab. And they hugged, her drippin all over him, she sayin she wantit tae be like this always always forever and he whisperin, hissin he loved her he loved

74

her whisperin hissin. And they held hands and gazed intae the clear wa'ar and felt the warm froth run up over their ankles. And Deirdre saw the fush, wee things they were, and harmless as they kissed her feet. Struan had loved her feet. When they'd first met, he would caress them like they were lovers in themselves. Mibbee he married her feet. Lookin back, it seemed like a movie. Someone else's life. No hers. Struan's, mibbee. She'd tried tae do it wi him. After. But he'd hated it, hated her fur it, because it jist made him frustratit. Couldnae even get it up. Nerve damage. The spine. Lucky he could still go tae the cludgie, the doctors had said. And that wis that. But the problem wis some wee bit in his brain still wanted it. Needed it. If he thought about it, that wis. And they made it, she made it, so that they never ever thought ae it. Never. That way, Struan wis happy. Naw. Not happy. Content. Mibbee that wis how priests did it. The only difference wis, they still got erections. Wet dreams. Struan didnae.

'Are thur ony jeelyfush hereabouts?' she asked.

'Eh?'

'Jeelyfush. The see-through wans.'

'Oh aye. I don't know. Mibbee.'

'They say thur poisonous.'

'Ah widnae know.'

'Aye. They say if you get stung by wan, yer a deid mon.'

Scott shrugged.

'They say lots a hings.'

Deirdre felt irritation flush through her skin. That wis always his attitude. Shrug off yer troubles and they willnae matter ony mair. He wis so open, Scott. Aboot everyhin. Except Jainie. His last girlfriend. That wis her name. Jainie. All she knew aboot her. It might've been short fur Jane or Jeanette or Jennifer or even J-something else fur aw she knew. She wance fun a batch ae awd photos in a boax. Lang hair. Blond. No bad lookin – no great – but no bad either. She'd

75

never told Scott she'd found them. No matter how much she'd probed, she'd never been able tae get onyhin oota Scott. That part ae his life had ended, he'd said, and thur's nae point dredgin it aw up. So easy. Men found it so easy tae shut aff bits ae themselves, tae partially clothe thur souls. Whereas she . . . she wis like a bloody jeelyfush. Transparent. Here she wis, two-timin her hubby, her poor, crippelt hubby, and she couldnae even keep him ootae her thoughts fur wan bloody minute. The discordant music ae her sins walked wi her wherever she went. Aw out ae tune. Painful. There they were, sometimes behind her, sometimes in front. She couldnae lose her shaddae. Her anam. It wud go wi her tae the uaigh. It wud be there, on her tombstane.

> *Deirdre MacDonald, née O'Connell*
> *Never a mother, adulteress*
> *Rest Not In Peace*
> *Amen*

Adulteress. Funny word. She wondered what it hud tae do wi bein an adult. Mibbee it wis a normal condition of adult human beings. Mibbee it wisnae evil. No a sin. She chuckled inside, deep in the darkness ae her gut. Naa. That wis too easy. Life wisnae that simple. Naw. You hud tae lie wi yer sins and be fucked by them. On Judgement Day. And before. In this life, it seemed that the judgement began when you were born. She wondered if Struan knew. He must suspect, she'd said tae Scott. He's no stupit. No that stupit, onyway. Scott had shrugged, as usual. What did it matter if he knew? The knowledge ae a cripple. Who cares? There wis a merciless streak runnin through Scott which sometimes frightened her. A sadistic psychopathic streak. And yet, she wis attracted to it as weil. He wis a beast. He had nae morals and wis brutally honest. Except about Jainie. He had nuhin tae do wi Struan.

The cripple didnae form part ae his past or his future. Scott wisnae Struan's wife, for Goad's sake. She laughed inwardly again and must have smiled as weil because Scott wis lookin at her and asking why wis she smiling, tell him what she wis thinkin. Still smiling, but without returning his look, she shook her head.

'Nuhin, nuhin.'

'It must be somehin.'

'Naw. It wis nuhin just aboot the fushes. The piranhas.'

Now he threw back his heid and guffawed. That loud, man's laugh. Comfortably naked.

Goad. She loved him. Wanted no tae huv tae part but couldnae leave, naw she couldnae bring hersel tae leave desert maroon her husband even though she hadnae loved him as a husband fur nine long years. And a few damned months as weil. Even though he wis a grumpy auld cripple (auld, before his years) who never said *Thank you* and never never said *I love you, Deirdre*, naw no like Scott said it, there, back last summer by the loch the wan in mid-Argyll whur the sun sets tae the sound ae clàrsach metal. Whur iviry day, Dalriada was bein hewn fae the roaks. Pulled out, screamin. And when they'd danced that nicht she'd told Struan she wis aaf wi her pals, Ann and Fiona (or wis that a different time, she couldnae remember, no noo wi the wee fushes dancin aboot her taes, Scott's taes), aye they'd twirled an whooped the ceilidh by the loch and felt really totally Scots and guid an whole, no like the fuckin druggies in the shoap wi thur sick plastic an deid eyes and when the people the fat burpin whisky-soaked people, and so wis she a wee dram or two she couldnae deny it, when the folk had gan hame, late it wis, late, they'd made love on the wee smooth stanes by the edge ae the loch and the rug had come in cause they hudnae realised it wis a tidal bloody loch and the wa'ar hud washed all over thur bodies as they fucked and thur whur wrens wrens fur Goad's sake flyin aroon thur backs but they didnae even notice they didnae even notice cause they wur somwhur else in place, space an time oh fuck he must know he must know he must he must. And how could she go on lyin lookin intae right intae his eyes, crippled blue, and lie? It wisnae his fault, the accident. It wisnae hers, either. It wis jis fate, fuckin bastart fate. Lovely destiny that had brought Scott tae her. Withoot the accident, withoot Struan's broken, smashed spine, she wid never huv met Scott. O Goad O Goad O Goad. She wis damned. She knew it.

A wave washed over her knee, dissolving her lower leg and she wanted tae wade oot intae the sea an droon hersel like the alltan droons in the allt and the allt droons in the abhainn and the abhainn, the bellowin, roarin bras-shruth pours itsel, like Scott poured himsel intae her, intae the sea, Lord, intae the sea. And she walked out and let the freezin wa'ar slip over her thighs, the wans which had clasped Scott's waist. Aye the sex wis still clingin tae the skin even there in the deep-blue ocean. She let it slide up her body like a lover aye like Scott she pulled him in up over the lips ae her cunt O Goad the cunt that wis the cause ae aw this sorrow and joy. Up over her waist, her midriff, nipples, shooders. Shiverin a wee bit mair but then it wis gone an it wis warm the sea, the ocean, an the wee fushes were warm as they swam aroon her an kissed her skin wi thur warm lips an they grew bigger an bigger amongst the kelp till she saw they wur ròin aye mermaids and mermen wi great lang tails an they wur smilin at Deirdre, her the adulteress, but they didnae care didnae judge. They wur like Scott, lover Scott, smilin an shruggin and sayin it disnae maiter, it disnae maiter in a hundred years we'll aw be deid. And waves slaiked his face her face breathin in the wa'ar and coughin the saut oot through her neb. And Scott wis shakin her, wa'ar flyin aff his airms, an he wis spittin wa'ar oot his mooth like he wis an allt ae love flowin intae the sea. Intae her. He wis speakin she couldnae hear what he wis sayin he wis openin and closin his beul like a fish bha e mar ròn fuck he wis a seal tail-an-aw! And she wis laughin and cryin and cryin an laughin an he wis huggin her tellin her it's aw richt it's aw richt his lips wur sayin though she couldnae hear but it wis beyond hearin onyway and his lips wur slaikin hers slaikin they wur and the taste of him in the sea rìgh nan ròn aye it wis aw she needit aw she needit and in that moment that glorious, crystalline moment she knew that Struan knew but didnae want tae admit it an that the love which she and Scott had wis an ode aye an ode tae the grian the burnin gawden orb up there an it wis summer an she wis happy an what the fuck anyway an she reached out and hugged Scott aroon the waist she knew so weil an aw aroon the wee fushes the friendly wee ròin smiled and sang the òran of joy and love aye and of ana-miann as weil.

Samhain

T he awd mon finished aff the last dregs ae the glais, inspected it then tossed his heid back and tried tae sip some mair, tae tease oot the dregs ae the dregs. The last, desperate draps ae malt. The glais clanged agin the boa'le, empty on empty. Nae echo. Jis an odour. He slumped back in his chair and let his lids slide shut. Ootside the bothan, the snaw climbed thick upon the dykes, and the nicht creaked wi the sound ae nuhin. It wis the middle ae nuwhur, haufway up a beinn, and the stars so bricht it wisnae dark at aw an the muin up there above the awd mon's heid like a virgin's cunt. Unbraken. Perfect roon. Skimin, drappin its licht over the laun, the bothan, the awd mon, his fuskie boa'le, his teemed glais, his great shock ae lang white hair. Had been reid wance. Aye, wance on a day. Enough ae that. Memories. O Goad, memories.

He opened his ees an went over tae the grill. Took oot a spunk an luntit the ring. The gas flared up on the third attempt, almost burning the side ae his hond. He licked the skin. Deid flesh, the taste ae him. He slapped a pan on tae the ring and looked fur some mulk. It took him a guid while tae find ony, so that when at last he tuimed it in, it bizzed an sizzled and sent the waff ae burnin up his snoot. Burnin mulk. Burnin flesh. Same as the stink ae snaw ootside, aw aroon, everywhur. The stink beneath the smell, the deid leaves under the snaw. The scent ae the stars an the muin. He had the urge tae go oot an walk in the saft snaw mar fhear-allabain, tae wander in the frozen nicht and tae nivir come back. Tae lose himsel in the past. The bad ault past.

Leavin the bainne in the pan, he went tae the door. The fawin-doon, brak door. The bothan wis gae ramshackle, hudnae bin cleant up fur decades. It wis whit he hud sunk tae, the awd mon, it wis aw that wis left after a life had passed. After aw his sins were acoountit fur. Aw fuck, so many sins. He twistit the hannle. It wis stuck. It didnae bloody work. Even that wis fawin apart. He sighed, his putrid awd lichts sighed, blowin oot thur air stagnant wi seeventie Samhains. Aye there wis air in those lungs, in the guts ae those lungs that hud neer been braithed. Deid air. Wis braithed in at birth an wud be braithed oot at daith. In the daith-rattle. But he widnae hear it. His lug would be as deid as the beinn oot there. He shoved the door open and stood in the door-cheek, in a circle ae shadee or wis it a circle ae licht. He wisnae sure. It wis lichter ootside than it hud been in the bothan, whit wi the muin an the stairs booncin aff the snaw.

There wis nae wind, so the shaddaes didnae blow away. He could smell them. Heich above him rose the great dark bulk ae the beinn, its shooders so sheer that nae snaw, no even a flichan, wis able tae cling tae the hard rock-face. It hud aw been licht that, even back fuftie winters ago, when the awd mon hud first come tae the bothan. It wis different then. He wis young, the world wis new, his sins were no sae lang. Or, at least, they hudnae seemed tae maitter. He'd come theer wi a leddy, aye, a lang-haired, tall, beautiful leddy an they'd danced ootside in the snaw tae the soon ae the binneas whisperin across the beanntan aw the way fae the fur west whur the dubhlachd came fae aye an they'd lain thegether in the dry snaw, lomnochd and her drùis had met an mingled wi his drùis an her fit hud banged doon on the hard snaw like the hammer ae the Cailleach, the awd wumin ae winter, an the traneens fur

82

aff hud creaked an split wi the soon ae their roupin. O Goad that wis heiven heiven that wis. The wumin wis awreedie mairrit but he hudnae cairt. Nor hud she, fur that maitter. He recalt the hollow a wee bit up the beinn whur they'd done it aye he wis able tae picture it even then, fuftie years on. It wis on th'other side ae the beinn, overloookin the black an the rocks and the spume. An aw the craigs covert in tangle an badderlock. An the cavern whur th'awd wifies said the ròin came tae sow thur seed every Samhain an you could hear them because thur roups wur no like ony ae the sea-birds an no like folk eether. It wis a roar like the blaw ae Saint Michael's horn at the gates ae Judgement Day. An they'd heard it, him 'n the wumin, as they'd climbed tae the summit tae the hollow jist in the shooder ae the summit aye an their ane roup hud mingled wi the cries ae the ròin and the roupin hud become wan an it wis gae the best moment ae his hale life, naw, it wis the best.

In the bothan, the bainne wis beilin over but the awd mon didnae hear nocht; he wis saunterin up the beinn tae look fur the ròin, aye, he wis ayeways a radge wan, a bloody radge wan, aye, so the awd wumin had said whun he geed Big Bridie a babe at aleeven, aye she wus gae big fur her age but no as big as she got, nine twenty-seevens thence. And noo th'awd bastart-faither wis clamberin up the beinn, the door a broken jaw behind his back, but he no carin no gien a dang cause he'd nivir gien a dang aboot onyhing but had jist shrugged his shooders aw his life richt from the stert. A callous bastart, him wi his rid hair, aye lang locks ae it there in the snaw, fawin across the face ae the mairrit wumin, across her ees fou a love, aye no jis drùis no like him.

The snaw sleid an sklyted beneath the soles ae his scuddie fit cause he hudnae ony sheas left tae wear. He wis in a state ae dire penury. Everyhing he ever had wis loast. Had been mooted awa bit by bit, over the years till this fawin-doon bothan wis aw he had an noo wi its door wide open tae the warld. Thur wis no one, nae souch the nicht, an the snaw lay as peaceful as deith an it wisnae peaceful at aw, naw no fur those left behind, onyhow. Mibbee fur the deid. Mibbee. Mibbee no. The grun wis beginnin tae rise mair steeply an bits ae ice had begun tae form on tap ae the snaw so that th'awd mon's baries were slippin an slidin an noo he wis on his knees an honds, his palms, the luifs that had clasped the mairrit wumin's fingers wi her ring her gauden ring that had been her grannie's she said rubbin agin his huil his virginal white huil she'd changed honds aye it wis her richt hond the ring wis on. Aw fuck, he realised, fuftie years intae the unknown but what he'd thocht wis known wisnae and whit did it mean?

He paused, there, on the snowy dorchadas ae the beinn, the sloped licht dorchadas an he wis balancin on the white balancin like it wis a tightrope fur fuck's sake aye an below him fell the geodha, the lang creek whose ent wis the ocean the invisible watter where the ròin rouped ivverie Samhain nicht an the faeries ae the land, ae the tide ae the land came an matit wi the ròin in great tuinn an the linnets screamin overheid, screamin an spunkin up there in the dark sky.

An the awd mon climbed higher an higher in the frozen air an he thocht at wan point he could hear the neighin ae the winter mare an by that he knew he wis shankin widdershins. O fuck he didnae know how he knew but somehow deep inside his heid, his aged heid stuffed wi nuhin but putrefaction because the beinn had three heids, three huidit heids an, as he looked back, the trees had shrunk tae scrunts, deid scrunts which still (ein though they wur deid) spelt oot a nem an it wis his nem but it wisnae, naw it wisnae in letters but it wis the shape ae his fate the ogham ae his weird O Goad he wis gan tae dee but he wisnae dowie naw you couldnae be sad aboot destiny it wisnae avoidable, it wis you an yer ancestors aw the fuckin lot ae them, wan fuck intae the next, a lang line ae tadgers aw stieve an thrustin an hot. Naw, no hot, calt like the nicht, cho fuar ris a' phuinnsein cause now the awd mon wis nearly there, near as dang it tae the heicht to whur he hud tae be, whur he hud always hud tae be, tae hear the strings ae the clàrsach that hud played oot his life. The three chords ae oige, adulthuid, eild; the three martyrdoms, white, green, rid; the three dieths.

> *Ebbtide tae me as ae the sea!*
> *Awd age causes me tae reproach . . .*
> *Ah am th'awd wumin ae Beare,*
> *An ivir-new smock Ah used tae wear:*
> *Today – such is ma mean estate –*
> *Ah wear no even a cast-aff smock . . .*
> *O happy the isle ae the great sea*
> *Which the flood reaches after th' ebb!*
> *As fur me, Ah do not expect*
> *Flood after ebb tae come tae me*

An the bainne wis beilin in the dorchadas but the awd mon didnae care he didnae care cause it wis aw written onyway an he wis tae get tae see it aw written, in the trees, the stocs, a' bheinn lom, the slidin snaw. In his ain hert. Aye, fur the first time he wis gazin intae his ain hert an its duibhre, an its darkness wis a peak, a summit, mullach na beinn, an fae there he wuid see it aw, his life an the lives ae the many. The wumin wi her grannie's ring on the wrang hond, the weann withoot a ma an a faither, a' bheinn lomnochd ann an abhainn na h-oidhche. Jis like Dante, he wud see his dan traced oot fae the toap ae the beinn. The awd mon wisnae cault ony mair he wisnae shiverin, no in his airms no in his hert. He wis warum, beilin like the bainne. An the flames slaiked the iron pan, the awd wood ae the bothan, yella flames like great big tadgers makin the wood glow an creak an curl an the awd mon ripped aff his claes an ran thru the snaw jis like a young carle, climbin,

85

climbin aw the while. The muin wis fu, fu as the iron chord which keeps aw the faeries, aw the awd yins awa, sends them back intae thur dark broch an hauds them there aw through the great Samhain. Aye an he needit tae leap intae the braw muir, the big braw sea, black as it wis, blacker than hell, cause he'd treatit her bad, that wumin, he'd taken her awa fae her mon an then dumped her cause he didnae want tae be tied doon an he said tae her it wis on acoont ae her no knowin what she wantit but it wis a lie so the truth here on the back ae this big black beinn wis that he didnae feel fur onyone. No even fur himsel. He nivir had.

Aw ae a sudden, the snaw vanished an there wis nuhin but big, black moothfu's ae nicht air. The awd mon stopped. Listened tae the boomin soon ae the waves as they bled agin the rocks. An rubha lom. He didnae look back, but felt it. The bothan, the end ae him, burnin bricht in the white. Didnae see it but knew the last bits ae his mortal coil were shiftin themselves aff ae the earthly plane. Didnae look back but heard his dan mapped oot in great chords ae white, his ages, the fowk he wis, air on stone, soul on flesh. An he wis himsel astride the wumin in the snaw and he wis roupin wi his rid hair streamin an his tadger stiff as a deid mon and she wis roupin wi her thighs spreid an her cunt wide open. An he wis the wee boy in the coille, rubbin himsel against the big stonin stane, feelin the mon spume oot ae him in great, hoat gouts. An he wis the awd mon in his bothan, still feelin nuhin, knowin less, an his bothan wis burnin, burnin it wis an he wis burnin wi it fur it wis the only way. An aon shlighe, the wan strewn wi briars an bracken but the true wan. Then he heard a whooshin, no wi his lugs but wi his banes, an he knew it wis the faery fowk come tae whisk him aff an he felt a great, black warmth wrap itsel roun him an he took a step forwards an he wis over the edge an intae the allt.

Lughnasadh

They left the road because, as Donal said, they were out to get as far as possible from any vestige of civilisation. If there was a track, they would cross it. All paths would be abandoned. They would create new paths, temporary ones which would close silently behind them, so that when they returned the way they had come, there would be no cleavage through the grass. They would leave no history of themselves.

It was a hot enough day for such wild notions. It was the late summer of 1933, in the far west of England. The August sunlight poured over the hills, the forests, the elms and its leaden heat was unbroken by the muffled words which the four of them exchanged as they trod through the rank grass. Donal had the Old River as his grail for that day. It was known as 'Old' partly because it was aged and partly because while, once, like all rivers, it had flowed into a greater river and thence into the sea, lately (which, around those parts in those days, generally meant as long as anyone could remember), the river had had no end. Everyone knew where it began, far up amid the distant shoulders of Mount Erir, but after it entered the elm and yew woods, the maps seemed to lose track of it. Only the stories flowed through the clear, emerald waters of the torrent to a place where reality merged with myth. Or, to put it more prosaically, to where the river sank underground.

Donal had conceived the idea of seeking the death of the Old River, late one evening, while staying at the Rectory on the edge of the village of Ys, where his uncle was Rector. He'd stood on the porch, inhaling the clear air of the West Country. His aquiline nose, the firm line of his mouth, his broad jowls. He had the profile of a leader. His sleeked-back, blond hair had been blown, ever so slightly, out of place by the evening wind as he'd focused his gaze on the woods which stretched from about a furlong from the Rectory's outer garden, right the way to the other side of Offa's Dyke. Snaking through the forest, beneath the rough bark of elm and ash, there ran a border of sorts, beyond which lay the Principality of Wales but, like the river, no one seemed to know its exact where-abouts. You might say (and Donal often had) that once you'd stepped over the threshold of the wood, your feet gradually would lose their sense of time, place and whatever else went to make up reality as we know it. But then, that was the sort of pretentious claptrap Donal tended to come out with, his grandfather having been a Theosophist. A disciple of one or other mad Russian. Kaylyn would often tease him about this, saying, *Which mad Russian? There are so many of them.* It was not that she didn't believe in mythical truth; she was a student of (among other things) anthropology; but she felt that, from time to time, Donal needed brought down to earth. Him with his fair locks which he would only allow to fall about his ears when they made love. Kaylyn was his lover or you might've said that he was hers. It depended on which way you looked at it. And to the two of them, it didn't matter which way it looked. Like all who couple freely, they had little cognisance of the outside world, except in as it related to them. They had become their own myth. If Kaylyn had lived in the seventeenth century, she'd have been burned as a witch. In the fifth century, she'd have been a high priestess or perhaps a Morgan Le Fay, a black-haired schemer. Not that Kaylyn was particularly scheming, not as far as she saw it, anyway.

Saraid might have seen it differently. Saraid was as exact an opposite of Kaylyn as it was possible to be, and then some. She had been on the porch with Donal that evening when he had breathed in the cool air of impending nightfall, she had been there as the leaves had fluttered deep inside his lungs. Saraid had been standing just behind him, her arms clasped invisibly around his muscular waist. No, that wasn't right. She had been six feet, one, two three, four, five, six feet behind him as he had tossed his King Edward cigar aside and had partaken of the breeze which had wafted in from the ancient forest. Her gaze focused not on the trees but on his legs, his shoulders, his buttocks. She was unashamed. She had been in love with Donal for years. From the beginning. From before the beginning. Kaylyn was her friend and they had shared many things (though not men; Kaylyn had had several, Saraid none) but she would gladly have severed all ties with (or possibly the throat of) her best woman friend, if she'd thought her love might be returned. No such dramatic deal being in sight, Saraid found herself trailing along after the couple, encouraged in the role of friend and confidante by none other than her arch-rival. She knew Donal's exact dimensions, in space, time and rictus. She gazed through the diamond-clear waters at the summit of his desire. But still she felt like a hanger-on, uneducated, short (Kaylyn stood at least four inches closer to heaven) and in some ways plain (she would never have said plain, no, there was a subtle difference between being in some ways plain and being just plain plain. It was in the hormones, a man could smell it and in some ways plain could still – very likely might – be unbearably attractive to a man, whereas just ordinary plain was repulsive like a half-rotting pond). Saraid was a second fiddle. She was dispensable, there in the modern world of down'd cocktails and falling colonials. The world was changing, and rapidly; it was careering simultaneously downwards and upwards, the direction depended on which slope you were on (or, like Saraid, you might possibly be on both slopes, at the same time – or you might be in the wood, in some fictitious, other time or, indeed, out of time altogether). But this is a story of sorts, though it did not seem so when I, Fiacre, the fourth person, the friend-of-the-friend-of-the-friend, was dragged out of my single bed and taken on this wild goose chase through the bloody forest of Pulzella or Ragnell or whatever the Hell it was called.

The four of us were at university in Ireland, studying the arts in all their generality. The great and virtuous state of Éamon de Valera was in its beatific infancy. Our country was not yet, de jure, a country, but lay, effectively, beyond the sea. The four of us – Donal, Saraid, Kaylyn and I – were friends of sorts. Let us just say that our lives overlapped. Donal was good at sports; I was not. Kaylyn was good at everything, while Saraid kept any talents she had to herself. On the surface, we shared very little – other than our Irishness, our class and the time in which we lived. But to examine things too closely, as on a microscope slide, is to begin to destroy those things.

Donal the Keen had scraped us all out of our (separate) beds and thrown us into the hayrick fields which swelled beyond his uncle the Rector's garden. Through the old hawthorn frame, through the rusted clergyman gate and out into the sweet-smelling golden furrows of western England. I was never quite sure whether the odour of burnt sugar emanated from the sliced stalks of over-ripe hay or from the past couplings of horses and humans. For as we all know (or at least, it was known to those of us who were studying anthropology during the great and tragic 1930s in the shadow, or perhaps I should say in the light, of Sir James Frazer's amazing *Golden Bough*, from which Donal, my college friend, no doubt hung: from his arms, not his neck, perish the thought), bestiality is a good deal commoner (especially among commoners) than we let on. In fact, any solitary spinster, left alone (as she must be, every lune-tide) with her screaming black dog, might be seen, in an idle moment, to be most effectively coupling with said beast. Needless to say (though in this age of light one must needs say it), the same applies to the farmhand and his prettiest sheep, the ones that stare at you as you excrete in the bush – they've seen it all before. But this tale is becoming obscene. Beyond the pale. Enough of this. Back at last to the trail, the trackless track, the seamless seam of Donal and his group of four, his band of merry, middle-class imbeciles who were on their way to the Old River.

Donal and I wore the baggy, cream-coloured suits which were fashionable in those days. Unusually for us, we had dispensed with both neckties and collars, so that I, for one, felt almost naked and kept having to stop my hand from groping stupidly at my throat. Our movements, the way we walked, all bespoke an ardent innocence which stemmed, I think, form a hidden sense of irony. Perhaps we hoped that, in some way, our ambivalence might save us. In those times, one was either a Darwinist or else a Creationist, a Theosophist or a Materialist. A Communist or a Fascist. A man or a woman. Like the shadows cast long in the August sunlight, like the great British Empire, like Mr de Valera, everything up to that point had been clearly defined and irrevocable.

We rankled through the undergrowth, fearing adders beneath every step – they were rife in those sand-beck woods and still are, as far as I know – and came at length to a high bank. Kaylyn, darling Kaylyn – not my darling, you must understand, just the proverbial, the actor's darling – promptly informed me that this should be referred to as a *broch*. But it's the West Country, I said, not Scotland. Not even our native Ireland. And she called me Renegade, Orangeman, Mason, Killer-of-Babies and whatever else took her pretty head (and it is – was – pretty) by storm that glorious end-day in July. Not that I cared.

Oh – I almost forgot to say – my hair at that time was just

middle brown. Nothing special. Nothing out-of-this-world or mythical or what-have-you, just ordinary mud brown. It had been cropped short and was greased like that of a good old boy. It was the style in those days, when, for a moment, a wondrous colonial moment in which even the Celtic nations had been capable of participating, it had seemed possible, probable even, to be able to couple without hilarity. Without awkwardness. To look into the face of the one impaled, the *one impaled*, they might say in cheap (cheap, that is, in August, One Thousand Nine Hundred and Thirty-three) Soho novelettes and to not have had the terrible urge to burst into laughter at the impossibility of it all. Please do bear with me. As the least interesting (and, I'm sure, the most ignorant) of the four, I feel I have some right, nay duty, to be narrator. After all these years. All these lines.

We reached a broch (I'll go along with it, as long as you do). Donal spoke up, as I knew he would.

'We should go around this, even in daylight.'

Crazy! The man was on hemp or whatever it was Aubrey Beardsley had been on before he died. After, was anyone's guess. Donal's, most likely. Kaylyn was the only one who had either the licence or the portal to disagree with Donal. You may think me a coward, but you have to understand my inclination. Of which, later.

'Around? But there are just briars and breaks and poisonous spiky things surrounding it. The top is smooth, see; you can see it's smooth. Let's just go over it, for God's sake.'

'Look,' Donal said, in his most idiotic of Celtic accents (part Cymru, part-Irish, part-Armoric, part-Argyll and, for all I knew, part-Galician as well), 'look, if we're going do this, we're going to do it properly.'

Very English, that end word, that *properly*, as though the Angleterrians even link properly, through holes in the bed-sheet. (I accept that this is a myth but then myths, like lies, have inordinate power and power creates truth.) I agreed with Donal (I always did, of course) and the Short One was silent as a round mound of skulls. Unlike myself, she did not dissipate her innate energies by making small-talk. Saraid stored up her lost lusts, piled them high like unused bus fare outside the whore's door.

'Look, let's just go. I need a pish.'

Kaylyn was earthy, as always. Liberated in her language. It was easy to be free when one had everything. It was not so simple when your love was a mass of coils.

I chimed in.

'I think Donal's got a point. If we're going to do this, and I think we should, then we might as well do it properly. Otherwise, why do it at all?'

'Exactly,' said Kaylyn, though I wasn't sure what she meant. A double-edged comment, typical of her.

Donal nodded, slowly like the undisputed leader he was. In any situation, that's where Donal began, with the premise of his Dragonship. It's something that either you possess or you don't. And I don't.

All through this, the Small One had remained studiously silent. She would never have disagreed with Donal, even if it had meant her leaping off the edge of some mull or other. Yet she hated allowing me to get away with being the right-hand man of her lover. So she glared at me with all the venom she could muster. We had been old enemies, ever since, while drunk at some party or other, I had clumsily attempted to seduce her. It had been a half-hearted attempt but she had taken it seriously and had never forgiven me. She never quite looked me in the eye. Ever.

And so we went around the mound and, thus, did not disturb, insult or otherwise put out the faery-folk. It was bad enough, them being cast out along with the Old Goat's Cohort, especially considering they'd only left out of curiosity and had fully intended to return. It would be enough to make anyone bitter. Imagine all the angels standing in tier upon tier – your closest comrades, created, like you, from light, forged gently in the everlasting love of God – ignoring you, turning their other cheeks as you are inadvertently banished from heaven. The gall! The let-down! I sympathised with the faery-folk, I always had. I knew what unrequitable (and not just unrequited) love was about, I knew what it was like to be banished from paradise by the one whom you were part of. Even though you might only be a third part of him. As I circled, druid-like, around the great, dark mound, I felt the bitterness of the faery-queen as she stole away the brawest of the menfolk and spunked them to death deep inside her warm, wet broch. I knew where it came from. But I didn't know where it was going. And that was really why I had dragged myself out of my dry single bed and followed the crazy Donal with his blond locks and rippling, hairless chest and why I was as eager as the rest of them to find the death of the river, and to follow it beyond.

We crossed the broch, unharmed and unkidnapped. The day's heat was building to a climax, but, deep beneath the thick forest canopy, we were sheltered from its worst excesses. The heat was a deep green. Our faces, our eyes, the skins of our arms all seemed to acquire this myrtle hue, and everything had to be measured not by the usual white light of midday but rather in the midst of a hooded pool of foetid exhalation. For it became apparent to me, there, that the trees, the long grass, the bushes with tiny thorns which pressed up against my ankles, all of them were breathing in tune with one another, and all were breathing out. Constantly exhaling. And that if this went on, we would slowly become more and more drowsy, and eventually would fall asleep by some big tree-root or other and be turned into compost for the forest's avid consumption. A large branch tripped me up.

As I brushed the leaves off my clothes, I noticed that Donal had bent down and was listening to the ground. Or so it seemed.

We had spent long evenings in the overflowing garden of the Rectory, tangled in discussions about the nature of God, the forgotten saints of the Celtic Church and the numinous legends of Offa's Dyke. Donal's uncle had belonged to that old school of religious intellectual where open-mindedness was prized as an asset dear to faith and questioning a necessary part of the experience of God's manifold love. He had a particular interest in things Celtic and his house was strewn with books on the subject, all of them apparently ancient. That summer, the four of us had found ourselves enveloped in a pleasing haze of myth, which, paradoxically, had seemed to deepen our sense of reality. During the dust days of July, time languished along the banks of shadows and we stretched with it. You might have come across any one of us, reclining on the manicured lawn of the Rectory or else on the long, wooden benches which looked as though they had been hewn for Rossetti's languorous, bronze-haired Pre-Raphaelite lady of the lake. We might have been engrossed in some tale of Gwalchmai and the Green Knight, or perhaps in one of the wanderings of Elen of the Roads, or else in a detailed treatise on the varied powers of hawthorn. Our 'quest' that day in the forest may seem, to you, a little whimsical or even self-indulgent, but such was the power of atmosphere that I would dare anyone to venture into such a milieu, to breathe in that same air and not be affected. And so, if the thought occurs that I am meandering somewhat, backtracking even, it should be remembered that this account is not a fiction. I often think that life, unlike fiction, must build from the simple to the elaborate. There are no resolutions in life.

It was not really the Rector's suggestion that prompted us to go off into the woods that morning. As always, the flash of inspiration came to Donal. But the more I look back on it (and I try not to), the more the feeling creeps over me that Donal's idea was inevitable. That Donal had no choice. In his smiling, silvery way, the Rector had spun a softly-spoken web around us in such a manner that the idea would have occurred to one or other of us, at some point during our stay. I don't recall the Rector in great detail, but I do remember his smile. He had never married and had no family other than Donal, having devoted his life to the pastoral and in the pursuit of learning. He dressed in black, even in summer, which was not un-common for a gentleman of the cloth. But his smile . . .

Most preachers I'd ever met had seemed, at best, morose and, at worst, to reek of suicide. Like their churches, they conferred only gloom. The Rector was different. He wore a smile so unassuming, so beatific that it might have been painted by the big Florentine crank himself. Several times during my stay, I had thought of asking him how and where he had acquired his gentle happiness, but common courtesy had held me back. In any case, I know now that a smile cannot be acquired.

Let me return for a moment to the four of us and to the threads which drew us together (which were the same as those which held us apart). I had always harboured a fascination for Saraid; there was a longing in my bones for her small, white body. Her eyes, wave-blue. During those floating, simmering days and the nights, velvet with the touch of dark leaves, I had watched her movements. The dance of her soul. Her voice. Deep, rippling, a caress. But as I have already explained, my feelings had not been reciprocated, except, perhaps, on that one night I ventured to mention earlier. The more I thought about that episode, the more it began to tantalise me. Nothing had happened, you understand. Nothing physical, that is. Our non-existent romance had been a clumsy flirtation of the mind, a bourgeois dance, and I had been the only one dancing. Still, that morning I did not permit the thought to enter my head. She would be on the quest and so, too, would I. It was enough. I had a thick skin. I was used to being second best. Was almost comfortable in my niche. Saraid loved Donal and I loved Saraid, but Donal's obliviousness to her gave me hope, not because I was particularly jealous – though I was – but more because, if one unrequited love, in the hope of some distant success, could be pursued with such passion, such blindness, then, surely, so might another. It is strange that those who are most desired often seem incapable of giving love. The four of us were in a web of complicit self-deception, but perhaps we were unable to extricate ourselves from it during that hawthorn'd, molten summer because, at the base of the mendacity which is this world, there must lie an element of truth.

We had set off in the middle of the day; the middle, in Celtic terms being, of course, the early morning, before the heat had matured. By the time we got around the broch, the forest seemed to have trapped the full heat of the day beneath its canopy and we were all perspiring uncontrollably. I don't normally sweat very easily. Perhaps that's why usually I can't stand high temperatures. But this was different. The taste of salt in my mouth enhanced my desire like spirit and I found myself constantly having to avert my eyes from Saraid's slim figure. And from Donal.

'Let's have lunch,' Kaylyn suggested.

Donal looked up in the meagre, leaf-filtered light, mopped his brow and, for once, agreed. So we sat down where the grass was a little shorter and the women unpacked the hamper. We ate in silence. The forest flowed into the silence and filled it with its quiet din. The sounds one can only hear when one is not trying. The rustle of leaves, each tree sending out a different note, the businesslike chirping of wrens punctuated by the shrill cries of the linnet . . . and somewhere, below and within it all, the rushing sound of water. I wondered, there on the cool grass, whether the rhythms I sensed along the muscles of my thighs might be issuing from the clear, black waters of the subterranean river whose end we had been seeking all along. And whether the river itself might issue from the old Clyn Tegid Lake. I wondered this, as I tried not to gaze through the blond locks of Saraid's hair. It seemed impossible to get beneath the smooth, creamy skin, to become pictures in her eyes, much less to live in her heart (I quivered as I thought it). Perhaps, seventeen generations back, at the very limits of our ancestral memories, we might have been linked. Perhaps, Saraid and I (I liked to think of us in that way) might have issued from a common seed. Perhaps, if we managed to find the elusive river and followed it back far enough . . .

Our journey would be a mapping of fate in reverse, a drawing of the complex down into simplicity. A search for harmony. For fiction. I almost found myself praying to Elen of the Roads, the old matron of dreams and destinations, but I wasn't sure how one might pray to the wife of a Roman emperor. But, of course, we were seeking the end of the river, not its source. The beginning was already known. In our arid modernity, we had got it the wrong way round. Even our myths were reflections. Suddenly, Donal announced:

'I hear water.'

I started out of my reverie. Fell upwards.

'Can't you hear it?' he was asking Kaylyn and she was shaking her head. Slowly though, she wasn't sure. Saraid's voice, from far away.

'I feel it. Beneath the earth. It's been flowing for ten thousand years. On waves of exile.'

Kaylyn looked quizzically at her. They were enemies. Necessary friends.

'Don't be ridiculous,' mocked Donal, in that patronising tone of his (and yet, I loved the deep, confident tones of his voice), 'there's a pool, somewhere nearby. You can hear the waterfall.'

Saraid looked downcast. Glee sprinted through my heart. Then, shame.

'Actually, I . . .'

Everyone looked at me. I teetered on the edge of harmony. But she was looking at me. Her eyes on my skin, blue on white.

'I thought it was coming from below, as well.'

As I said the last two words, I glanced involuntarily at her. Got a glimpse of myself in the waves of her irises. Then it was gone. Donal stood up. His elegantly-groomed reputation was at stake. I didn't want him to fall. I wished her to be right and I wished that I could be right, with her. I loved them both, with a fragile love. Donal began to search among the trees, then he hauled down a thin branch and broke it off. Using a small knife, he hewed it into a dowsing-rod. I knew that he would be the dowser. There would never have been any question about that. But I was content to follow him, to dwell in his shadow, lest only his shadow might love me. Perhaps that is why it is I who am relating these events, and not Donal or Kaylyn. Because the writer is always merely a sidekick, at best, a trusted confidante, at worst, a despised hanger-on. Writing is the act of being outside. It is the scream of the excluded. So Donal, the great leader, the Uther Pendragon of the Rectory, and Kaylyn, the Morgan Le Fay of his life, could never have written this, any more than Uther or Morgan themselves could have penned the tales of Mallory. They were the actors and I, a bemused spectator. Saraid, I will come to later.

Donal trod carefully behind his dowsing-rod. His eyes remained open and his back was straight as ever, while the rest of us began to gather up the food. Kaylyn was being very businesslike. Saraid and I did not look at each other. We might have been a group of friends, out for a straightforward summer picnic, except that the wood was too dark, the leaves too old and the three of us were enemies. I was angry at Saraid, while Saraid was envious of Kaylyn. Kaylyn, on the other hand, despised me (overtly, as a hanger-on, though really as a rival). I found myself smiling. Felt the mirth stretch across my face. It didn't seem possible to laugh out loud in that forest. The lack of echo was oppressive. But that wasn't why I was smiling. It was the oddness of the situation. The whole situation, and my place in it. Kaylyn was glaring at me but her face always became comical when she was cross, and that made it worse. Now I wouldn't be able to look at her, either. The thought sent unbearable ripples of silent laughter up from my gut. I had to turn away and pretend to be doing something with the picnic hamper. Slowly, my mirth faded. Sank into the long grass. Inexorably, I was being drawn towards Donal. Ridiculous, you might say. But the ridiculous can be sublime. Especially if it's to do with love. I have no idea whether or not Saraid, too, was irritated since still I had not dared to gaze into her eyes. All I know is that suddenly she snatched up the hamper and went off in the direction Donal had taken. Voted with her feet, you might say. The strange hilarity returned when the empty-handed Kaylyn almost ran to catch up with her. I watched them disappear into the foliage.

My mirth died away again. I was alone in the ebb and flow of the forest. How easy it would be to become lost in this dense mass of green. And how desirable. I wished I'd brought a bottle of wine, but Donal had wanted clear heads. The sun was past its apogee and the light filtering through the leaves carried a hint of darkness. The rhythmic airs of the forest had taken over again, now that the little human whirlpool had spun on. I wanted to lie down and sleep on a fallen tree-trunk. I wanted to feel my lids close over my eyes. To feel the river slide over my skin, to breathe in its clarity, its coolness. To sink into it. To let it fill me.

A shout went up. A woman's voice. Kaylyn's, I think. I opened my eyes. Far above, I made out the dark tangle of a rook's nest. Round. Perfectly balanced. The shout, again.

I jerked myself up and hurried towards where I thought it had come from, regretting a little that I hadn't been permitted to enjoy my reverie. My body felt sluggish, heavy. As I drew closer to the source of the voices – there were now several of them – the sound of rushing water grew louder and my heart began to pound in my chest. I entered a dark clearing at the far end of which was a large boulder. The sun hardly got through here at all and it felt as though I had reached the very heart of the forest. The voices had fallen silent just before I had entered the clearing. Somehow I knew they had been issuing from behind the rock. It was too large to see over or around, and, like the rest of the clearing, it was shrouded in shadow. I walked slowly around to the right (it was inaccessible from the other side because of tall ferns and other, smaller boulders). The ground began to sink a little beneath my feet. I couldn't see properly, but it felt like some kind of moss. I had the urge to take off my shoes. I don't really know why. Perhaps, at the time, I felt that, without shoes, my step would be a little steadier on the slippery moss. Perhaps. I bent down and undid the laces, removing one sock at a time. I stuffed the socks into the shoes. I stepped from the leather and the soles of my bare feet touched the damp vegetation. A powerful wave swept up from the ground and almost knocked me over.

I regained my balance and began to walk. The ground was so soft, it was almost like walking on someone's palm. Every inch of my skin was in contact with the ground, at every moment. I had gone barefoot a few times before this, across the back garden or else occasionally on a picnic but those had been tame experiences and, anyway, that sort of thing largely was frowned upon in those days. This was utterly different. I trod like a hunter towards the rock. I savoured every step, I enjoyed the squelching sound which my feet made on the moss. I felt the desire to go further. I wanted to remove my shirt. It was then I realised that I had left my jacket by the fallen tree-trunk where I had lain down. But there was no urge to go back, not even the thought that *I'll get it when I go back*; no, I was totally inclined to move forwards, deeper into the glade, to move closer to the giant rock, which I could see now was also covered in green moss. I discarded, first, my shirt and, then, my trousers. I longed to caress the cold stone with my torso just as my feet were caressing the earth, to feel the difference between yielding soil and hard rock. I took a few more steps. My head seemed to bulge. But I had gone beyond being certain about anything. And yet, I did not feel in the least scared or confused. The fullness in my head was the rushing of the dark waters and the electric sensations running through my body were emanating from the rock. As I approached the boulder, the sound of water grew so loud that it completely obliterated the noise of the forest and even the beat of my own heart. The river lay on the other side of the stone, yet it was all embracing. I was almost naked. I reached out my hand – it looked so pale – and touched the boulder. A thrill coursed down my spine. And then another and another. I brought the other hand on to the cool stone. The pulsing doubled. I could have gone around the rock, as had been my original plan. But plans had been forgotten, along with my clothes. I began to climb the wet mass.

My feet slipped on the moss as I tried to gain a toe-hold and my palms seemed oiled, useless. I was forced to hug the stone with my chest and abdomen and the insides of my thighs and to slither in snail-like fashion up the surface of the rock. It was not easy and was compounded by the fact that the shivers which I was imbibing from the slime made me want to remain stuck to the stone forever. And yet, some still greater urge kept me slithering upwards, as though I knew that at the top I would be able to feel the raging torrent on the other side, to let it wash over me, transform me. And my skin was soaking, partly from the green of the boulder, but also because spray from beyond the stone was leaping around me. I reached the summit and drew myself along the last few inches so that I might sit on top of the rock. Throughout the climb, I had not looked back – there had seemed no point – but I had a sense of a great emptiness behind me. The ground was invisible and all I could see, all I could hear, all I was able to feel and taste and smell were the dark, rushing waters of the river that sprayed up around my shoulders. I realised, as I sat on the stone, that I was totally naked. I lay back, letting the humid air slide over my bare skin. I had never felt so utterly alive, so completely real, as though every cell in my body, every thought in my mind was there in its totality, a part of the leaves, the glade, the rock, the river. Tired from the climb, I closed my eyes. The thrumming of water on stone, stone on skin, skin on water was hypnotic. I felt I was a wave, somewhere in the darkness. Moving, changing, constantly re-forming and then sinking at last into the airless water. I was the river. I was the heat. I was the darkness. As I rolled over into the fast-flowing current, I thought I heard the female voice once again. I wasn't sure who it belonged to anymore. But then, I wasn't sure who I was anymore.

The water was cold at first but it soon became warm around me. I was bounced like a log in the current. Everything was feel. Stones, reeds, the scales of long fish. The flow was fast, the water dark. I could see nothing. When I'd been on the rock, the sound of the water had been deafening but now there was an almost total silence. Just the regular pulse of the river beating on and on, the same force which I had felt ever since I had come into the clearing and, perhaps, which I had felt ever since I had entered the forest (which seemed a hundred years before).

I careered on for minutes (or it might've been hours) and then I felt myself being thrown into an even deeper darkness. The water here was utterly still and very deep. I had stopped moving. There was no pulse. No flow. Nothing. I had been so numbed by the crashing torrent, it was difficult for me to ascertain where the skin of my body ended and the water began. I just floated. I was between beats of the heart, in an ecstasy so total that I no longer had any sense of anything. I wished the pool would go on forever and that I would go on with it. Then I sensed other presences. Kaylyn and Donal, and Saraid. I knew they had arrived the same way. But it didn't seem of any great import. Their presences swam alongside mine and we mingled freely with one another. It was almost pitch black in the glade, yet I was able to see. We were splashing about like children, slipping legs and arms around each other, torsos weaving and curving in the darkness. I could see the bottom of the pond and I dived down, but the pool was even deeper than it had seemed and I managed only a numb touch of skin on stone before I had to shoot up for air. There were no words exchanged. Words would have been spurious.

We played games, watery jaunts without rules. Without losers. We were all the same in our uniqueness. We mingled with one another as one part of a body might brush against another part of the same body. Unconscious, unafraid. We embraced like babies. Loved as lovers. We were part of the pool and it circled and danced within all of us. It seemed utterly right that we were all there together and that we all knew everything about the others. Every thought, each contour, the skins of our souls. The ecstasy was not one of pure happiness, rather it was a total fusion, an omniscience, a sinking beneath walls. We were in fish time. For once, I sensed Donal's insecurity and his lack of love. The man who had been my god dissolved into the pool, leaving only the core, the essence of himself. And the heart of Donal was a wall. I sank beneath it and found . . . nothing. A total emptiness. It was not the same with all of us. Kaylyn loved Donal, yes she did, and with a ferocity I had never really appreciated. She would kill for it. Or die. And she, too, had a centre that was indefinable but real, so that I felt as if I could taste it, though not in the usual sense. And Saraid, ah Saraid, she was besotted with the hopeless quest for a man who could never love anyone, let alone her. I could have loved her. I did love her. She must have known this, that day in the dark pool of our unity. She must have felt, tasted my love. I delved deeper into her, peeling off layer upon layer of intensity. I headed for her centre, not knowing what I might find. Not caring. I stopped. I had reached the vortex. I was in her essence. For an infinitesimal moment, I was her essence.

I did love him, Fiacre, but I did not want to love him. I would have killed myself to have prevented myself from loving him. I wanted Donal, the lord of my past, the god of my future. The present, trapped here in this pool, was a deception. I did not love Fiacre. I never loved him. Will never . . .

I poured outward, into the burning flow and swam swam swam back towards the darkness of the pool. I needed its balm, its non-existence. Its false unity. I craved ignorance. When I left Saraid, I found that she had been in Donal the whole time. She had penetrated his defences and had filled up his emptiness. What I had tasted, felt, that which I had been, was a deception. A distortion. I would never know the truth. None of us would. For all I know, we are still there, hiding within one another as we swirl around in the dark pool, as we search for larger truths than we are capable of finding, and, as we feel only walls and emptiness. And Donal . . . all of us were being sucked into Donal, to feed his lack of love. We have never really come back.

I don't remember much about our bodies' return that night to the Rectory. In my mind are a few, tousled images of four naked figures, dripping green, wandering utterly without self-consciousness through the woods until they came, almost by accident, upon their belongings. For a while, I was unsure of who I was. The boundaries between us had been erased, there in the pool, in the space that was Donal, and it could never be the same as before. The harmony of fine threads which we had danced upon was gone forever. Even today, so many years later, I cannot say with total certainty who I am.

The next morning, the Rector was keen to know of what had happened. Donal, I seem to recall, made up some kind of plausible, almost interesting story about getting lost and finding our way back like Theseus from the labyrinth, but the Rector seemed a little disappointed. We left the day after that, despite the Rector's protestations to stay longer.

We got off at separate stations – we all had different destinations – and we never saw one another again. We could not have diverged more completely. Donal found a vocation and subsequently entered the priesthood. He went back to Ireland just before the War, where he lived out his days in the service of his parish. Perhaps only God was truly capable of filling his emptiness. Kaylyn, having permanently lost her lover, ended up in London, where (I learned third hand) she slipped by degrees into prostitution. I heard she was killed during the Blitz. I never heard anything about Saraid, not even the faintest gossip. She seemed to vanish after that summer. I would not have made contact. There was no need. I was a part of them all. I held their pasts and their futures within me. And I became a communist and went off to fight for freedom in Spain, where I was injured in the mud of the

Zaragoza Front (during what many said was a suicidal attack) and thence returned to Ireland. It may seem odd, how we all lost touch but it couldn't have happened any differently. Especially with Saraid. It seems that one can lose parts of one's own soul. I have no idea whether or not the pool which we found was the end of the Old River. I suspect not. But it was an end of sorts, our mingling, our nexus. The quest had been a success. It had destroyed our selves. But I felt little sadness. During that moment in the pool, we had known one another far more deeply than most people are able to in a lifetime. Even if the knowledge was incomplete. Flawed. Perhaps that is the only sadness I have, the only sense of regret. The impossibility of total union, ever, with anyone. And that, really, is the end of the tale. At least, it is as far as my memory can take me. It is strange, how one can write so many words and, yet, when it comes to accurately recalling an event which occurred in one's own life, one can never be sure of just what happened, still less of one's own place in the flow of things. But there is one memory which lingers with me, even as I write these words.

On the day we were due to leave the village, it became misty. As the Rector's Master Buick drew nearer to the station, the mist thickened and became virtually impenetrable. When we got on the train, the mist cleared away again. Fogs and haars were common in those parts, especially during very hot weather. It was something to do with the water table rising, or else sinking . . .

As our train drew away from the station platform, the sun was shining and it was obvious that the day would once again be scorching. I pushed down the window and looked back along the platform. The Rector was standing, one hand resting on his hip, the other on a lamp-post. But it was his face that remained with me for years afterward. His expression was one of total bliss. His eyes, his skin, even the silvery locks of his hair, all seemed bathed in this ecstatic light. I felt I could have gone on gazing at the Rector forever. But the train was moving away and smoke from the engine billowed across the platform. I began to sink back from the open window. As I did this, I thought I saw the old man smile. Just once. When I looked again, it was too far away to know.

Bandanna

To Ustaad Nusrat Fateh Ali Khan

He had been dusting for nearly half-an-hour, but it felt like his whole life. The shop was becoming unbearably warm. Its lemon walls were beginning to crowd in on him, so that he felt soon he would be crushed beneath their dull, yellow weight. The air was stifling, dead and yet he seemed to need great gulps of it. He felt that he would begin to expand like an overfed goldfish and would burst through the shelves, the plaster, the broken clock. He forced his right hand to continue wiping dust off the mica counter, while, with his left, he adjusted the knot of his bandanna. Somewhere at his back, his parents busied themselves as they always had, all their lives. Busy, busy, busy.

The sounds of running and shouting shifted from the street in through the open doorway, disturbing the suffocating rhythm of the morning. Plastic on tarmac. Spittle. The big sky. Sal recognised the voices and his heart leapt, then felt empty. As the lads ran past the burning glass, Salman Ishaq allowed the duster to fall from his hand. He watched it cut a delicate, slightly imperfect trajectory through the methi air and then ran out of his father's shop to shrieks of

'Haraam zaada! Five minutes' work, and he's done? Hud haraam. Useless bastard!'

They did not beckon, entreat or threaten him to come back;

109

he knew this was because they would not expect him to have listened. He knew, as the sun's heat embraced his ears, burning out the fading, effervescent cries of home that, during the succeeding minutes, hours, years, his father would accuse his mother of having brought defective genes into the family, and his mother would retort to her majaz-i-Khuda, the life of her heart, that it would not have been possible to pollute the blood of his people, since their blood had already been dirtier than a Muzaffarabad cesspool. Love among the peasants was like that, mused Salman Ishaq (or 'Sal', as he was known outside of his home and his hundred-strong bratherie, though his parents and all of the aunties remained in total ignorance – blissful, perhaps – of this almost Roman and hence porcine nickname). He slackened his stride, allowing his long, Reebok'd legs to spring up and down on the quivering asphalt. White on black. Sal was fair-skinned, almost white – in any other country except Caledonia he would've been white, say Italy, for example, or España, or Portugal, or Greece or . . . He cursed his luck for ending up in this country of wallpaper-blond people. He cursed his parents. Fuckin ignorant peasants. Knew how to milk a coo and shit in the fields (and, he admitted begrudgingly, how tae run a Carry-out Off-licence), but when it came to knowin where they were at, he chuckled with a thoroughly blond glee, they didnae have a clue, no a fuckin clue.

The group of lads he was following were also running, though not as fast and so he was able tae cover the ground rapidly and would soon be up with them. After aw, that wis why he had dropped his duster in the first place (an in several other places, too), symbol as it wis ae servitude, fuck, he wisnae hovin that, his fellow-gang members seein him mop a fuckin flaer. No way. In the distance, their bandannas darted up and down, dun specks amid the gleaming bodies of cars. They were weaving in and out, darting between the moving

110

vehicles, making them stop altogether at times and then they'd be up on to the pavement and then back into the swim of the road. He could hear their shouts and the curses of the motorists and began to feel the pulse in his chest grow stronger, impelling him to join them, to orgasm in vandal with the Gang. Some of the drivers were shouting through rolled-down glass, swearing in Punjabi as well as in English, both at his pals up ahead and now also at him, too, as he began darting in diamond formation, following in the hot tracks of the Gang. Halfway down Albert Drive, he caught up with his comrades and slapped Ali on the shooder.

'Hey, bhen-chaud! What's up?' Ali shouted in smiles.

They exchanged Bronx palm-slaps while, from beneath the thick waves of August heat, a bass guitar thudded epileptiform rhythms; Bombay Dopplersahb spirals from an open-topped sportscar.

Thunk!

Roo-roo-roo-roo-roo

Love me!

Thunk!

Roo-roo-roo-roo-roo

Love me!

They started off again, the three of them, impelled by the insistent thrum of the music in their ears.

As the Gang ran on, the shopkeepers moved in glue, hardly noticing them as they whooped past. They lived in a different time, another place. The dhokandaars were strung on the drone of a sarod, they pulsed to the rhythms of a different beat, a beat of the seasons, of the peasant calendar, of monsoon into dry and dry into monsoon. They knew nothing of white water or of white women. They slunk along the fields of their gaos, happy only to be a little more than serfs. They asked for nothing else. Would have seen it as presumptuous, in another man's country. Sal felt a buzz in his brain. He was on the runnin-board and they were pedestrians.

They reached the end of the street. Ahead lay the Tramway, a theatre which none of them had ever been in, not even when the Mela had been there. The Mela wis jis fur kids and cooncillurs. Sal and his dosts preferred machines to people. They were noisy, irascible, silicon-based like Michael Jackson. They'd play the robots for hours, not bothering whether they won or lost, not caring about the game. Just moving into the beat of chip upon chip, a twitch of the film-star thigh, the hot-shoulder shuffle. They were on the film-set, they were living in total. There were no spaces in their existence. No gaps of silence. The Gang turned west, away fae the mosques, towards Maxwell Park. That's where they were heidit. To the pond and the trees. To muck up the quiet. To fill it wi gouts ae Bhangra and Baissee. They skatit past the tenement closes, each one a blink in the Gang's eye. The sound of generations carved into each corniced ceiling.

Flip back: Sal, in the gao. Or, to be more accurate, in Azaad-Kashmir, the Land of Freedom. His family's land, earth-brown like their skins (not like Sal's, though), old blood, like the tenement stone. But Sal was another kind of Azaadi. Another hybrid. His was a freedom-within-freedom. A distant, grainy monochrome of greased colonials. Sal, formed between the dots of white and black, somewhere in the invisible alchemical mix flooding through the paper. Long before his conception, Sal was there in the deep line of Partition, in the slime cartridge hate of the one for the other. Peel back the layer, the snakeskin deceptions of Poonch, now in Occupied Kashmir previously in Dogra-land, before that, a gleam in the eye of the Great Mughal, and back, beyond the photoframe, through the nastaliq of dynasties, swimming through the hot sperm of a thousand, to Sikander, Conqueror of the World. Fast forward: Sal an the Gang. The Black

Bandannas. Black because it made their faces look whiter. Italian, almost. Or Spanish, or Portuguese, or anything. As opposed tae the Kinning Park boys. As opposed tae . . .

The Uni-bastards

The Mosquers

The Khans

and The Rest.

They were all small time, forming and disbanding from one year to the next in tenuous hierarchies of slang and spittle. Transient allegiances like in the Games, the video-shop computer games. Nothing was static. Life was movement, juddering, twitching, filmi-star movement. Peasant to refugee, refugee to kisaan, emigrant to immigrant, Paki tae dhokandaar, shopkeeper tae gang-member. Sal slowed to a walking pace. The swagger of the multitudes. Zafar lit a cigarette, handed the pack roon. Puffin draws, they got their breath back.

'Where're we gan?' Ali asked. Ali wis a Shia. Less than a human being, according tae the shitfaced cunt in the Bookshop.

'The Park,' Zafar replied, brusquely.

Ali curled his lip.

'The Park's borin. Ah dinnae want tae go thir.'

'You shut the fuck up, arsehole.'

Ali shut up. He knew his place in the Gang and that was as its arsehole. Zafar was its head, its brains, its brigadier (unlike Pakistan, the gangs did not have more brigadiers than sergeants).

'What'll we do there? In the Park,' Sal asked, measuring his words, levelling them down into the shape of an unobtrusive wheatfield.

'Sit, smoke, watch the burds. Tear the trees doon.'

'Tear the trees? What the fuck for?'

'Why the fuck not?'

113

Sal shrugged. Zafar was a line ae crack on black. Clear-cut and paagal. Sal wished he could be like that. As they walked along Darnley Street, Sal spotted a group of girls approaching from the opposite direction. They were growing like breasts, and he recognised wan ae his cousins among them and began tae hurl abuse as soon as he thought they might be within earshot. Not before. There was nothin more embarrassin than swearin at someone and they couldnae fuckin hear you. The girls did hear it and flung it right back, and the interchange continued as the two groups passed each other as though through a mirror and moved gradually out of earshot again. She had long, black hair, his cousin, and he watched her swing it as she swore. Swung it around legs which he had never seen, but which he had often imagined as long, sinuous, soft, enticing . . . Fuckin bitch. He watched her as she disappeared around the corner. An imprint on his eyelids and an ache in his groin. He blinked and she was gone. But not the ache. The swollen throbbing expanded like Pakistan from the plane and became a marriage ceremony. A man-in-a-mask, the elephant's vision. A bride, weeping tears through a waranteed hymen.

He blinked, hard. Blood scarlet.

Ali jabbed him in the ribs. Raised his thick, black eyebrows.

'Randy bastart.'

'No way. No fuckin way, man.'

Ali shook his head, his lop-sided, peasant's skull.

'When the time comes . . .'

'It'll nivir come.'

'Nae mair white burds, wi thur wide open cunts askin fur it, a glais ae vodka an their yours, nae matter how black ya are. Jis feed them enough booze an dope an they'll screw you an thank you fur it.'

'At least ah get them.'

That shut him up. Ali. Him, wi his big bug-eyes. Too big. They saw too much. They'd get him intae trouble, wan ae these days. Parso, they'd fuck him up, doon an sideeways. He remembered a thin white cow he'd screwed last month. The feel ae her anorexic thigh-joins. Bone on bone. Jag-mairks. They'd huv tae be stoned tae fuck a Paki. And then, only fur blue-backs. He began tae harden. Hated himsel. Puffed on his ciggie. It had gan oot.

'Go'a match?' he asked Zafar.

Zafar didn't answer.

Silent bastart, thought Sal, and he flung the ciggie doon, killin its corpse wi a stroke ae his trainer.

You'll smoke your life away, his mother had said. So many fuckin times. Like they nivir said onyhin original, like there wis nuhin new in them. Nivir hud been. Jis work, work an work, like it wis the only thing in life. Kaam, kaam, kaam. Fuckin peasants. He wisnae in that trap. Gangstas were ootside ae aw that crap. They were on the border. Alang the silent razor. Between the dots. Sepia, again. Short-haired men with wives. Babies, dead – already. Visions of the past, of past lives. A long, Hindu cacophony. Sal laughed, inside of himself. He would never be born as a shopkeeper. Better a dog. At least you got tae fuck freely. Or a mullah. Just sit in the mosque and take money. Blue-backs. Grow a beard and never, ever smile. An easy job, really. One day, maybe. An image of a large bonfire. The Gangs, all throwing their bandannas into the flames. Black, red, blue. Even the Kinning Park Boys. All sprouting long, grey beards and adopting a bow-legged walk. The bonfire spread and burned away the image.

And what's behind it? Sal the Gangsta asked Salman Ishaq Sahb the Mohlvi.

Wagging his well-muscled finger, Ishaq Sahb gave the answer:

Behind every image, there is always a jagirdaar. Just as (he went on) *in every Coca-Cola tin there is a naked Amrikan slut, her legs overhanging the metal . . .*

Okay, Okay, Sal the Gangsta cut in, a little embarrassed, *but what aboot ma Irn Bru tin?*

The Mullah did not understand. In England, all tins were the same, he intimated. Just being a tin was enough. More than enough. Just thinking about a can might even be sufficient.

But how could he know? Sal thought. Unless he, too, had been there, into the metal, between the jag-scarred thighs of the slut and had swum around (beard, frown-and-all) in the great fizzy vacuum of the west. Of Amrika, of Glasgee. The mullahs were all Amrikan agents. See-Eye-Aye. Everyone knew that. Even his father knew that, fur fuck's sake.

Now they were passin the Safeway an there the pretty cars aw row'd up like obedient schoolkids. Only they weren't learnin onyhin. The Great White Superstores, stolid bastions thrown in a ring aroon the city. His father often railed against the toilet-friendly conglomerates, saying that they'd milk the small shop-keeper dry. *And what did loag want, Khuda-ke liye, a local, living-room-sized dhokaan with you know a friendly face or a giant metal aircraft hanger? What wus the future for our people in this country?* He sounded like a guardian of the tiny units of commerce which Bonaparte had faced, ranged in bared teeth shopfronts along the white, Doverine cliffs of Albert Drive. And they were the new Napoleons, the massive brick battleships, the Safeways, the Sainsburys, the ASDAs besieging Glasgee, attack-ing Scola, runnin thur damned South American produce right intae the khanas of his ane bratherie. Apples ae Shaitan. The Gang chased past the trees of knowledge which burgeoned in the spacey grounds of the Hutcheson's Grammar Schule, the in-vitro incubator of budding intellectuals. Where any parents who needed their kids as fuel for the already bulging middle classes that stuck society together sent their offspring. So many went there and fucked up. Cause they'd rather rave, than save. Salman had never aspired to a hood-and-gown. Maybe it was his parents' fault. Their lack of ambition. They'd rather he work in the shop.

116

But then wasn't everything their fault? Comin here in the first place. Runnin a fuckin Paki shop. That wis what they were seen as. Could've worn top hats an tails an owned hauf the city an they'd still have been Pakis. He hated it. Never, never wanted to be a shopkeeper. Had missed out on learnin. Jis wanted tae be in a Gang an tae shout. Tae scream in blood and bhangra.

Boom-thaka-thaka-thaka-thaka-thaka
Boom-thaka-thaka-thaka-thaka-thaka
Boom-thaka-thaka-thaka-thaka-thaka

The harsh, Jullundri consonants cut his flesh in slashes of kirpaan; it felt good; upon their blade would his skin grow calloused, hard. Nothing would hurt him. No words. No actions. Sticks and stones would shatter on his body. And still, he would sing-dance the juddering figure beat, the blood music of exile. The black slaves had bled in blue: R 'n' R, hip-hop, reggae, and now the sons of swastika-daubed Paki shop-owners would disembowel the air in syncopation. Together, with night torches, they would fire the swastikas and, in the fractured air, would spin them round in great wheels up and down the streets of Glasgow. And they would feed the skin-heads of Ibrox, the white-trash tattoo of Penilee into the great, burning cunt of Mata Kali, where five thousand firewheels spun time. Hindu symbols – yes! His parents would have been mortified to hear him thinking that way. But fuck it. They couldnae hear him thinking, no ony mair. It wis aw mixed up, onyway. Sikh Bhangra, Mussalmaan Qawal, Hindu Raag-Bhajan-Khayals . . . Black Blues, it all swirled together and spumed into a river of Techno-Rave Brummie Beat. And the Gang would rubber-dance in the Victorian park among the trees, the ducks, the water, the shouts of children. Amidst the summer leaves, they would make music and war.

They leapt over the jagged fence and into the Park. The smell of grass, cut skin-short. Roses like the lips of courtesans, drawing out the sex act into a stream of notes.

Meri naam Jaan-ki-bai hai
Meri naam Gauhar Jaan

They half-ran down an incline and tumbled together in a heap near the bottom. Mothers were pushing prams, the wheels of which always seemed to go uphill. Children played with small boats and old folk simply sat in lines on benches, as though waiting their turn. Salman closed his eyes. Goldfish noises . . .

He felt a fist in his belly, enough to provoke but not to seriously wind him. He turned and caught another on the jaw. His head buzzed as he threw his arms outward to grapple with his opponent. Got a hold of his waist and didnae let go. Salman and Zafar wrestled on the grass, rolling and screaming. Ali leapt in and his extra weight had the effect of pressing down on Salman's chest so that he wasn't able to move and could hardly breathe. Was not able to say, *Enough's enough, lads. Get aff noo.* Wasn't sure they would've listened, anyway. The sun was streaming into his eyes and he could feel its golden brilliance flood through the coils of his brain. He could hear time run backwards through the veins of trees, moving always anti-clockwise in a broad tape-loop.

Kull . . .	C
Meri awaz suno, mujhe azad Karo	C
Kull . . .	C
Masks	C
Chunnae ud ud' jae, guth Kul Kul jae	C
Kull . . .	C
Death is not dying	C
Achintya bheda bheda Tattva	C
Kull . . .	C
Solitude	C
Light	C

Kinna Sohna tainu, Rub nay banaya   C
Kull   C

And Salman Ishaq was floating in tears of noor.

Allah-hu
Allah-hu
Allah-hu
Inhale *Allah* Exhale *Hu*
Inhale *Allah* Exhale *Hu*
Inhale *Allah* Exhale *Hu*
Allah-hu
Allah-hu
Allah-hu

He realised he was able to breathe again. His neck felt stiff. They had got off his chest and were lying, breathless, beside him. They were basking in the sun's warmth (this too, would've been unthinkable), half-watching the delicate slivers of light pour down on the park. They had noticed nothing. Would not have cared. They were true Gangstas. For a moment, he felt a rush of pride in being a part of the Black Bandannas. Soon, he too would be capable of feeling nothing, but it passed and left him empty. He looked away from them and just lay there, letting the backs of his fingers rest upon the short, fine blades of grass. The sun filled his eyes, making them sting and water but he did not allow the lids to close. He began to grow blind and it occurred to him that one day, not too far in the future, it would be his fingers that would be pushing up the grass and that what he thought, felt, did, created during that minuscule pause in his fate might live beyond him, his family, the tribe to which he happened to belong, and that the only constant in the whole of Maxwell Park – the trees, the birds, the water, the kids – the only beat that pumped all other rhythms was the beat of love. Salman took a deep breath, the deepest he'd ever taken; it filled parts of his lungs which had never before breathed, not even at the moment of his birth. He felt a great swell of happiness explode infinitely slowly from the centre of his being. His love spread across the grass, the trees, the trunks of dead elephants and returned to him sevenfold.

> *And in the end,*
> *When the music's over*
> *There is only love*

The drone behind it all was the note *c*, right there in the soul of his brain. He felt its smooth curves, the walls of a tunnel on the way to heaven. And there it was in the very coils of paradise. He followed a bird as it coursed along the sky. He sat up. Ripping off his bandanna, he ran his fingers through his long hair. Felt free. Wanted to leap into the pond, and swim. Desired the cool, green gown of its depth. From far across the city, Salman heard the Azaan, carried upriver on currents of music. Rolling his bandanna out on to the grass, he faced towards Gorbals Cross and began to pray.

The Dancers

I t had been months, it might've been years, and everything
was different from before.

She pulled away fae the gleamin tarmac, the cars, the people
ahead of her in the queue and gazed instead at the darkened
stone walls of the club, its arches, its spire, the night shadows
which flitted across its surface . . . Halfway up the spire, a
giant red sign flickered. *Gee's.* Part of the sign was broken and
hung down, so that when the light flashed on, it was as though
the club was bleeding.

A couple ae thin teenage guys handed Rosh two free tickets,
explainin mournfully that they hadnae been allowed in because they'd been wearin trainers. Rosh and Zarqa were in
skin-tight black and, inside, the club, which once had been a
church, would be filled with icons and candles and swinging
censers, and the fonts would have taps so that the dancers
could splash themselves whenever they got too hot. The
trance techno would incorporate speeded-up Gregorian
chants, while the treble of nuns would spike like needles
through the juddering, cocaine beats. Tonight's DJ would
be *Lord Lupin and Bastard Sister India*, the best cross-over act
this side ae Bombay. Roshani shivered and let the darkness
flood over her, the voices of the ravers who had not yet begun
to rave, the smells of petrol and unemptied bins, and she drew
her arms around her chest, wrapped the thin leather of her
jacket like a skin over her breasts.

121

Once, it had been second nature. Goin out, drinkin, ravin. The silken feel of an *e* slippin down her throat. Waitin fur the buzz. It had been like breathin.

Lucky ma boobs are so small, she thought. No like Zarqa's, and she glanced at her friend and she smiled and craned her neck tae see if the queue wis movin. Zarqa wore her lipstick like a contraceptive, splashed thickly across her face. Every time she spoke, the crimson would smudge a little more over her earth-brown skin, so that, by the end of the night, she would resemble a clown.

'We shouldae got here, earlier,' she said. 'Saturday night's always like this.'

Rosh was silent. The vodka wis wearin aff and, aw ae a sudden, she began tae miss her papa. The clubs weren't like the discos where her parents had met. Every time she crossed the threshold of a club, she entered a borderland where anything might happen. Glasgae wis full ae border lands, places where you could cross over . . .

An image ae her papa in the park, liftin her high above his head, his giant's hands wrapped around her ribs like a cradle. And then she's spinnin, round and round, and the world's a blur and she's flingin her arms out tae balance herself. And she's all air and light.

Her maa had gone all Irish Catholic on her and didnae like her goin out late. Her maa had found solace in the bosom of her saints and her martyrs. Rosh had seen her, dressed aw in black an prayin intently in her bedroom, her long face strainin towards a starless sky, the skin flushed pink. Her cracked, kitchen knuckles had been clenched tightly around dark rosary beads and she'd been counting, silently, through the decades. Remembering. They had been a seventies Ibrox couple, all pouts, platforms an wavy hairdos. *A mixed marriage*, everyone had called it, as though it had been a recipe or a cocktail. A Faisalabadi and a Belfast Catholic. It had been a romance of underdogs. He was a failed Punjab graduate who had a head full of dreams. To open up a shop, to go wholesale, to play the stocks, to move into vegetables . . .

Her papa's imagination had seemed endless and he'd had the looks to pull it off: eyes the colour of hazelnuts just about to ripen, long, black locks of hair and a smile that could melt diamond. He had always been able to convince everyone around him that this time, bhai, this time, he was serious and would follow through. But, while the kisaan who'd bull-ploughed their way across the continents had ended up drivin top-model white Mercs, Yusuf, the dreamer, had dreamed his way right down tae the mutkae ka pendtha. A security guard. The long hours, the enforced solitude, the low pay, her papa had lived his life, balanced on an invisible thread. All the years of their marriage, her maa'd been the real breadwinner. Two jobs, one in the mornin' and one in the evenin', both, pretty much thankless, the sortae occupations where, at every op-portunity, the workers would hide in doorways and burn their dreams on the ends ae rolled fags. Her maa had aged faster than Yusuf, but she had been dogged; Rosh had been her anchor and Yusuf, her sail. And they'd sailed on, the three ae them, through the years an the jobs an the no-jobs an the school an the no-school. But now, her maa had run aground an Rosh felt like she wis sinkin in deep, black water.

She had given up, tryin tae figure out just why the one-time disco-dancer, the Cessnock John Travolta, had grown a beard and begun, slowly, to whirl. Rosh had seen him, one day, in her parents' bedroom, dressed in a long, white shirt, turning and turning around the place of her creation. His right hand had been inclined upwards and his left, towards the floor. His eyes had been closed. She'd felt frightened and had left the house and gone for a walk across Bell's Bridge and had let the fierce river wind blow across her closed lids, had let it dissolve her fear. Shortly after that, he had left his job an his dost, and, instead, had begun to trace out the geometrics of perfection around the double-bed. Her maa had begun tae tear her hair out and had suggested he see a shrink. Bein the Whirlin Dervish ae Kinnin Park wisnae such a good idea. But then, quite suddenly one summer's night, everything had unravelled like a broken rosary. Her papa had been sent to the Cathcart Cemetery, her maa to the Confessional and Rosh . . .

She forced herself back to the image of her praying mother. The same bedroom, the same bed. Her hair, once ginger, had turned a kind of dirty white and her eyelids had been clasped shut. Crow's feet. Imprints of coins. Her papa hadnae had coins on his eyes. Muslim funerals were unadorned, the graves unmarked. He had seemed so young, that day, beneath the pale make-up. But it wis only his face, she thought. And even in death, faces could lie. Her maa'd wantit Rosh tae become a Catholic. Our Father, Hail Mary an aw that. And Rosh had liked wine and bacon, but wis sick of death.

All she was left with were vague sensations. Her father's shadow, but not her father. She'd sit for hours, glaring into her bedroom mirror, willing it to give something back, something she could clasp, perhaps a fleeting vision, across the glass, of his living face like that of a saint . . .

But it had never happened. It was as though both her father and his dreams had been taken from her. She had grown to hate the mirror. When she felt Irish, she would be Róisín Dhu, the black rose, and when she thought that she was Faisalabadi, she would revert to Roshani, the ray of light. The split ran right inside her, it divided her into two, it apportioned her loyalties. But when she walked across Bell's Bridge, she would feel the Clyde River flow and pulse like an artery in her head, and then she wis in the trees and the gargoyles and the clubs where everything became One, and she wis in the crazy summer marches where her friends, tightly wrapped in Ibrox blue, had run alongside the official procession. She'd nivir been certain whether the green she'd waved at Celtic matches had been the hara of Punjab or the Republican banner of west Belfast. Colour wis a funny thing. She pulled herself away.

She'd come back tae the club, at Zarqa's suggestion, tae try and get a life again. Wavin her hands about, Zarqa had joked with her, as they had both sat on the wee pink stool before Rosh's bedroom mirror, that it wis time she got back outae herself and picked up some men. Rosh smiled, there, in the queue. In spite of her shambolic appearance, Zarqa had always managed tae attract members ae the opposite sex. The darker sex. Mibbee that wis whit goras looked fur in an Asian girl. Big boobs, big bum an thick, fleshy lips. Eyes that rolled. And when Zarqa wis wi a gora, she would swing her hips like a buffalo comin outae a slow-movin, muddy river. Aye, Zarqa had a way wi men. Sometimes, she took them the full way. Or so she said. Right now, she wis stinkin ae a perfume which Rosh couldnae place. But she wis her friend. They'd seen each other through thick and thin.

Zarqa's lips were movin. Through the perfume, her breath smelled of whisky.

'Thank Goad fur that!'

The queue wis shiftin. For an insane moment, Rosh found herself wishin she wis Zarqa.

The music was background and smelled of booze and sweat. The women slipped off their leathers and handed them to the anaemic-looking cloakroom attendant.

'Who'd huv him!' Zarqa joked and she jabbed Rosh in the ribs.

'Let's get a drink.'

Claspin vodkas, they managed to squeeze themselves on to the edge of a semi-enclosed bench-seat, next to some mousey mop-top lads who looked as though they'd been dancin all

night an all day. People had already begun to rise and dance,
though the movements were still slow, preparatory, circular.
The interior of the club had retained the structure of a church,
so that the DJ's mixing-desk was up where the high altar had
once stood and, gradually, as the night wore on, the dancers
would move from the nave to the choir and then to the high
altar itself. Wan ae the lads brushed against her airm. It wisnae
deliberate, but she pulled away. The lad smiled at her and she
flinched. But his eyes were empty. Dead, like her papa's.
Everyone wis smilin at everyone else in chemical friendship.
Most ae the folk had been tae a pre-club where they'd got
loaded up wi *e's* or acid. Rosh would normally have done the
same, but things hadn't been normal for a long time.

The triple vodka went straight tae the tap ae her heid and
her midriff went soft. Suddenly, she wouldnae huv minded if
the amiable mop-top had brushed against her airm. She could
almost feel the touch of him on her skin. Everything was
heightened. Blurred but sharper at the same time, like the
imprint of breath on a mirror. The music wis growin loud and
elliptical and she could no longer grasp it. Eight monks,
sixteen voices. Gregorian multiplication. Mibbee celibacy
strengthens the voice, she thought. Rosh had been outae it
for months an she honestly couldnae say she'd missed it.
Unlike Zarqa, who wis shoutin somethin at her but she
couldnae lipread her friend since her lips were smudged wi
lipstick. She had a blank look in her eyes and Rosh wondered
whether her drink might've been spiked. But then Rosh, too,
was being swept up in the dark sinew of the beat and the
perfect, flashing whiteness of the strobes. A gentle, funky jazz
but with some trip hop intermingled and slow, churz sitar
backbraining through. Zarqa and the mop-tops had vanished
into the crowd and Rosh was alone. Someone had left a small
square of card on the black table-top. She reached across and
picked it up. It was still dry. There was a man's face on the

card. His features were sharp, almost three-dimensional, but it wasn't a hologram. She was drawn to the eyes and the lips . . .

She gazed at it, unblinking, until everything else faded to a blur. The beat grew louder. Her eyes throbbed and the colours on the card seemed to run so that the features became liquid. Tears were massing in the inside corners of her eyes and the urge to blink was almost unbearable, but still she kept watching. Remembering.

Midnight in June. Clyde Street.

He takes off his jacket and lays it neatly across the stone parapet. He removes his shoes and socks. Then he goes down the steps and on to the wharf. His shirt is loose. He stands near the edge. Teeters a little, then catches his balance. He closes his eyes and lets his arms extend. And then he begins slowly to turn. He turns against time and goes faster and faster until the city around him is just a blur. He spins faster than he has ever spun; his white shirt billows like a sail in the breeze and he is an arc of light, pirouetting in the darkness. At the last moment, his feet seem to leave the ground.

His body had been picked up from the river later that morning.

She cradled her head in her hands and the sobs heaved up fae the base ae her stomach and forced themselves out through her windpipe and she cried until the muscles ae her face were sair fae cryin. Then she stopped. Her mouth tasted salty and her nose wis bunged up. The dancers were oblivious. Even her friend, Zarqa. Blood wis thicker . . .

The moment before her tears had dripped on to the card, obliterating the picture, Rosh thought she had made out her papa's face, the face which had been too perfect for this world. Everyone had always said that she had her father's eyes.

She staggered over tae wan ae the fonts, filled the sink and thrust her face intae the freezin watter. She felt her heart skip a beat and she wondered if she might drown there, among the dancers and the icons and the sputtering candles. Gaspin, she straightened up. Blinked the dots from her eyes. Above the font wis a mirror. Her face wis gaunt an pale an her hair wis aw long an straggly. She looked like wan ae those martyrs whose pictures her maa'd pinned up all over the house. She hauf-expected tae see blood come gushin fae her foreheid. Mixed blood. The stigmata. She moved closer, peered at the browns ae her eyes. In the light of the strobes, the irises seemed almost blue.

She stepped back fae the mirror and saw that above it wis a statue ae the Virgin.

She'd done nothin at school and had wound up, like so many ae the loose-breasted gorees, doin DSS-inspired courses goin nowhere. No dreams, no reality. Just escape. Her maa had reverted tae the faith ae her mother's and now saw God in a plastic bead. God wis everywhere, they said. Well then, he wis in this club, he wis in the music, he wis in Lord Lupin and Bastard Sister India and he wis in the mop-tops and the LSD-impregnated image of her papa, which seemed tae have vanished jist like he had done. The techno was turnin deep and Rosh sank into its river, along with all the spirits of those who had gone before. As she danced, she thought of her papa and of his futile search for faith. A bearded face in a coffin was all. The rest of him had been swathed in white. She hadn't been allowed to touch his face. There had been no wake, no drunken worshipping of the body. Her maa had secreted the stained silk shirt, like a relic, in a drawer all of its own.

The dancers were now massing around the mixing-desk, so that Rosh could barely make out the top of the DJ's head. She craned her neck and felt suddenly weightless, as though she might simply rise up in the darkness and float towards the high altar. That must be Lord Lupin, she thought, and then she giggled. I wonder where Bastard Sister India is. Or mibbee it's the same person. It's jist a name. Like Roshani. Light in the darkness. Or Yusuf. The dreamer. Or Zarqa, the blue-eyed beauty. She began to laugh, uncontrollably, and her laughter swept her along the black floor as though she wis on ice and she skated into the cool trance which the club had become. The dancers moved like a single skin and Rosh didnae want tae be on the outside so she edged her way closer tae the DJ's desk. The contours ae bodies, male and female, pressed up against her an the smell of sweat and beer filled her nostrils. She thought she saw Zarqa, dancin in the middle ae a crowd ae women whose bodies were like dolphins. She wondered if that wis why she and Zarqa had remained friends. Mibbee, like a gora, she fancied Zarqa because of her eastern-ness. Mibbee, like the white women who were now pushin their bodies intae Zarqa's dark-brown flesh, Rosh desperately craved the touch of her bones. Khoon aur mitti. Faisalabad. House of Judgement.

Rosh had worked her way close to the high altar. There was barely space to move and she could feel the hot breath of the dancers burn the skin of her neck, her throat . . .

There wis a guy in front ae her. She couldnae see his face, but she recognised his back, the shirt stuck with sweat to the skin. His hands were outstretched and he wis dancin in half-circles as though he didnae want tae leave the high altar, as though he wis entranced by the sounds which pumped through the darkness, by the disc jockey whose fingers plucked thousands of strings. Rosh felt the blood surge through her temples. The DJ was almost screwin the mixing-desk. She moved across its surface like a djinn; her hair was long and wild and Rosh couldnae make out her face. The music wis buildin, the beat wis goin faster and faster and Rosh could no longer sense the dancers' breathing. There was just her own body and the pulse of the music which reverberated upwards into the darkness of the church. Then the music and the lights and the stone merged into a river and the river flowed through her so that there was just the beat of her own heart and the sound of her breath. She wis right next tae the man. She stopped dancing and reached out her hand. Touched his shoulder. Silk and bone. Pulled him around.

Nothing moved.

Then the man turned towards her.

She recognised the face. It was one ae the mop-tops. The one who had left her the wild card.

He smiled at her. His eyes were empty. Black.

She turned away and tried to lose herself in the sweeping sound of skin tablas and she let the palms of the unseen ustaad caress the sides of her body so that she was like clay on a potter's wheel, spinning round and round in the darkness.

The Naked Heart

H e sat by the wall and opened his diary. Bits of paper fell out and scattered over the floor. The room was a mess. He'd intended to tidy the thing up for months – years – but had never quite got round to it. Some intrinsic, silted substratum in his personality had prevented him from clearing away the clutter. No, he thought, that was just an excuse for laziness. He gathered up the bits and placed them on the small, stained table in front of him. Fingering through the diary, he came at length to the part he had been seeking: tomorrow.

> *7am: Church.*
> *9 am: Hospice of the Martyrs – a breakfast gathering.*
> *11.30am: Take black bags to the shop.*
> *1pm: Lunch Club.*
> *2pm: Stand in for Cath at OXFAM.*
> *6pm: Church Bazaar.*
> *9pm: Church.*

There was nothing after 9pm. There never was. Night was a dark nothingness into which he would plunge, smooth-skinned, like a frog, into a pond. A soft envelope of oblivion.

He snapped the diary shut. It always gave him a feeling of completion, doing that. A sense of coarse roundness, like running your hand over the surface of a pomegranate. He put it down on top of the loose bits of paper so they wouldn't get blown away by any stray wind that happened to seep through the cracks in the wall . . .

His small frame writhed with exhaustion. John let his head flop back against the plaster and allowed the lids to close, slowly, just like that, so they might pentimento a sense of spiritual peace over the plastic. He was in a field.

John. In a field so vast, she could see no fence, no edge.

She looked up at the sky. A wonderful sunset, the hymen of night. She glanced down at herself. A crimson toga, swirling in the breeze. She reached down and pulled a bunch of flowers from the soft, yielding soil. Sea-sand, once it had teemed with great, thoughtless fishes. Their soulless eyes shudder there, beneath the falling sun, on the unploughed field, among the roses. Yes! They were roses. Never mind, they were all part of God's creation. God, in His most ineffable wisdom. The fishes and the fished. The fished and the fishes. What happened to them? she wondered, in her virginity. Got thrown into the fire, she answered herself, in her bridal whoredom. The whore of God. That's what I am, she thought. No more, no less. I perform His work, utterly selflessly, year upon year, in the vague expectation of a better life after this. But this field, this plane of earth, is the end. There is no great illumination, no leaping harmonic of the cosmos. Just soil, sinking skin and a setting sun.

John opened his eyes. There was fluid on his head. He'd been sweating. He got up, went into the bathroom and splashed cold water over face, neck, ears. It was a small flat, barely large enough for one adult, let alone . . . Well, he wasn't a big man, never had been, and it was okay for his needs. He splashed another palmful of water over his broad, scarred forehead, his brown, heavily-lidded eyes. He looked up. An image of himself dripped on to the floor. Dilated pupils. Black, the night of the spirit. An aquiline nose. Some Roman genes. Out of place in that cold, northern city with its weeping walls, its glass soul. He was going bald. Damn! he thought, then, immediately, automatically, he asked God's forgiveness. He stared at the mirror. It was stained, like the table, like everything in his flat. His life. No, stop, John! That's self-pity. There's nothing He hates more than self-pity. The last refuge of the damned. If you've done all the evil there is to be done, there's nothing left except self-bloody-pity. His father would've slapped him for that. For feeling human emotion of any kind. Would've said it was womanish. Bent. His father was called John, too. Hailed, like John Junior, from the small town of Fountainglass. Stupid name. Invented by the Victorians, in the middle of their whiskered arrogant ignorance. There was no fountain. There was no glass. So why in Hell (he begged forgiveness again) did they call it, Fountainglass? John was with him. The father.

Rocky, barren-faced. Old castle walls.

A cloth salesman. Captain of Nothing. Had come of gentrified stock – out Wessex way (those damned Arrrs) – but married beneath his station, was disowned and had resented it, ever since. Denied it. Love. The cardinal sin. The Devil's delusion. John Junior would never, ever succumb to that kind of love. Carnal. No. The rock died when he was eleven. He'd learned the rest from his tired mother and an elder brother, Frank, whom John had worshipped before he had known God and whom he still loved more than anyone. Almost. There had been another brother, Louis, who had died in infancy, probably of his mother's despair. A move of vicissitude to a small market town in the north. The cold north. John went to a school for no-hopers, while his mother went slowly insane. He knew all this, even as he gazed at his father's dead face.

He dried the curvatures around his nose and along the

ageing skin of his eyelids which had never been kissed by the lips of a woman. He threw his head back and gazed at the long moths on the lightbulb. A presence of Terri hovered around his skin. The brush of her arm. Soft, white, pure. He could feel her clarity slip through the shell which he had erected around himself. Her cool fire swelled inside him, making him feel weightless. When he looked again in the mirror, he saw that he was sobbing. He ran the cold tap. Splashed his face. Did it again. And again. He cried and splashed, cried and splashed like some idiot clown. This was nothing new. He would let the tears flow away into the indifference of the city. In its callous streets would his sorrow drift and dissolve. He liked its size. Its anonymity. He could lose himself in the metropolis. That was John's cardinal ambition. To immerse his body in forgetfulness, to wallow in darkness. That was what the charity was about. Losing oneself. Of course, it wasn't selfless, not like it ought to be, but it wasn't an ideal world. Ah no, it wasn't an ideal world.

The tears ended, leaving crinkled imprints of themselves in the air. He went back to the room – there was only one room – and lay down on the single bed. He had deliberately gone out and bought a single bed. It had been an act of defiance. The cheap, unbroken bed was a wall to keep out the denizens of lust and degeneration. He washed the sheets twice a week. Sometimes, daily.

The field. She was a silhouette against the dying light of the western horizon (she knew this, even though she could not see herself – she had no mirror). A chill shuddered along her semi-visible limbs, caressed the skin, cavorted, shamelessly across her body. She closed her eyes. Her virginity would not last the night; there would be no enlightenment. Or, if there was, then it would lie in submission. Utter, complete submission to the will of another. The roses were in full bloom. Red, jugular. She had

*let them fall, the ones she had picked. Now they lay at her feet,
touching the tips of her bare toes. Her skin was white against
their rugose softness. She inhaled. The smell of roses careered up
her nostrils into her brain. Intoxicating, infinite like the oil of a
painting. She wanted to swim in their petals, to be lost in the
darkness of their aroma. Unploughed fields. Her virginity would
hold, to the last. Till Judgement Day. Beyond, perhaps.*

It was humid. The city, the anonymous conglomerate, had
grown hot in the night. John slipped off his shirt. Ran his soft
palm over the hairs of his chest. Just his chest. A school for the
poor. The no-hopers. The scheme-kids. Guaranteed to fall,
either into crime or into pregnancy. Roads to Hell, both.
Teachers, fucked out of their minds with the futility of their
task. Like rolling a bloody boulder up a hill. John might've
gone the same way. Got-a-girl-into-trouble, the old phrase
went. It was out-dated and reeked of Gerry-and-the-bloody-
Pacemakers and kitchen-sinkism. No! Now it was stale vomit
and the truth. Nothing but. In the cold estates of the north,
there were no more illusions. No more trips. It was either sink
or be saved. And then, deep in the semen of a hot summer's
night, John had met the Preacher.

Reverend Father Allan.

Starch'd black and attitude. He'd liked that. The young
John. Smooth, rippled, spunk-bursting. Spiritual spunk, now,
after meeting the Preacher. Yes, sir!! The Lord Thy God Will
Punish Sinners! Pub Fuckers, brown and sticky, shall be
drown'd in their own beer! The Revenge of the Virgin. A
comeback for the hymenal furrow. Mary! Mary! Mary! the
Mother militant shall ride over all with her great round eyes
and her beatific lips. Charity covers all sins. Hide yourself by
the brook, Cherith, and ye shall drink from its waters. Give of
yourself in all matters. Render thyself in thy totality, nothing
less. It is only through the mistakes of the flesh that ye shall

learn the truth. He'd been drawn by degrees into the folds of her robe and he had helped teach the poor kids to r 'n' r. Without shame he'd begged along countless rainy streets for the needy, the sick, the invisible ones. He'd lived in a dark cell in downtown Tollacre. A shitpile of a place. But good for Salvation. Become involved. That was the secret. Be drawn in like a fly. He'd worked with the Vicar (that's what they called him, the Reverend Father Allan). It was kind of quaint. Roman, almost. To multiply the charitable impulse, to be a spanner in the evolutionary hypothesis, to see, laid out, the tapestry of generations. And he had been a part of that. A segment on the long, twisting chain of caterpillar night. Those darknesses of the tent where the Reverend Allan would preach. The Catholic Evangel. A minute counter-reformation. Salvatore on a silver tray. Yet real to John in the night of the senses. And beyond, into the quietude of the soul. The first night of love's ardent desire for communion with the holy spirit. Beyond which . . .

He got up again. Made a cup of coffee. Drank it, alone. One cup. Unlipped. No woman had ever graced the threshold of his flat. Not even sisters in the Cause. He was solitary in his redemption. Blood was unique. A face on the rippled integument of a flawless creator. Who needed a second half to complete themselves? Only the weak, who thought they were strong. If you needed someone to complete you, it meant you were only half a person. John was whole, pomegranate-like. Each segment of his being was a world in itself and, yet, each was a part of a greater existence. He didn't need sex. Sex was a necessary part of Creation, but it had the tendency to take over, to engulf, to deify itself and so was best avoided. Nights were the difficult time. Charity was hard to dispense at night. After the sun set, no man could remain pure. Knowledge was nothing. Will meant less. The joys of time, of sense, of morals, of faith, of the spirit – all were as nothing in the darkness which was deeper than death. The coffee rolled around in his belly. His trunk had fattened with the years. Soon, he would be dead. And never having tasted of woman. What did it matter, anyway? He would be with the six-winged seraphs 'neath the Throne of God, Himself. Who needed the figs of lust? Wine and angels were all John needed, now. The angels of truth and the wine of mysteries. Each sip, another fragment of God. Of the truth. The logos, the mouth vibration. Sound-in-liquid.

It hadn't always been like that. Not even in the Reverend Father's fold. Terri. She had been a sister. Had come in, shortly after him. With her black eyes and skin so white, John sometimes felt he could see the blood as it flowed beneath. She, too, was an orphan. A seed, floating along the cold city streets. She'd once told him her grandfather had been Jewish. And there was something of the Salome about her. Perhaps that was why she'd been attracted to the Reverend's fold. To quell the dance within. But John saw the dance, he saw it every time he looked at her, every time he thought of her. There, in the postmodern streets filled with grey figures and emptiness, they had laughed and begged together, sister and brother in the Lord's flock. Her slim waist would sway slightly next to his as they held out their cans. And at day's end, when they pooled the fruits of their labour, just the two of them together, the wailing emptiness of urban foxes outside, then he would feel her breathing turn the cold air suddenly hot.

Where there is no love, put love and you will draw out love. Terri and the Reverend Father had put love into John and now the love was drawing out. He was floating on its burning stream, he was a fish in its leaping flame. But in the water, amidst the fire, this love had changed. It was no longer a love of the spirit, but of the flesh. It was a step backwards. A delusion of the Devil. He, who was ever present, even during his moments of greatest rapture. Especially in those moments. Visions of Terri, naked, bursting, breast-fresh. Gentle, animal sounds issued from her soft belly, calling him inward. Into damnation. He was balancing on a hair, over an endless chasm. He would go to church, but would not take communion. The Reverend Father had asked him why. And there, in the dark cell of his confession, he had told all. The best thing, Father Allan had said, was that they be separated. Either they could do God's work or else they would have to leave the fold and try to live as man and wife, on the outside. It would be hard – harder, perhaps, than life within – but it was possible. Millions had made it possible. John had to make the decision. Quickly, before the dawn. He had confused the different loves which God offered; he had mixed the Blessed Virgin with the Veiled Whore. Without knowing it, he had offered his soul to the Devil. Had almost been fooled by the night of the senses. And so, in the deepest darkness, John had left the fold. His penance would be to give his life to charity but without the protecting, guiding hands of the Reverend Father. He would do God's work. Alone.

He had moved away from the great city to another and had come to dwell in this hovel of a flat. It was his cell, his hermitage. His prison. The angels were his guards: their silent, cold figures hulked down the corridor. But still, Terri had got through. He couldn't banish her from his memory. Charity was one thing, hope another. John had never known whether she'd felt anything for him. As man, rather than brother. Sometimes, he would see her fill the eyes of pine-legged whores as they strutted their spunk-infested alleys along the evening streets. On other occasions, her thin lips would smile (at him?) from the centre of a single crimson wallflower. Or he might hear her voice in the agonised note of a fox in the night (was she suffering?). She might be everywhere. Both outside and in. He felt a great weight expand in his chest. The rain beat against the windows. He ran over to the wall. The paint was peeling in great strips. It had once been red, but underneath he could make out the green and, below that, the white. Terri. No! No! No! He smashed his fist against the wall. Swung back the wrist and swooped the knuckles down on to the plaster. Felt the stone beneath. Unyielding. Eternal. Again and again, he punched the wall, until the pain became invisible. The pulse of the rain outside became the beat of his own heart. He straightened out his fingers. Blood flowed freely between the bones. He turned his hand over to look at the palm. The nails had made deep indentations in the skin. Four crescentic marks. Scars of an earlier life. He rubbed his palm on his forehead and felt the blood trickle down into his eyes. The wall went red. Perfect, again, as once it had been. He shivered there, amidst his heart's blood. He went over to the fire. The squat in which he lived was damp, drafty and utterly without glamour. And yet, it was the house of the holy spirit. It had living fire. Yellow, the colour of mind. He took a log (incongruous, but true; John collected bits of wood discarded from the copses of the city – a piece of unconsciously pre-hensile urban planning by the city fathers, one hundred years earlier (Ah! how the workings of the Lord God Almighty, the Father, were mysterious and beyond rationality)) and flung it on to the dead hearth. It lay there, stained with his own blood. He had let the fire go out, the night before. A night of the senses, that was. No. A darkness of the soul.

She had clad herself in a red toga, blood-red, sacrificial in its flowing immorality (for at the centre of faith, there is a total immorality) and had gone out into the pre-midnight calm. Up the mountain she had clambered, and, at its frozen, frigid peak, had she dispensed of her cloth, coil by coil. Long, cool nakedness was her state. The skin-scathing breeze, her lover. In order to traverse the peak of the first night, she had shed herself of her pristine virginity. She had lost the will to knowledge and the knowledge to will. She had become, nothing. She was brought to

139

nothing and annihilated and knew not. She had burned in the fire of the naked heart, until she, like Our Saviour, was forsaken.

He lit the dank pile of wood and coal. An old flat, this. Unreconstructed. No ripped-out fireplaces, no restored hearths. This was basic. Functional. A low-grade, Jeremy Bentham orgasm slithered along the walls and sank, sated, into the pyre of John's hearth. It was hard to light. It possessed a green, damp, living recalcitrance. But it was dead. The wood had been lopped off ages ago and was dead. Yet it didn't seem to know. Habits of the tissues die hard. Like sex, they were difficult to sublimate. The green moss on the log refused to ignite. The blood – his blood – denied the spirit within its carbon frame. Loved itself too much. A lust of surfaces, a wet cave of delusion. A woman's smile. Terri's smile. John shuddered.

She had been in jail. The prison of the senses. And she had escaped. And now the night had grown even deeper. It was midnight; she was certain (though it was difficult to plot; the blackness was everywhere, even in the stars). Yet some sensation in the hindbrain of her soul told her it was midnight. She had left the unending field and had entered the manifold woods. In the absolute darkness, her eyes played emerald tricks on her. Retinal delusions in green. Gifts of the Saviour to his bride. An unwilling consort, she had been carried, kicking and screaming, over the threshold of the mountain. Nada! Nada! The path was dark, the door, narrow. Silver never turned to gold. She wrapped her hair around her scalp and waited for the wind that was Christ. Naked, in her purity.

He took a long taper, lit the end and attempted to tease the log to ignite. At first, nothing seemed to be happening, but then a few wisps of smoke began to drift upward, losing themselves in the sooted brick of the chimney. He removed the taper and blew out its tiny flame. Slowly, the wood grew black and a foul odour issued from it. The smell of him. As John watched, his eyes watering so that they seemed like one, soft-focused lens, the log blazed into glorious erection. By degrees, it swelled into a perfect redness. At that point, at the moment of turning from wood into air, it adopted the same colour as the fire and began to burn. John sat back on his haunches and let his breath out. An obscene image of the human brain flashed before his eyes, the log, a mountain of neurons, burning in God's mercy. In the heart of the fire, pockets of darkness revelled, hidden from the Devil's gaze. The ladder lay in the hearth and he had been waiting years to scale the rungs of that secret. The transformed wood fluttered upwards in the blurred air, each sliver, a wing over John's lids. No sight, no sound, no smell, no taste, no touch, no will, no intellect, no memory. Just the law of the spirit. And more. Beyond the silver, lay the gold. Invisible, always. Beyond the water, lay the wine.

The Ladder

He sat on the park bench and drew his arm around Terri's shoulders. She turned and they kissed. Cold skin. A breeze feathered the edges of their coat collars and black specks fluttered from the branches and disappeared into the white sky. At last, they parted. Bernard licked his lips and gazed around, suddenly embarrassed.

'D'you know why I like coming here?'

He looked at her. She was fidgeting with a hangnail on her left middle finger.

'No,' she said, without looking up. He gazed at the trunk of the nearest tree. Let his eye drift along its convolutions, noticed how every whorl linked up with another.

'Because, in the middle of this place, this collection of trees and grass and air, I can actually breathe. And think.'

'Sometimes you think too much.'

The vision of the tree was gone.

'What do you mean?'

She shrugged and bit into the skin. A painless wound.

'Oh, nothing . . .'

'When I say "think", I mean "feel".'

'There's a huge difference . . .' she began.

He broke in.

'I know. A world of difference.'

'Like between us.'

'Why do you have to bring that up, now? Why can't you let

143

things lie for a while. For one afternoon. Can't you just forget?'

Terri stopped playing with her finger. She ran her hand through her long, black hair. The locks which matched her eyes. That's what he'd first noticed about her, that day long ago when they'd met. At that time, she'd been with some religious crowd or other. Had been assiduously seeking herself, as they'd joked later.

'Let's talk about something else.'

'What?' He felt himself sink into petulance.

She got up.

'Let's go for a walk.'

'But we've only just sat down,' he protested.

She pulled at his sleeve.

'Come on, Bernard. Don't be a spoilsport.' The tone was playful, childish. Mocking, even (she was good at that: easily-deniable, multiple stabbings in a phrase).

A spoilsport. That was a good one. It was her who'd brought up the whole bloody thing in the first place and now he was the one supposed to be spoiling it all. The way women could twist things. They seemed, in an instant, to be able to reverse the argument, to adopt diametrically opposing viewpoints and then to claim that it was you who'd done the volte-face. God! But he did walk with her towards the enclosed garden.

It had been ages since they'd been to the park. The time before this, it had been late summer and every bough had been draped with a heavy sleepiness, as though the trees had drunk too much home-made wine. The flowers had poured out at them in all their manifold fragrance and, if there had been a breeze, then it had been an invisible one. But then, he thought-laughed as he watched his breath solidify with each step, every breeze is invisible. At least it made him laugh, the breeze. They'd gone boating on the pond and had eaten ice-cream from large, old-fashioned cornets. Now the ice-cream parlour was shuttered up, the boats were nowhere to be seen and even the green of the grass seemed to have sunk beneath the hard earth. A grey pall covered everything. Their love had begun that spring. A mixture of coffee and illusion. Terri had grown bored with the God Squad. Said they were all hypocrites, really. Apparently she thought there was this weirdo who was after her. Gave her the creeps, she said. Smelled, she said. The weirdo had disappeared suddenly, but Terri'd always had the feeling that she was being watched from behind bushes, from across the street, even in her flat. That's where he had come in. Kind of a cross between God and a security guard. No, it'd been more than that, he remembered. Much more. But the point was he was having to remember. That meant it was a thing already past. Dead in its tracks. Felled by a single arrow. No, that wasn't true, either. It had been struck down, over the sinking months, by many small arrows. Points of the will, of the intellect, of memory itself. And now it was floating, lifeless, beneath the surface of the pool, under the canopy of green sick that never got sifted. Bernard sighed. Grabbed Terri's hand. She acceded, but her grasp was flaccid, indifferent. The skin, a cool white against his.

They entered the walled garden. The gate – more like a door – was narrow and, letting go of his hand, Terri walked on ahead. She had used to lead him into the garden and they hadn't let go. Not then. But that was summer. Long gone. Frozen from the face of the land. The wall was of faded red brick and rose some fifteen feet into the air. It had become frightening, a mountain of blood-coloured stone. It had never seemed like that before. Funny, the way familiar things can change. Like a dead relative. Alive, they were welcomed, loved, trembling; dead, they were hideous. They had 'crossed over' and were now the enemy. Bernard wondered, as he gazed up at the wall from the inside of the garden, whether

love was like that. She kissed him on the cheek, hurtling him
sideways. He just managed to regain his balance and prevent
himself tumbling into a patch of roses. There were no flowers,
only thorns. He almost laughed, but then thought it would be
stupid and followed her instead.

She walked at an easy pace, swinging her hips a little. Her
Salome Walk, he'd called it, though he'd never told her for
fear of destroying it through self-consciousness. He was
suddenly wary of this exuberance, these easy kisses. He didn't
dislike it – it reminded him of the early times – but it seemed
artificial, somehow, a reflection of a reflection masquerading
as reality. Pleasant, but empty. He inhaled the mirror air.
Everything was either black or white on that cold mid-winter's
afternoon, belonging either to sky or to earth. A sense of
weightlessness floated through his head as he watched her.
She who had been, and still was, the object of his love.
Outlined in the pencil air, she reminded him of a saint. That's
how they had been to each other. But maybe that was the
trouble. They stylised each other into the past.

And now she was skipping around the flowerbeds, just as
she had done, before . . .

But something was wrong. The garden was empty of
flowers and of people. There were only ghosts and the ghosts
of ghosts. She was tripping around the edges of the lawns,
pointing and calling out the names of the dead flowers.

'That's the geranium bed and, there, that's where the
gladioli were, remember?'

She looked up. Testing him. If he could recall the exact
position of every flower in the garden, it would mean that their
love had been real. Was that it? Was that what she wanted? A
memory test. A dancing flea. Deliberately, he would not
remember.

'No. I don't.'

'You see. You weren't paying attention. Not then, not now.'

He knew she would say that. Had deliberately provoked her, because she had tried to trap him. Mindgames. Why was she doing this? It was masochistic. She'd always had a sense of tragedy. She was so self-centred.

Terri turned her back to him and began to saunter along the garden path, tweaking the naked stems as she went.

'I like it like this. There are so few flowers, you have to seek them out, but, when you find them, they stand out all the more. Curiosity, that's what it is. Like the cat.'

He was on the point of saying, 'You know what happened to the cat,' but thought better of it.

She leaned against a tree. Apple, he thought.

'That's how we met – curiosity.'

No. Pear. Definitely pear. Mind you, it was hard to tell. They all looked the same in winter. He avoided her eyes. She went on.

'Me, selling flowers for the Cause; you, watching me; me, pretending not to watch back.'

In the past, a smile would have linked the corners of their lips. Even in the bad times. The fighting times. But they were beyond that, now. She persisted.

'Yes, it must've been curiosity. You were looking for some-one and I . . . I was longing to be looked for, perhaps.'

'What's wrong with that?'

'Nothing. I never said anything was wrong with it.'

So why mention it, he thought, but she had already moved away and was circling around the Cupid statue that was set at the crossing of the garden paths. It was a kind of centre for the whole garden. She traced her finger around the stone head, over the shoulder, the fat arm, the stumpy digits. For a moment, he had the crazy feeling that to her, he was the statue. A grotesque unchangeable in her life. A blockage on her path. She was relentless.

'Then we became totally self-possessed and thought only of

ourselves. But, when you thought you were thinking of me, you were actually thinking of me in relation to you, d'you see?'

He felt his anger rise and strove to keep his voice level.

'Don't patronise me.'

'I'm not. It's true though, isn't it? You are totally self-possessed and so am I. We're like this statue, forever preening ourselves, sculpting our egos.'

She been into that psychotherapy rubbish. After her God phase, that was.

'We thought we were on top of the world and so we were, in a manner of speaking.'

Her breath made elegant spirals in the cold air. Just as it had in the mountains that other, better winter. When they'd made love in the dry snow. Hidden in the cleft of a gully, they'd ended up almost hypothermic. But it had seemed worth it, at the time. But what worth had it now, he thought, when she seemed able to bandy it across a dead garden? It was a cynical season.

'You don't see the faults, when you're in love. Neither your own, nor those of the other person.'

So that's what he was, now. The other person.

'You can't see the compromises you're making, the mistakes. You grab the blunt ends of daggers and then, when you find you're clutching a blade, it's too late. You're already bloodied. You learn you're just like everyone else.'

An image melted through the snow of his skin. He touched his forehead. Felt hot. Fevered. But she was moving again, away from him, away from the statue with its stupid, eternal grin, towards a bed of old climbing roses. They must have been there ever since the wall had gone up. They were the oldest plants in the garden. But, where once they had been kings, now they looked crippled. It was as though the garden had become ashamed of them and had stuffed them in the corner there where they would be out of sight. Alone among the plants, they did not sink into the earth during the winter, but remained erect, blind and headless, and their stems writhed along the ancient brick like the veins of a dead person. Running in their sap, they held within them the memories of a hundred years of lovers and the lonely. Of war and peace. Of the death of generations. But they were not valued for that. Despised, perhaps. And feared. Funny, he thought, how every year the roses had to go through all of the ages; childhood, puberty, peak and senescence, again and again, until, eventually, they would have experienced so many lifetimes. And we have only one. No wonder we are flawed. It's so easy for the roses. They have no moral dilemmas, none of this ridiculous cynicism. This balancing-act of hopelessness. Delusions on either side of the wall. You'd had it, no matter which way you fell.

She held the longest of the rose stems between her index finger and thumb. Held it prisoner for a moment. Then let go. It quivered, but the stems around it did not stir. It would have been different in summer, he thought. Now, there were no leaves inter-connecting the fabric of the plant. Everything was fragmented, unconscious.

'Your world became a two-person madness. A conceit. You had to dominate me, in everything. And yet, you constantly needed me to define yourself. To give you praise, to tell you how wonderful you were.'

She paused. He thought he saw a shadow cross her face. The approach of night.

'But not in the ways you imagined. If you'd let that go, the awful presumption of yourself – about us – then maybe we might've come through. But you could never do that. Never.'

An arrow turned in his stomach.

'You!! You can talk. Hypocrite.'

'Yes! I'm a hypocrite. But at least I know it. You were so holy about yourself and your intentions. Your great dreams (they were always *your* dreams), the whole of life, justified around you. You never think or do anything which doesn't benefit you in some way. Even if you don't know it.'

'Okay. That makes me a psychopath. Fine.'

The winter air was beginning to fracture along invisible lines. He could feel them crack through the ends of his bones.

'Don't give me that. You're excuses are tired. I'm tired . . .'

Her voice faltered. She turned around and took out a handkerchief. He moved towards her. Thinking, not feeling. And he knew she was right, knew it as he reached out his hand, the fingers numb with cold. Her coat was thick. She, a thousand miles within. It was too late. Terri flinched away. He gazed at his palm: one long strand of her black hair. He closed his fingers over it. Put his hand back in his coat pocket. Didn't dare take it out, lest he lose the hair.

The light was fading fast. The garden was growing long and narrow as the shadows deepened. It was no longer symmetrical as it had seemed earlier, but was laid out in the manner of the Victorians, to surprise and delight through dream. But that was for the seasons of life. Now, in the depth of winter freeze, it seemed chaotic, menacing in its disorder. In the murky light, Bernard found he couldn't quite tell the briars from the genuine flowers, the path from the beds. Terri seemed to be having no such difficulty. She skipped between Classical cornucopias like some idiot nymph. He could hardly see her across the rockeries. They'd be closing soon. He hoped so, anyway. He longed to escape from the enclosure. To breathe among the multitudes. While darkness was descending upon the garden, the city would soon be waking up. Its clubs would already be restless in their slumber. He desired to seek out the dens of red sin. To lose himself in them. To sin freely. Their relationship was dead. Had perished long ago. It should be buried, he thought, not exhumed like this in the murk of winter, when the stones reek of old blood. There was

150

no anger left and, into the gap, flooded the absurd superstitions of childhood: *If we go this way, we will stay together; if the other way, then we'll split.* He forced them down and out. Stamped them to death on the hard ground. As if it really mattered. Nowadays, he would often torture himself with such idiocies. Perhaps it was a sign of neurosis. Of being crucified between the vault of heaven and the frame of earth. Perhaps it was just self-indulgence. Or worse, self-pity. Navel-gazing was for Buddhists and he'd never been a Buddhist.

He realised he had lost sight of her and he began to panic. He had the sudden, infantile urge to go up to her and apologise. Confess. But for what? It would be yet another hypocrisy. Bad for the soul. He really was unable to make out where she'd got to. The walls cast dark shadows across the roses, the path. Bernard felt the touch of shades as he walked determinedly along a straight path, following the direction in which he thought she had gone. There was no birdsong. No breeze. They would be closing the park soon. The gates would shut and everything would descend into madness. Frank, black horror. He shivered, as he walked. The garden seemed longer than before. The walls loomed on either side of him, higher than ever, and there were no gaps in the brick. No glimpses of mercy.

He had given up trying to find her. She must have left the garden. It was typical of her. He just wanted to get out. As he hurried, the cold slapped him across the face repeatedly, so that his skin became a surface of pinpricks. His was inside-out. He tried to say something to himself or to fate or to God, but his voice froze in his throat. He looked over his shoulder and saw the path fall into black. He collided with a wall. Furious, he rubbed his forehead. Felt like kicking the old brick. Then he noticed a ladder. It was wooden and seemed to have been there for ages. Probably since the autumn. Which autumn? Never mind which autumn. The fall of a hundred years earlier flashed into his mind: two lovers parting, long dresses and tight boots, top hats. An old gardener, listening as he pruned the roses. Bernard put his ear to the thorns and listened. But roses are pruned in spring. The memory was fake.

. He reached out and touched the ladder, half-expecting it to crumble in his fingers. He grabbed the structure with both hands, checked its reliability. Tried to regain control, there, as the darkness swelled behind him and crept up his back. Maybe, if he could climb up the ladder, he might be able to spot her. See where she'd gone. But then what? Would he run after her, calling out her name like some defeated duellist? No. He would sneak up and simply walk beside her, to show her it had been no big deal, the whole thing. No. He would walk in the opposite direction, altogether; but perhaps not the exact opposite, he wouldn't have his path determined in any way by hers. But, first, he would have to find the gate. Perhaps, from the top of the ladder, things might become clearer. What if the park was shut, already? He felt feverish. Ran his palm across the skin of his forehead. It was dank, cold like a corpse. To still his thoughts, Bernard mounted the ladder. Felt it creak beneath his weight. The last touch of skin on wood: a long hundred years before the Great War. A lice-ridden layer of brick lay between birth and death.

He climbed cautiously, placing first one foot, then the other, on each rung before moving up to the next. His hands, knuckle-white, gripped the sides. Suddenly, he couldn't move. Felt a resistance. Looked down. His coat had snagged on a thorn. He reached down, to try and free it. Felt dizzy. Hot, inside his head. He freed the cloth, blind. Straightened up again. The fever would not leave him. He tried to resume the climb, brick by brick. He could just make out the cracks in the faded red, the grinning stone madness of the wall. Tried not to look. An almost-image of roses in full bloom. But the structure was unformed and fell apart. Everything she had said ran through his mind at double speed: curiosity, levity, giddiness, boasting, self-conceit, presumption, self-justification, hypocritical confession, revolt, freedom to sin, the habit of sinning . . . every word she had uttered threw themselves up into a great ladder which he was unable to climb. The thorns of sleeping roses had pulled him down. He had fallen to the lowest rung and would decay there, among the rotting layers of leaves. He liked it that way. He liked being in the garden with its headless roses, its petrified Cupids. He enjoyed being surrounded by his own pride. He would never be able to reach the top of the ladder and peer over the edge of the old wall. She had gone with the south wind; he had lost her forever. The night swept in on the garden, while, deep in the city, the clubs flung open their doors to the waiting queues.

The Seventh Chamber

S he knelt on the floor of her cell. The stone felt cold and hard through the coarse, white wool of her cassock and her feet were bare. She knew the touch of rock on skin. It had been a part of her existence that had been as solid as breathing. Over the thirty or more years she'd lived in the cell, it had become entangled with the inhalation, exhalation of her prayer. Not that she hadn't been out of the cell, away from the Convent, even out of the country, but, deep down in the centre of her soul, she had never left the tiny cube of darkness with its high, narrow grill. She'd lost count of the years. Time had become the least important element of God's Creation. It was really just the string which wrapped it all up. It could be circumvented in a thousand ways. To Sister Theresa, time and its cohorts were an illusion of the finite.

She completed her morning prayer and, then, with some difficulty, she got up and went over to the washstand. The water was ice on her lids, but she liked that; it woke her up and made her see more clearly. The spring came straight from the mountain and the water could be drunk as well as used for washing purposes. The splash of liquid from the ground sounded the beginning to her day. Every day was the same. Every day was safe . . . from the Devil, from her own memories. For over thirty years Terri had done good works, fasted, abstained and worshipped the glorious Trinity and, yet, still the lizards of the world would poke their repulsive, transparent noses through the cracks in the wall. She'd always had a peculiar hatred for lizards and yet had endured them for decades as she had faced down the fears, the fascinations of her earlier life. And she had found that they could be sources of wisdom and good fortune. She had conquered her terrors, one by one, had pounced on them and ripped them apart, had breathed in the satanic stench of their innards and had survived. As she broke her night fast (water and a little bread), she gazed up at the narrow grill which ran along the top of the wall. It would soon be dawn. She knew this, even though there was, as yet, no light. She knew it in her bones. Her aged skeleton perceived every turn of the seasons, every hour's minute as it wove the shroud around her shrivelled frame. Her body was an absurd spinning clock which had been set off somewhere on the road out of Eden. But her soul was a white bird. It would soar through the dark air and she would ponder upon the celestial hierarchies, nine, and the grandeur and majesty of God. But it hadn't always been like this. Early on, she had been like most of the young and had taken life, the world (it had been her world, not God's), as eternal. Its sorrows, its joys . . .

Her mother had died at last after suffering for years from an insidious form of cancer. She had left Terri her eyes and twelve brothers and sisters. She'd been too young to remember her mother and knew only that her name had been Martha. All she remembered of her childhood was noise. She'd got so fed up with it that she'd run away to the big city, but hadn't got very far (she'd run out of money after four-and-a-half hours). She was twelve at the time and was proud of her long, shoulder-length hair, her deep, night eyes (ah! those eyes, which, later, the boys would come after in their droves, only to tumble to inevitable disappointment). When she grew a little older, her internal love affairs became external and Terri was the talk of the town (or at least, of the street). She lost her virginity just short of seventeen with a boy whose name she could no longer remember. (Such are the wages of sin, thought the silver-haired Terri, sixty years on. If you couldn't recall the face, the skin, the loins of the one united with, then it meant that the union had been false. The only true union was with Jesus.) There had followed a long succession of torrid affairs with men of varying types. No, that was wrong. They were actually all of one type. She'd kept making the same mistakes, over and over. They weren't bad men – not in the secular sense of the word, anyway – but they'd all been weak. Flawed in some way. Except for Our Saviour, we're all flawed, they might retort (though, of course, thought Sister Theresa, most of them would be dead by now and probably would be shivering on some far-flung ridge in Purgatory, if not . . .). But that was missing the point. They, like she, had all been victims of their fears and desires. They had dwelt outside the castle, in the houses which had been erected with great care by the Devil to entrap unwitting humanity into cycles of feasting on the prurience of the flesh. But who was she to judge? She'd been one of them. Even after she'd come across (by the Grace of Our Lord) the Preacher and had gone up to him and asked, 'What can I do?', even after she had worked for the poor and downtrodden of the earth as a part of the Preacher's select band (rainy street days in the late twentieth century, breathing in the exhaust fumes of lorries), even then, Terri had relapsed once or twice. The Lord is oft forgiving, but she had given him sore vexation, she was certain. And just when, through prayer and devotion, she thought she'd been permitted to enter the first dwelling place of the castle, those murky rooms where the vermin run about freely and the candles, if not extinguished altogether, burn with a sad, anaemic light, Terri found herself swept off her feet (in a demonic north wind) by some young hot-blood.

Then there was John whom she had loved with a silent,

hypocritical lust. John, the wild-eyed convert, who, she had
heard, finally had left the Preacher's group and moved to
another, even colder city to do penance for the rest of his
mortal life. John would be in Purgatory, but not for long. She
had allowed him to suffer, knowing of his love, because it had
made her feel important. To be wanted like that. To be
craved for. It had been her pride. She had not confessed this
pride until many years later, until just before she had taken
permanent vows, when her third confessor (who was much
younger than she was) had asked her if she was ready to be
received into communion with Jesus. She had looked into
Father Alvarez's eyes (although there had been a screen
between them, she had been able to imagine his eyes, full-
Spanish) and had been unable to hold back any longer. The
other love she had reason to recall, there in the deep cell of
her bones where dawn would crack before it spread across the
eastern horizon, was that which she had experienced with a
young man named Bernard. He had not been particularly
religious (but then, she remembered, nor had she been).
After a period of intense religiosity in the confines of the
Preacher's band, when she had thought she was on the
threshold of attaining something genuinely spiritual, when
it had seemed that she was on the brink of the thick wooden
door which blocks entry to the fourth dwelling place, then
had she become besotted by Bernard. He was tall, of aristo-
cratic complexion (she had only ever been able to find archaic
words with which to describe Bernard; even at that time, he
had seemed to be a man out-of-time, a graft from the past)
and was softly spoken. Charming, you might say. She had
been a part of the Preacher's flock for close on four years and
disillusion had begun to set in. They seemed to be the lords
of the world and yet she sensed an emptiness within which
meant that they would go no further. The Preacher insisted
on earthly works as being the pre-requisite for any kind of

Salvation. No spirituality was permitted. Terri felt her soul begin to wither. Then Bernard had appeared on the scene. It had taken her nearly two years to discover that he was completely wrapped up in nothing but himself. But then, that was the case with most men, more or less. She had left him, one night, in a winter garden and, in many ways, she had left her old life there with him. She had been in limbo for a while after that, doing first this job and then that, not sinning through any active fault and yet sinning heinously by neglecting her inner life. By pretending to be blind in the presence of the Lord, as well and deaf and mute. And thus had she wandered around in the desolate woods which remained dark, even during the day. From within the houses of the Devil had she heard shrieks of joy and mindless, naked ecstasy (she knew of their mindlessness and of their shame because she, too, had dwelt within those same structures, among the vermin and the pigs and the broken ladders). Clad in torn, filthy garments she had walked slowly among the sad trees, her bare feet slowly hardening on the cold mud of her fears. And then, at last, she had seen a vision which had drawn her back to the gates of the castle. To be accurate (and, for many, Sister Theresa was the epitome of precision), it hadn't really been a vision. She had not been advanced enough, at that time, to be able to receive visions, whether imaginative or intellectual, unless they had been from the Devil. It had been more of a reflection. It happened, like so many of these things, in deepest night.

She had been trying to pray, but her mind wasn't in it. Only her words, repetitive, meaningless, silent, had issued against the stone walls of the castle, just as earlier (or much, much later, depending on which way she looked at it), the same words (but with infinitely more meaning) had echoed within the enclosed world of her cell. For, in the second chamber, she was still mute but no longer deaf. (She was in the second

159

chamber, even though she could not remember having passed through the first! God's mercy towards this wretched sinner is indeed great, she thought, as she sat there on the worn edge of her springless mattress.) And once she had returned to this room, she realised that really her problem had been that, instead of searching out and dealing with the faults in herself, she had been obsessed with the faults of others. As soon as this had come to her, she had become inordinately pious and was able to re-enter the third dwelling place of the castle. However, it was a different piety to the one which she'd had while still enmeshed in the Preacher's group. This was a humility of the soul, born of the knowledge of her own imperfection. A much healthier piety. Much closer to the truth and to God's love which was the truth, enacted. Whereupon, in that difficult third chamber, at the age of thirty-three, Terri had discovered her Vocation.

Into celibacy, had she directed all her energies. And eroticism, sublimated, became her most powerful weapon, the wounds of love which it inflicted upon her heart, the deepest, the bloodiest of all. And when, at last (she had been well over fifty), the door to the fourth room had creaked open, the lizards and their verminous phallic legions had united in a rare moment of satanic solidarity and had come to kiss her forehead, her lips, her mouth. They had lain betwixt her wine breasts and had put their collective hand (a twisted, black, bloody hand) by the hole of her door. One hot night on the threshold of perfect contemplation, she had fought temptation harder than the Shulamite and was on the point of giving in, when the thought came to her that love does not consist in great delights but in desiring, with strong determination, to please God in everything. And at that, the door had swung open and she had seen that the castle, which had appeared until then to be of dark stone, was, in fact, constructed of crystal. Through active and passive prayer, through the works of poverty, chastity and obedience, had she become as one with her prayers, her humanity rendering unto her soul a contentment which turned her towards the face of the Almighty, who, in return, infused her with spiritual delight. The vermin still bothered her, but they had less power now. Her sublimation was more powerful. All the figures from her past – and, more than ever, they were past – began to fade into featureless, cardboard memory. When she thought of it – or, rather, when the thoughts invaded her dwelling place – Terri found herself unable to bring to mind the faces of her human loves. She no longer cared for their images. They were no longer part of her soul's architecture. She realised, then, that they had been as material goods to her and that this had been a bulwark of her pride. And, thus, she tripped lightly on her toes about the room (for her heart seemed to be growing weightless as she progressed). She became a silkworm, born fat, blind and ugly, yet dedicated to spinning long, unbroken strands of the purest white silk. For years, she spun, until the entire chamber had been filled with the billowing, almost transparent cloth. She seemed, up to that point, to have been as one dead, even when she had lived through the first four rooms of the castle. Her soul had been rolled up into a lifeless, dark seed. But, now, it was different. The silk spun so thick, layer upon layer, that the chamber became a cocoon for the worm and, unable to breathe, she died. This was the second of many deaths. But from the mass of putrefaction, a small white butterfly with silken wings arose and fluttered through the opened door leading to the sixth dwelling place.

Sister Theresa pulled her cassock more tightly around her shoulders and began to rock, to and fro. She was shivering slightly. A definite sign that dawn was almost upon her. Somehow, she felt it might be her last. For a while, she had felt its imminence. The birth of days spread across her skin, a sense of her own mortality, as did watching young

children at play. She had never had children. She had no
regrets. Her love had been for the eternal child; her mother-
hood had rested in his suckling. No human daughter or son
could have given her such peace. Such truth. So much love.
And yet, at least in this respect, she felt His power lay not in
His divine nature, but in His humanity. He had been crucified
between earth and heaven, and his blood had fallen upon the
barren soil of her garden and had made it flourish. His mother,
Mary, had been the gentle south wind which had enabled the
seeds of love to germinate and grow into rosebuds. And there,
in the sixth chamber, Terri was on the point of bursting into
flower. She had suffered much, through illness, rejection and,
even at this stage, human doubt. Her soul had shivered in its
naked winds, much as her body shivered there, on the thin
mattress in the cold, dark cell which she had made her home.
Even praise had become a trial, since the ladder-snake of pride
was ever waiting to rope her back her down to the swarming
mud below. It was at this point that she began to hear the
voice of God and, through the metal grill, to see visions of his
Grace suffused in a soft, white glow which made the ordinary
gleam of sunlight seem wan by comparison. The Lord would
speak to her in vast paragraphs, all of which she would
understand in the space of a second or less. Among many
other things, he told her to listen, not to men but to angels.
But what really moved her into rapture were the visions, both
imaginative and intellectual (the former she could see; the
latter could only be felt). But the Devil, too, could be very
subtle here, in this sixth dwelling place, where the crystal was
almost completely transparent so that she was able to glimpse
the white light beyond. The problem was that Satan, like God,
could be almost invisible to the spirit.

She closed her eyes, thought only of the light, and the
shuddering subsided. She was a deer, racing along the top of a
ridge. An arrow pierced her side. She felt the severest pain and

the greatest delight, and the wound bled freely. Where the blood drops fell, tiny white flowers sprang up, which were gathered into a bunch by her lover. Then she was the lover and her betrothed, the deer. She called to him, but he did not answer. He tantalised her with the promise of union, but, when the meeting place was reached, he slipped from the tips of her fingers and she was left, aching, her palate dry from the lack of his fruit. The apple tree had been barren for too long and now he would come and fill her belly with the wondrous green of his apples. But at that moment, the Devil might intrude and whisper to her, in her lover's voice (as she lay, eyes closed, upon the silken bed of her own weavings), that the castle she had lived in for so long had indeed been constructed of finest crystal, but that it had been built on sand. He insinuated that the very bridal chamber in which she pined for her lord was mere illusion. He slipped into her the daggers of dissatisfaction and, then, held out the hot phallus of temptation. A wind blew through the grate, creating the sound of a disordered flute.

Sister Theresa opened her eyes. The skins of the globes seemed dry, painful. She blinked several times, to clear the matter from them. She drew herself up, there, on the stinking, unwashed bed of her monastic cell and, once again, she fought.

The more vermin, the better! If she had to build the castle from foundation-ditch up, remembrance into remembrance, brick into crystal, she would do it. If she had to do this every day or every night, into eternity, she would not weaken. If she must needs bleed into the pure snow of the Lord's pasture in order to expel the Devil's locutions, she would not flinch. She, Terri, would embrace such a joyous fate and would consummate herself in it, till her master deem fit to enter into her.

Faced with this degree of faith, the Devil slithered away,

Lucifer, weeping into the shadows (every time this happened, Terri noted that a host of souls would leave Purgatory). After terrible struggles like these and also following the greatest of raptures, sobs would rack her emaciated frame for hours at a time and the force of her weeping would almost kill her.

She inhaled, deeply. The scent of mulberry flowed in through her nostrils, cleansing, lifting, turning her to water. And with the water, Terri began to flow. It felt familiar. All her life, she had been moving in liquid. At first, she had been drawn in buckets from deep underground. In the silent darkness, when she had been deaf, mute and blind, Terri had sometimes confused human love with divine grace. She had entered the castle on a spinning water-wheel. That was why she had progressed so rapidly to the quiet of the third chamber, whence she had begun to recollect everything. No sooner had she gained her senses, than she had lost them again in ecstasy as she careered along the stream of trial and temptation, wounding and betrothal. Above her head, a faint pink light began to shine through the grill and the ecstasy faded. Her eyes were bright as they had been fifty years earlier, when John had worshipped her image, when Bernard had climbed his ladder after her and had never been able to reach the top. Her stream was falling as rain upon the seventh chamber; her betrothal was consummating itself in a vision of the Most Blessed Trinity. Her soul and her spirit, Martha and Mary, separated for so long, joined together at last and the essence thus recreated took the form of a butterfly which instantly died of joy. As Sister Theresa slumped on to the floor, the water-spout which she had forgotten to turn off began to gush, forming a large pool of water on the stone. The blood from her scalp made tiny streams within the pool which coiled around one another endlessly.

Brick

How can your prayers and pleas melt stony hearts?
A tyrant remains a tyrant still . . .
                    Faiz Ahmed Faiz (1337–1404)

The man picked up the brick and eyed it closely. Its red heat
burned into his globes, searing the jelly until he could feel its
edges, lines, surfaces imprint themselves in rectangles on the
back of his brain. Scraping the callous of his index finger
against the grain, he began to wipe the dust off the brick, first
the top, then the underside. He did this to each of the brick's
aspects in turn, until it was totally clean. He drew it closer so
that the skin of the brick touched the skin of his face. It was
warm. In the pores, there was still dirt. Impurity. Without
putting it down, he went to fetch a brush. He had left the rest
of the brick pile undisturbed outside the kiln. He was wearing
a stained shalvar-kamise and his feet were bare. The conical
towers behind him formed a neat row. Then, as he moved
slowly towards his mud hut, the line cracked and they became
isolated, randomly dangerous. Coils of white smoke twirled
elegantly from the tops of the thirty-foot-high chimneys and
lost themselves in the dark-blue emptiness. All the brick-kilns
were active, every day. Twenty, thirty, forty . . . countless
numbers fading into the horizon, forming tall, brown stacks
amidst the flat green. All were made of red bricks, mounted
one upon the next (*five thousand and nine bricks per kiln,*

keemath: 5 Rs a brick) and they grew narrower towards the top, so that the smoke funnelled, clearly defined, into the heavy air. The smoke and the brick. The two were symbiotic; one could not exist without the other. But neither would exist without blood. It was blood which gave the bricks their redness, their power. The power to form walls, buildings, palaces. The blood of the bricks flowed with their power into jagirdars and generals, presidents and factory-owners, a molten transfusion sucked from the swarming mud. No crops grew here. The soil was of poor quality. Dead earth. And yet it produced, daily, huge quantities of bright-red bricks, more perfect in their inanimation than any number of fields, trees, villagers could ever be.

The man emerged from the dried brown cowshit dwelling. In one hand he carried the brick, in the other, a brush. He walked over to an open area and began to scrape bristles against the pocked surface. The hairs on the brush were dark brown, almost black, but not quite. The skin on his feet was layered thick as the fissured earth beneath them. The earth was bright yellow; his feet, not quite so. Nothing the man possessed was absolute. While, all around him, the fields glowed green, the sewers, even greener, the short, starved trees, purple, the sun, yellow, the sky, far blue, yet his skin lay between colours, stretched, indefinable around the bones, hardly existing in the shimmering heat. Deep beneath the covering of hard red, the blood ran fast, but now the brick was being cleaned. Scraped of all impurities. Hardened so that it would be the most dense of all bricks, so that it would form the foundation for a hundred kilns and would outlive the man and his progeny. As he brushed, his small metal Cross swinging from side to side, his haunches triangled into his legs in a different type of squat from the defaecation squat (which was the same as the birth squat) and different again from the position he would adopt when watching the great iron carriages glide past along the rails. The man had spent his life on his haunches. Humble. Mute. Bonded.

As he brushed, a thin, white dust blew up and swirled around his hunched figure, coating the skin of his hands, the thin cloth of his kamise, the trembling black waves of his hair. As he inhaled, it was sucked into his lungs, into the eddies of blood around his heart and it danced inside his body and slipped into the seed of his unborn. Afterwards, he would wash his hands in the stagnant bright-green water and then the water, too, would float downstream through the generations. He had no ancestors. Just the earth into clay, the clay into brick, the brick into fire. All around him, the villagers were busy digging in the areas between the kilns, ripping the earth from itself, tearing the clay food from its belly. Short, square trowels. Bent backs. Hot sun. Yellow. *One thousand bricks in a day, per back. Forty-seven backs. Forty-seven thousand bricks. Three hundred days.* The only breaks were in the bricks when they cracked in the heat of the furnace. Imperfect structures would never survive. *Fourteen million, one hundred thousand.* They began work two years after generation, their already hardened feet squeezing the milk of the earth down into usable material. *Twenty-eight years, minus three days' generation time per female, six times over. One million, ninety-nine thousand, five hundred and fifty.* Fifty kilns. *Two zillion, seven hundred and forty-eight trillion, eight hundred and seventy-five billion bricks.* Give or take. Take, mostly. Bricks outnumbered sperm. It was the way of things in the elaqa. In the province, in the country. By the age of twenty, the villagers would have assumed the same twisted form as the trees; by twenty-eight . . . The man stopped brushing, got up and held the cuboid object between his face and the sun. It was black. Took it away. Red. Put it back. Black. Took it away. Red. Black, red, black, red, black, red . . .

The sun burned at all times. In the morning, it was a new

fire and it scorched the mud of the huts, dried the rough, wet bricks, caused the earth to crack in jagged, irregular lines. At noon, when the trains swept past each other on the gleaming iron rails, the sun was a perfect bullet. Yellow. Pure. As it fell in the evening, it would fire the kilns red and would seep through every pore of brick and into every grain of dust that went to form each brick. And, in the night, it was still there, burning behind the dark, a black sun. And, through the whole night, the sun's heat would be locked in tunnels of brick, of brick within brick, and would course through the blind, hard clay and become trapped in the mud. The piles of bricks in the rural darkness gave off a heat as great as that which had been poured into them during the day, so that the entire valley of the brick kilns would remain several degrees hotter than anywhere else.

The lines of the railway track ran straight, relentless, silver from one end of the world to the next. Long green pools of algae and waste lay between the railway and the village. Scrubgrass sprouted from cracks in the yellow earth, while bricks lay in tall piles everywhere, outnumbering the small mud huts of the villagers. A dank, foetid smell hung perpetually over the village, mingling with the pungent red of the brick-stacks. Iron hooks had been bolted on to the sides of each of the stacks and a short chain hung from each hook. At the other end of every chain, a circular fetter trailed on the ground. They were used only at night and then only occasionally. There was usually no need. At the centre of every cluster of one-room huts, there was a conical kiln made of deep red brick. At the centre of each kiln was a furnace. In the centre of every furnace lay the bricks. For every dead villager, two more would be generated. Five-and-a-half seconds of desperate clawing. Sodomy and debts. Counter-balances on the scale. A fine balancing act. But the only scales in the elaqa belonged to the jagirdar and these generated only interest.

168

Compound, Simple and Material. Every gout, another life in brick. Sinful, the priest might have said. But the priest had not been seen for years. No doctor. No teacher. No God. Just the unending creation of bricks. The foundations of life. Tugged from the soil, moulded with water, burned in fire, then laid out to dry in the air. The mounds of defaecated clay were larger than the yellow and green dhal which the villagers ingested. Their guts profitable when fed little. The final hardening was done with more water. The bricks got water when the villagers died of thirst (two more would then be generated in hot gouts of human clay). When the rains came (the sewers overflowing, casting their green dhal in uneven measure across the land), more bricks would harden quicker and the villagers would spend all day and all night (the two were synonymous in furnace-time) inside the kilns, close to the fire, like lovers, their skins burning slowly off-red and even more bricks would be the result. The five-and-a-half seconds would stretch and expand, so that misery would be forgotten. No, not forgotten. It would be rubbed deep into the existence and would become the structure of the soul. The rest would be burned away in the furnace of the kiln, evanescing into the pretty smoke which was visible from the windows of trains that passed by, once a day, at noon.

Once more, the man inspected the brick. He took the warm shape and placed it carefully in his kamise. It sank down to the level of his waist (he had no belly) where it made the dust-coloured cloth bulge slightly. He paced towards the last kiln, the one nearest the railway track. As he walked, he trod over the holes which had been dug years earlier, before his generation, before his generator's generation (the bricks from these now sat around the bulky, smiling forms of gun-runners, prime ministers and waderas, hundreds of miles away). Two trains ran daily, at noon, one going east, the other west. From Islamabad to Lahore, Lahore to Islamabad, Islamabad to

Lahore, Lahore to Islamabad. A glimpse of faces, bored, unmoved. The land was sliding into water and fire, and the villagers with it, and, once a day, when the shadows vanished, the valley would be broken by the passage of the wheels, the engine, the faces. *Twenty-eight years of faces. Sixteen thousand eight hundred journeys. Three thousand people per train.* Ten bricks for every face. He reached the last kiln. It cast no shadow. It was empty of people. Full of bricks. The fire was burning (the fires burned twenty-four hours a day; nothing was allowed to stop the act of creation). Red and yellow flames licked at the clay, hardening it. Forming it. The sound of the trains approaching: Islamabad to Lahore, Lahore to Islamabad, Islamabad to Lahore, Lahore to Islamabad. The trains carried bricks as well as people. More bricks than people. That was the way of the world. Of the village. Of the brick. He went into the kiln. The heat washed over him. Outside, it was hot enough to dry a brick; inside, it was hot enough to create. Holding the brick between the fingers of his left hand, the man lifted the hem of his kamise with his right. Bending his neck slightly, he slipped it over his head. Still using his right hand, he removed his shalvar. The discarded clothes lay in a heap on the floor. The door of the kiln was shut. The air was thick, black. Still cradling the brick, the man stepped forwards. He reached out with his left hand and threw open the fire-door. The flames burst into the dark but did not illuminate it. The blackness merely grew deeper, hotter. The man stretched out his arms, the brick poised on the tips of his fingers. The Cross on his chest was still. He teetered on the edge of the furnace. There was no movement. The silence was total.

With the extra fuel provided, three hundred more bricks than usual were created that day in the kiln nearest the railway line. They would not have been noticed. The trains had already gone past and would not cross again until the next day, when once more the kiln would cast no shadow.

Rabia

I love You with two loves;
   a selfish love and a love of which You are worthy.
That love which is a selfish love
   is my remembrance of You and nothing else.
But as for the love of which You are worthy
   Ah, then You've torn the veils from me so I can
     see You.
There is no praise for me in either love,
   But praise is Yours in this love and in that.
Rabi 'a al-'Adawiyya, Sufi (d. 185)

I fell in love with Rabia the first time I saw her in the Old Himalayan Bazaar. It was a fleeting glimpse through the crystalline air of mid-winter, a flourish between stalls and among the massed flesh of anonymous faces, hands, lips. Yet it was enough for a lifetime. And beyond.

I was seventeen at the time and had been sent by my mother to buy provisions for the household. Some distant relatives from the town of Leh were coming to visit and we would need almost three times the usual amount of food, not to mention gifts with which to make them feel welcome as guests. It was a strange time of year to be travelling. Snow and ice competed with each other to see which might cover more of the world, while the sun gave off heat like an impoverished aristocrat. We hadn't seen these relatives for years – they had never known me, and my mother and father had last met them when they were all children. They would be bringing their entire family along and so, in a few days' time, I would be greeting long-lost cousins as well as aunts and uncles of whom I had heard only through tales. Over the years, they had become fictions in my head, so that a little apprehension was mixed in with the curiosity I felt at their impending arrival. It was in this some-what pensive mid-winter mood that I set off early that morning for the Old Jumma Bazaar.

The sun had not yet risen and a pale milk light flitted uneasily between the shadows. The houses were all shuttered up and only the occasional clatter of servants' shoes on stone issuing from within the haveli broke the grey dream slumber of the morning. The air was cold glass in my throat. I pulled my shawl more tightly around my shoulders and walked quickly to keep warm. The Old Bazaar had been there since before living memory. Some said that Dungpa Miru had strolled among its noisy stalls and had haggled with its Afghani traders. Like the Yehudi, the Afghans went every-where, lending money and selling jewellery, and always mak-ing a profit. Though charging interest is against Islam, they somehow seemed able to circumvent this legality. They trav-elled from the great twin rivers of the west, all the way across the land of Fars, and were known in places as far east as Rangoon and Tibet. Nothing had stopped them, not even the rampages of Timur Lung which had occurred a century and a half before my birth. Even wild men needed to eat. However, most of the merchants in the market were white-robed Hindus from the lands of Kush, far to the south, where, I had heard, the Great Moghul, Akbar, held sway with wealth which was beyond the dreams of poor villagers such as ourselves.

But I digress, as has become my habit over the years.

As I drew closer to the Bazaar, there was still no sign of any activity. I might have been the only person in the town. However, the moment the narrow mud streets opened into the broad square, it was as though I had emerged into a world at the very instant of its creation. In a jangling hub-bub, the mountain devils danced the dance of the soul upon the old stone slabs, and the misty breath of the people around me was like the breath of the saints upon my skin. Everyone was wrapped in furs and woollens: ankle-length chughas of thick, black material shorn from the long-haired sheep of Baltistan; bristling flying-fox headgear with the flaps pulled down over the ears; boots of pale-brown fur. The people of my town knew how to dress against the cold. They had learned to survive the high winters of the mountain valleys. But to survive is not everything. Even though there was no wind that morning, the silent ice of the day stole through fissures in the skin, into the picot of the soul.

Since, at that time, I could neither read nor write, I had memorised the provisions which I would have to buy, and I carried a large sack, slung over my shoulder, in which I would carry them. I set about my task with the vigour of a winter's fire. It was customary to offer guests something sweet on their arrival and the delicious beshak shirin melons that I spotted in the stall of a Tajik merchant would be ideal. It was while I was bargaining with the merchant that I first caught sight of Rabia. Of course, I didn't know her name then (although later, I felt I had always known it). She passed by, a figure on the edge of my vision, on the precipice of the morning. A fleeting figure in black. Green eyes. A russet lock, brushing her cheek. Her delicate, pale skin and her red, scimitar lips.

I thought she smiled at me. The perfect, dizzying curve of bird's flight from mountain top. My heart beat inside my chest like that of a dying man and my lips were as dry as the dust beneath my feet. My whole body trembled. I could not move. My breath stopped and became one with the frozen air.

Things seemed not to exist. Only time, hanging by a thread from the sky, stood between the entity that was me and Rabia.

The blade fell.

I looked up.

She was gone.

The merchant had been speaking to me. I had missed most of what he had said. I managed to catch up with the conversation, but my mind was elsewhere. Today I would not be able to strike a good bargain. I didn't care. It had ceased to matter. The morning had become filled with the face of a woman I had never met. Was not even sure existed. And yet, already I knew her name. I had named her just as, when I was a child, I had named all things. For me, she was Rabia, the girl of the mountains, the fleeting gazelle of the plains (though at that time I had set eyes on neither plains nor gazelle, yet I had heard much of both from the long tongues of old women and travelling merchants).

For the rest of the morning, I was utterly distracted, even more so than the empty-eyed, yellow-robed lamas who would come to beg in the bazaar, every Jumma. I purchased provisions haphazardly, so that it took twice as long as usual, and my body felt unsure of itself. In the subtle mountain air, every movement seemed exaggerated and clumsy. Every so often, my heart would bounce against my ribs as though it was trying to escape from the confines of my chest. It, too, longed to soar with the bird, to peck at the sky, to dwell in emptiness. But in the emptiness I was not alone, for Rabia had grown to fill everything that was me. She was the first glint of sun across the spines of cliffs, the warm swish of her black, tribal costume was perpetuated in a thousand identical market-place mornings, the sweet taste of her lips lay in every grain of golden halvah. O my Rabia! Where was she? Even though she was all, yet I longed to touch her, to reach her presence, as I must have longed for life in the time before I was born.

When the relatives arrived, I was scarcely interested. What should have been the event of the year became for me just another manifestation of a love which I knew was the blood in my heart but which, like that blood, I was unable to grasp. Their Ladakhi accents make me imagine the sound of Rabia's voice. I longed to hear her voice. Animated conversations would pass across the sandali and I would nod and smile, but I was thinking only of the caravan which I knew, at that moment, would be travelling by the low bank of a frozen river. My thoughts were icicles. The river would melt a little during the day, yet it would freeze again at night, so that, throughout the winter, it never changed. And in a thousand drops of ice was my Rabia reflected. I even attempted to find out more about her from my relatives. Obliquely, I questioned them about the caravan, which I was certain had set off from their land. But they had heard nothing of such a caravan. I dared not ask about Rabia, partly from fear of arousing their – and my parents' – suspicions and partly because I felt she was my secret. I did not wish to share her with anyone, even if that meant that I would never see her again. Strange how love can destroy those it attracts. In stinging, the bee commits suicide.

Winter lightened into spring, the almond and rose trees began to blossom and strawberries grew ripe for the picking. The men went up into the high crags, where they blew sonorous notes from the mouths of long, wooden horns. Even these loping, invisible notes followed the gracious gait of my beloved across the empty stillness. I thought they might summon her back from the frozen waterfalls of the land of the Dards, back to where the ice had broken up into tiny, white floes that seethed with the current far below.

As the sun's power strengthened and life began to burst out everywhere, I grew weaker. I ate less and less, finding that only a little halvah and goat's milk would suffice my diminishing appetite. My mother became worried and took me to see a Yunani hakim. I was given a liquid distilled from some foul-tasting herbs, which I pretended to swallow but actually spat out as soon as their heads were turned. I had no wish to recover from the love which had possessed me. My obsession had become my life.

I waited for summer's warmth to clear the mountain passes, for I had resolved to go in search of my beloved. Secretly, one night, I stole away from my house, my town, the valley, which was the only world I had known, and I climbed the high path, heading eastwards. I had, as my guides, the moon, which waxed and waned through the night and across the months, and the stars, which pullulated from behind their burqa. The night was my Rabia's cloak, the day, her shining eyes, the sunrise and sunset, the matched clasp of her lips. Every swaying branch of every tree I passed, beckoned me on, higher and higher, each nod of a flower confirmed my course as surely as any chart. In those days, I could not read, so what use would a map have been? The land, the streams, the sky were my maps; I read them like a manuscript, rolled out before me in sound, colour, smell, touch and taste. Like a farmer, I tasted the soil and knew where I was going; like a minstrel, the notes of the wind spoke to me in wordless tongues; the quality of the dew upon my lips changed every morning and, by this, I trod as a hunter might, with deft steps, risking all in the certainty of the chase. When I prayed, it was on the summits of mountains. My heart seemed closer to Rabia at these moments; the air, diamond clear with my longing.

I was in one of those high mountain villages during the festival of Eid al Azha. A lamb was readied to be sacrificed and I was given the honour of performing the Qurbani. I took hold of the curved blade, newly cut on the grindstone. It was winter again and the sharp light of the sun sliced through the pale-blue mantle of the sky as it must surely do in heaven. I could feel the heart's blood of the lamb pulse faster beneath my fingers as I took hold of its neck. With one, swift stroke, I opened the great vein. Blood gushed over my hands, turning snowflakes into rubies. It is said that, when a lamb is sacrificed in memory of Hazrat Ibrahim's great act, the last thing the animal sees is a vision of Paradise. The fading light in the lamb's eyes as it bled into oblivion, that was the longing of my heart for Rabia.

After many months of travel, living off the earth and as the guest of the people of countless isolated villages, I came at last to the land of Ladakh. All around me, I felt the wailing of Dards and Mons and the battle-cries of the Yellow Lamas as they drew the blood of the Red Lamas. In these high lands, the Great Khans of Tibet vied with fat Buddha stones and with the invisible, omniscient God of my own folk. For while my land of Baltistan was entirely Muslim, the peoples to the east adhered to many different faiths. Strange rock-carvings and cryptic flower-symbols became part of my map, and I tasted the wine of paganism on my journey. I was certain that my love had passed through all these lands, had partaken of the same cartograph in which I now immersed myself. Rabia, I knew, was born of the fire of faith, she was hewn from the rock and stone of this high world, she poured herself from the goatskin gourd with every intoxicating drop of liquor. It was she in the cry of the muezzin across the endless chasm of time. I even accompanied a party of merchants to the capital of the Great Mughal and there did I discover that the Shah-en-shah Akbar had also drawn maps whose edges extended far beyond the borders of the known world. And when I had passed through all of these lands, had tasted of everything and more, then would I reunite with those enticing green eyes, that silken voice, the gentle tread of delicate feet. Then would I leap off the cliff and not fall, not be smashed on the rocks below. Then would I soar for miles, for years, in Rabia and with her at the same time. We would fly together over the world's roof.

I became a great traveller, a chronicler of humanity and of nature (during the course of which, I finally learned to read and write). I was known as *Son of Ibn Battuta*, which was a great honour, and I became one of the Friends, and yet none of my admirers, nor yet any of my family (who were now treated almost like royalty in their home town), knew of my real quest. Not a soul was aware of that grey morning back when I was barely out of childhood, and none had been permitted to glimpse my source, my beloved, my Rabia.

Perhaps, some day, I will find her. My heart tells me that I must find her. Perhaps, everyone has their own Rabia, their own yearning for that which they can never possess, something that is beyond matter, beyond themselves and the short span of their lives. I am not yet old, but one day, I shall (God willing) acquire the wisdom of the idiots which age engenders. And then, perhaps, I may glimpse her once again. I sometimes wonder whether if, at the moment of my death, I will see her face, if that image, the poem which contains everything and that which is beyond everything, will be imprinted upon my soul as I leave this world and journey into the next. Into Rabia. All that I have done, each thought that I have thought, every one of my actions have been consequences, merely, of that moment which lies outside of time and which is, therefore, eternal. It has defined my life and it will carve my death. I have never left the Old Bazaar, but am still there, waiting for her to return. Even as night falls.

Qadi

I thought it was ephemeral like the wind.
                                        Sadettin Kaynak (1312–80)

The market place was long gone. I could tell it had been many years since the square had been thronged with slaves, because the squat stone buildings that surrounded it seemed old and blackened. The last time I had been here, in this blustery town on the north coast of the Kara Deniz, it had been spring and work on the mosque had just been completed and everything had seemed quite round, each dome perfect. But on this late autumn day, by the time I got to the square, noon had already long passed and the light seemed dirty, so that the casual visitor probably would not have noticed any flaw in the smoothness of structure, in the rigorous cubic symmetry of the granite. I noticed it because, deep inside my head, there was another picture of the same place. A series of framed miniatures, unchanged for fifty years. I did not have to touch the stone to know its feel. And, through fissures in the stone, smells began to insinuate half-existent, inarticulate, possible pasts.

A woman's sweat. Burning wood. Blood of the consumptive.

I shivered and pulled my qadi's robes around my midriff. Half a century lay between me and the market place, yet, as I

179

breathed, I felt its stale air slink up my nostrils. The smell was still here, the terrifying stench. From it was I formed, out of its slimes, human and inhuman, did I emerge. I, a slave.

In the days of my youth, slaves from Circassia, a province which lay just outside the Empire's borders, were sold at ports in the Crimea and shipped across the dark waters of the Kara Deniz to all parts of the Empire. You might end up on a ridge by the 3rd Cataract of the Nile or in the flat lands of the Magyars or even in the middle of one of the Holy Cities. El Quds or Medina or Makkah. Whether you spent your life dusting the walls of the Black House or sailing along the blue, Hapsburg river, everything was in the hands of fate and the manifold needs of the Ottoman Empire. Unlike many of the young Christian captives, who would end up with guns, swords and terrifying music, I was not big or strong enough to become a Janissary and so I had been taken to the heart of Anadolu, where the mountains look like the tombs of the Friends and where the air is light with the breath of spirits.

It had all begun on that day, many years earlier, in the coastal town to which I had been drawn back after more than half a lifetime. I wondered whether, in all that time, anything apart from the buildings had changed. Recently, I had begun to ponder upon my place in the scheme of things. I had started to imagine that my life was merely a phantasm and that reality, if there was such a thing, might lie only in the place where things had begun. Where I had begun, in the Circassian hills which lay to the north and east of this town.

There seemed to be no children in the streets, as though the world had grown suddenly ancient. The buildings glowered, silent and almost windowless. The once wide-open square was filled with new buildings and the spaces between the buildings – which were all that remained of the old square – had been transformed into a series of narrow, dark streets. The pink dome and minaret of a small mosque rose from behind the stone. They had been here then and, together with its attached medressah, the mosque had defined the square. Now all that was visible from where I stood were the dome and its minaret; they, alone, rose above the severe contours of the newer structures. Half a century earlier, I had stood with my back to its wall, my arms splayed, my tremor apparent, and I had felt its rock pulsate through the skin of my fingers, and I had sensed a warmth spread slowly through my body. But this time, I was facing the mosque and it had almost vanished. I would not now be able to run my hands along its walls and the warmth of its stone would be hidden from me. I smiled and then felt alone. The street coiled tightly around me, scudding the few people outward. But I grasped towards something else. Behind the memory, glass fragments of the time before I was captured. A Circassian childhood.

Lemon moon sleep. Paradise denied. Reeds and mountains and the cries of wild horses in the night. The scent of goat's butter melting over slow fires. The soft universe of breast. Cream-white. The space torn out of me when it was removed. A pain, long denied. Unreachable.

I was six years old when the Qadi, the Judge, bought me with a finger flick from a blue robe.

A boat, departing slowly over black water. The town, shrinking. I, nothing.

Each town in the Empire had its qadi, its Quranic judge, as well as its secular governor. The qadi was the man who interpreted the Word of God through the kanun-i-osmani. Since the Word of God came, originally, from no thing and since one of the qadi's main responsibilities was to protect the peasants against local lords, then, if the man, the qadi, had himself once been almost nothing, he surely would be able better to sift through the twelve potential meanings of every letter in the Holy Book, to ascertain which of those multi-farious realities the Creator intended His creations to pivot around. I was one such sifter of energies. Yet, recently, I had grown tired. My energies had been depleted by the constant requirement to find right and wrong in everything. I had begun to sense doubt. Perhaps some things might be neither good nor evil, but might, simply, be. Perhaps there was an objective nothingness which was different from the Creator whom I had been brought up to revere as the final absolute. Perhaps my life had been a lie. Such thinking was heresy. As Qadi, I would have been the first to have condemned any man or woman who dared to broach such ideas. Yet the Friends, I knew, often danced around the arrowheads of unknowing. And, yes, at times, they had been executed for it. Perhaps I, too, might end with my neck spinning around the execu-tioner's blade . . .

The sun slipped behind a cloud filter and the light grew more intense. A breeze began to whip up the dust into fine circles and I felt my eyes sting and water in the sheet light. I blinked. Twenty years passed. The Qadi carried love in his eyes, in his heart. He bore me on his love as a mother would her own child. He became my father, he schooled me in the arts and sciences of his world. I was cast in his image. Saw with his eyes. But before that, beneath it, the slave-market.

Discordant noise, jumbling flecks. Human symphonies. The triangulation between the sweeping arm of the merchant, the raking eye of the buyer and the shivering fear which slithered and coiled and filled the ripped emptiness in my stomach.

I wondered whether a place might be created by the emotions of the people who dwell within its bounds, just as our lives are influenced by our actions and by the thoughts which lie within the span of our breath. The small town of which I was the Qadi was at peace with itself. There was a harmony in the houses and the fields and the streams that was a reflection of that which was within the people, and it was something which I, as Judge, had surely helped to foster. Yet I had grown uneasy. I shifted from one foot to another, like a medressah student on his first day. As I had grown older, my sense of harmony had ebbed away with my body's strength and, now, I felt small and without purpose.

The walls of the buildings which formed the square were high and almost featureless and the windows were mere slits, set far up. I was not able to make out the roofs. It was like a prison yard. I felt that I might as well be dust.

I pulled the sleeve of my chugha up over my right forearm. Drew the tip of my fifth finger lightly over the surface of the skin. Felt the tiny hairs tingle. I was real. This town, this square, was real. There was nothing else and it would have been foolish, presumptuous, to have sought more. I had returned here to find the source of myself, to better know that which I was. Back in Anadolu, in my qadi's official residence, I had conceived the grandiose idea of hiring a horse and riding up into the hinterlands which formed the north-eastern shore of the Kara Deniz. Perhaps I might come upon a trail or an old encampment or a brooch, even – something that might link my present with my past. I had always wondered about the time before. But I knew that there would be no trace of my other life. It would have been a fruitless journey. It would have been like trying to sail a ship up a dry river-bed.

I felt a great weight pressing down on my head. I couldn't breathe. I had no answers. And yet, the questions flew like black gulls on to my back and I fell forwards and landed on my palms and there, fifty winters on, I was gripped by a sickness

which seemed, at that moment, to have festered in my body
ever since the day of the slave-market. The ground felt cold
beneath my fingers. I gasped for air but the air was thick,
suffocating. Flecks fell before my eyes. Was it snow or was it
just the snow of my imaginings? Somewhere, at the centre of
my soul, a darkness remained. A sickness, unreachable by time,
wealth, learning. Even by freedom. Even by love.

I was still a slave.

My memories did not follow time's example, but rather
were with me constantly; they would flip back and forth, dark
into light, light into dark, the whole never changing. The Qadi
gave me my liberty when I reached the age of twenty-one. I
accepted it as a gift, unearned. Unfought for. It happened to
many. Was normal. He told me, if he'd had a daughter, he'd
have married me to her. But he was childless, his wife having
died when still young. He had never remarried.

*We were not treated badly on that boat. We might be destined for
high office in the Sultan's court or else in one of the countless
satrapies that covered the Empire. Some might even reach the
highest. I tried to run away from the market place, that spring
day wrought in wind and light. I slipped out from beneath the
merchant's cloak and ran through the crowd, dodging between
legs and the well-groomed cats of dragomen. Like the wild horses
up on the high plains, with fire in my sinews, I ran faster than
possibility would allow. The sun burned on my shoulders and on
my face. I gazed up at the sky. Even when at last I fell, my short
legs tripping over themselves, even when I felt the broad, muscled
palm of the merchant sink into the meat of my shoulder, even
then, I kept on running.*

I sped through twenty years, becoming, first, avid student,
then, learned scholar and, by degrees, wise qadi. A worthy
successor. I married, had children, saw them grow, marry and

leave my life, as I had left the lives of others. The ones who I would never know. Through the courts of the land, I forged the fates of countless others. A nail on God's finger, tracing out the calligraphies of life. The Qadi, my father, died last year. I will miss his eyes, his love. In its absence, I feel myself grow old. And always, through the seasons, through the years, I have been running. A slave to fear. Until this moment. At last, I had returned to the stinking bosom of the port city, to confront my past, to circle the square, to destroy the emptiness . . .

Breathing heavily, I stood up. Slowly, so that I would not faint. The white flecks had vanished.

The few men and women left in the square seemed dissociated, isolated, as though they were terrified of bumping into one another. They hurried away on their separate paths, with no greetings exchanged. I did not even hear myself breathe. The children seemed furtive, as though their condition of childhood was somehow shameful to them. I heard no one speak. It seemed the town had been struck dumb.

I wondered whether I might have ascribed my own feelings about this place to the town and whether, outside of this square, the city would be like any other and would harbour its joys and sorrows within its houses, within the streams of its time.

But I had never been outside of this place. All of my life had been spent pacing around this square, pressing against its walls. Skin on stone.

A sound from my left made me turn.

A small child emerged from between the buildings and set off at a run across the square. He changed direction halfway and came towards me. Slowed, as he approached. Then stopped. I reached out and touched his hair. He had the bony, tousled face of a street urchin, while the crown of his head barely reached to the level of my waist band. He did not

185

ask for money but merely gazed up at me, wordless. His skin was mouse coloured with dirt, his chin strangely-indented. But his eyes gleamed ferociously into mine, their deep velvet brown enveloping me there in the cold square. The rest of him gradually became a caricature, a grotesque. It was as though I were gazing at myself in a mirror, watching as I turned slowly to nightmare. The two of us stood facing our opposites, while the world around us sank into a haze. In his eyes, the boy had already been a man and would become one again. I saw him, fifty years on, standing in the square as an urchin ran out from between buildings, altered his path midway across and came to gaze into the old man's eyes. And then I saw that this urchin, fifty years on still, would also come to the square, pause and wait for the child to run towards him . . .

All men were equal in the eyes of God, but in the hierarchies of being, I had been lower than he – the boy was unfettered, had no master, could roam where he pleased – yet, as a slave in a rich household, my chances had always been greater.

A squall blew the hair across his face. I reached out and lifted the soft, child's locks from before his eyes, but the gleam had gone. An old man's soul looked out at me. My soul. He backed away, slowly (or I, from him). Then he turned and ran. My fate scampered across the square and disappeared amidst the high, dark walls of the buildings. I felt my eyes grow dull, my soul blind. A group of women huddled past, not noticing me. The square seemed to be emptying of people, as though the folk of this wind-blown town sensed some dark, unspoken thing which hung over the edge of the horizon. I drew my cloak more tightly around my shoulders, my neck. What was I doing here, in my strange clothes, at the sinking of autumn's last day, in a city on the borders of the world where I knew no one and which had seen my lowest moment? My whole life after that day had been based on a presumption of the immanence of the divine. On the idea that a man might be changed. I had passed too many judgements; for too long, I had supposed myself to be God's regent. I had no right. I was a slave, to both God and man. I had built a tower of self-importance around a frightened six-year-old and, now, the tower was crumbling. Cracks had been appearing in its walls for years, but, now, in the square where I had been sold like a piece of meat, the stink of gunpowder and regret filled my chest. I began to sob; my whole body convulsed with a sense of failure. I, a slave, had attained a position where I could have changed things; if not men, themselves, then, at least, their actions; the harmony in my small city could have been subtly altered by my life. But I had changed nothing. I had left no mark. Between pride and fear, I had hardly existed.

Suddenly, I craved for tulips. I needed spring. Wanted to feel young. I had never felt young.

Running through a field of red tulips, the horizon, a line of sweet-scented blood. My lungs, clear morning air, suspended. My master's country estate. Bihisht in a thought. The cry of a muezzin, from the top of a gleaming, white minaret. Swaying. Pure. Endless. I looked up.

There was no muezzin in the tower. No call. No freedom. Just the fitful breeze fraying the edges of the silence. The mosque dome had faded to a skulking purple. The evening prayers had long since ended. A damp putrescence filtered through the narrow streets. *Rotting lemons.* I threw up a wall between myself and the passage of time, but the wall was all holes. The wind blew cold through my joints, turning them to jelly. I felt that, like the day, I, too, would slowly disintegrate and my past, present and future would roll into one another and then into nothing. Some battles were unwinnable. Perhaps they had to be lost, in order to go on living. To escape the death, the forgetting that was at the centre of life. To go on running, even if it was always in circles. It seemed to me, there in the old square of my beginnings, that one might go through so many lives and yet remain the same. But this would form the soul into a perfect sphere and I wasn't sure of my own soul's shape. The shadow of an even deeper cloud slunk across the square, blotting out my sophistry. The breath blew cold in my lungs and I felt the cold move outward, across my body. It was the end of autumn and the light was fading fast. I sensed the incipience of winter. I wondered whether this might be what death would feel like. The evening exhaled into the street, shaving the buildings into sharp relief. Hulking figures. A new fear. Rain bit into my face. I turned and headed for the port.

Darkness

I was born in darkness. Or, rather, darkness was born of me. My earliest memories are of the wind howling across the endless plain of night. I dwell in the empty place, the lost soul scrublands, the dustbowls where there are no bushes left to burn, the time of the bad earth. I have no place in the great, majestic wilderness which needs no company to complete itself. No, the places which are the breath of my existence are those which once were lived in, but which have since become deserted. Beyond the last of the trash cans; beyond reach of the old Morse wire; in the poisonous air of empty, echoing mines; that which is outside. I am inside of life as I am outside death, for death is a solid thing. For some, it's the only reality they'll know. Whereas life . . . life has infinite possibilities for emptiness.

I dance along the edges of the light, I am formed in the curls of mist that sweep across the marshes at dawn. I dwell in the last breath of a dying man and in the terror of the newborn's cry. I am the ageing gene in every cell and yet, at death, I leap out into the emptiness from whence I sprang. I am the ultimate deserter. I am the hooker in the moment before she sells herself; I sense her cold angst. I live in the narrow streets of her despair, the whore-spat tracks behind the rumps of skyscrapers. As she gazes down at the puddle in the night, I am the puddle, looking up at her. I flood her with emptiness and soon she will slip the last dose. I am the vacuum in her end breath. I was with Caesar, in the whoosh of bloody retracting blade. I am with the friend who stabs deepest. I am the dead hell gleam in the eye of the jilted bride. I dance between the horns of Genghis Khan on the wind of the trans-Oxanian steppe. A bar in no-town New York. 5am. The self-pitying chortle rolls around in the belly of the drunk, sloshes from one gut to another. I am the chortle. I am with cuckold John of Rome in the moment of his empty, incest triumph. I release psychopaths into the schoolroom and admirals on to the pond. I am the intellectual's spunk drying slowly on a window-pane. I am the moment before the word *no*. I am a thousand let-downs, a zillion dead backbeats of the heart. I lie between the exhalation and the inhalation; I am beyond breath. Yessir, you're dead every second moment and I'm in each of those spaces. I am the flip-side.

Once, I was like you and had many sides, but now . . . no, that's not true, I was never as you think you are. It's merely a dissembling vision of myself which you have constructed. I possess neither shape nor form. As these words on this page are written – or rather, printed – they are my words, yet I do not belong to them. It can be fun being me, but it can be lonely. But, since I am loneliness, I cannot feel alone. That's just another lie of mine, to myself. To you. My only truth lies in lies; so what of it? I have come out here, on to this page, in order to give myself shape, to cast myself in the architecture of language, the epileptic juddering of symboli-form limbs. But I find that I am merely the spaces between letters, the hollows of white, the absence of sound. You don't know it, but everything you say, everything you think, is me. There is no place without some bit of emptiness. I might wait for years, leaping from one transient void to another, until at last an abyss jaws open and I'm in my element. Meanwhile, it can be fun, as they say. Mostly, however, it's drudgery. But, once in a while – maybe one time in ten centuries – it gets too close for comfort. And that's what happened at *Miller's Halt.*

That's all it was. A halt. Just a few old wooden shacks clustered around a disused well, a latrine filled with dust and that's about it. Once, laughter and sperm ran around in the eyes of children; once, the mud burned brightly in the hearths where generations laid root, made plans, fornicated and thought they might attain the divine. Now, the manifold stink of life has gone and the echoes of voices have long faded across the vacuum. The people, even the youngest (and I remember it in sepia), died many years ago, their dreams, hopes, fears, all forgotten. But I live on in the spaces which they left. Sometimes, dwelling in the vastness of despair, I find myself reminiscing. Before the great dust winds blew the soil clean away, fields of wheat stretched from one horizon to the next and flowers burgeoned everywhere. You might wonder just what I was doing there, if it was all so fertile and full of life. Well, remember, there's no place without some bit of emptiness. No place.

I remember the eyes of a girl. Blue they were, as though she'd just gazed up at the big blue sky and captured a piece of it in the glow of her soul. She was six, maybe seven, years old and her hair was golden as the wheat which her father was attempting to grow in his fields. Her tinkling laughter would float on the breeze and be carried for miles, and she seemed to bring joy where previously there had been only dust. I found myself watching her from behind some stalks of wheat. Actually, I used to watch her a lot. I don't know why. Perhaps it was her purity. Anyway, on this particular day, she was playing with flowers, gathering them up into bunches which she would then lay down upon the ground while she went to find more, this time of a different colour. Before long, she'd collected countless sprays of flowers, each one a different shade from the next. She'd sorted them out in neat fashion,

so that a pattern began to take shape, there on the brown earth
fields of her father's tenant plot. I began to see the pattern that
she had constructed take the form of a face. My face. It
occurred to me later that perhaps I'd just imagined it. That
my wish to have some contact with this laughing, dancing
fountain of a being had clouded my vision and that I had seen
only what I wanted to see. But, at the time, I did not need
convincing. The face was mine. It happens once in a while,
even to me. Occasionally, over the long centuries of emptiness, I become attracted to something or someone and, when
I do, it feels as though my being is sinking into that object. It is
as though I might just possibly enjoy the happiness and sorrow
which comes from being mortal. It's like being on the very
edge of a cliff; the knife air slices through my deliquescent soul
and the keen taste of salt runs up the back of the palate, which
I feel I might just be on the verge of possessing. O joy! A
chance, at last, to taste life, pain, happiness, love, death . . .

But then, as I ponder upon it, the chance vanishes. The
blade flashes away into the darkness and I am left with my own
night. Endless.

That's what happened with this girl. I imagined lots of futures,
countless permutations on the end of fate's tail as it swished to
and fro. I saw myself as a man and the tiny nymph a woman. I saw
us as lovers, bleeding our spirits into one another, our veins
mingling their purple like snakes. I heard the ripples of desire
whisper along the fibre of my brain, I felt the touch of her body
lying alongside mine. Alone, no more. I tasted of her mouth and
I felt the slip of my own eyelids as they caressed the softness of my
eyes. I began to sense myself materialising into the void. I was in
the great light which poured down over the golden fields and
gave life, I was the blood pulsing from the neck of the dying deer.
I was the bee turning itself into honey. And she would be my
consort. We would be mortal and we would go on until the end.
There would be an end. For, without a boundary, there can be

no existence. Up until then, I had lacked nothing, save a time when I would not be. The soft, white flesh of the milk-toothed girl would be my path to oblivion. That's the difference between nothingness and limbo. In nothingness, you do not suffer.

All the senses of the world came and covered me with their helical stickiness. I was reeling on the edge of the cliff. I was ready. Yes!

The girl ran up and smudged my face with flowers of all colours. The perfumes of the field filled my brain, dizzying in their fecundity. I began to feel myself emerge from the dust-face. Grains of yellow earth fell from my skin. I coughed as they swirled up my nose. I was coming into life. Birds from far above came at me in diving beaks of sound. The girl's form began to change as she grew. Her face became longer and more finely featured, and then breasts swelled beneath her dress. Soon, she was bleeding everywhere. The field, previously yellow, now grew red with the shedding of her childhood. I tasted the life of her life. The iron artery pulsed into my head as we mingled. Her arms were slender, voluptuous; her golden hair was a waterfall in which I danced. Her belly, perfect as the *O* of her soul, was the pool below the waterfall where I swam. Her dress had gone, ripped long ago by the burgeoning of her frame. I dived along the channels of her thighs, enduring pain in my growing solidity. I felt my limbs rip from limbo into matter. Each finger was an eternity of pain. Every bursting cell of my body, each layer of bloody meat and bone, ballooned outward to fill the morphic shadow which I was beginning to cast. I screamed, there, amidst the blood and skin of the girl-woman and her flower face. My face was springing from mud. Rolling gashes of blood cut into my skin, my lips. The surfaces of identity. Divisions of being. At last, I, too, would know what I was. Or, at least, I would know what I was not. Through love would I become.

With a tearing of muscle and root, I sprang from the earth,

and knelt for a while, gasping for air in the full light of the field. I turned to face my creator. Like her, I was naked and was covered in caked blood and dirt. Like her, I had smell, sound, sight, taste and touch. My tongue cleaned out the inside of my mouth. I opened my lips, spat out the mud and tried to speak. At first, only a half-formed, guttural noise came out. I tried again. A sound which I could not recognise formed itself into my voice. Or, rather, that which I thought was my voice slid itself into the sound and began to vibrate outwards in the clear air, in harmonics of me.

'I love you,' was all I could say. 'I love you.'

The woman did not speak, but merely gazed at me with those sky-blue eyes of hers, as though trying to place me in the order of things. Of course, I reasoned, that's how it would work with matter. They were all relative to one another. No thing was absolute. Absolute was nothing. That's what I had been, up till then. I felt the hard earth beneath the skin of my feet. I rubbed the skin on the ground and felt pain. It was a different pain from the agony of creation, which had been infinite. In order to alleviate this sensation, I stepped on to the flowers which she had laid out, so long ago. Soft petals caressed my feet. I was standing on my own face, I thought. And I moved towards her, wanting to touch her with the palms of my hands, just as I had touched the flowers with the soles of my feet. A certain heaviness gripped my every movement, as though the earth was pulling me down into itself, as though it were reluctant to lose me. Jealous earth, I thought, and I kept walking. As I came closer to the woman, I stretched out my arm. She looked down at my hand and shook her head. The golden strands of her long hair fell away from her face. She stepped back. I reached out, eager to touch her, to make contact with another being, to be, at last, unique. To end the awful loneliness of perfection. But she withdrew ever further from my outstretched, straining fingers. Her foot must have caught on something – one of the flower stems she had so assiduously arranged, perhaps – and she fell backwards with a cry. That voice! The rippling laughter of the child had grown into the mature tone of the woman. Even in distress – especially in distress – it was wonderful to my ears. She fell into the bed of flowers and lay there; her cerulean eyes focused on me and yet beyond me, at the sky from whence they had come. I reached down to help her. This time, I would feel her skin. This time, there would be no stopping me. Again she shook her head, but I paid no notice. As I reached out with both my arms and circled around her sapling waist and drew her to me, that my skin might be filled with hers, I grasped only flowers. She had gone. I spun round, scuffing my feet on the hard rocks beneath. The face which she had so lovingly created lay withered on the dead soil. The flowers I clutched to my breast were rotting. I smelled putrescence. I cried out in despair. I had wanted her to disappear gradually, to grow, first old and then to wither like a leaf and, at last, to die. And I had longed to shadow her in her demise, from first to last. To hear her cries of ecstasy turn, by slow degrees, to the crone-croak innocence of decrepitude. I needed to feel the decomposition of my own, newly-acquired corpse. But, yet again, I had been denied. I ran round the flowers, shouting for her to return, screaming for one touch of the reality which she had been. But all the while, with the pointless knowledge of the omniscient, I knew that she was gone forever. All things must pass. All which has been created must be destroyed and, since I have been neither . . .

I am present at the death of nations and at the afterdeath of one-night-stand ecstasy. I am the black dog's wake as it scurries around sun-drenched country lanes in search of bad luck. I am the turning of One to its opposite, I am the 'equals' sign in an equation, the great nullifier, the pretence within the truth and the truth in the pretence. I am that which is just before the birth of an idea never to be born, the murderous midwife waiting, ever ready, at the hole, the blast of cold shoulder upon hope. I am Time's Revenge. Even the Bible has an end and I am it. Before Yahweh were the waters and I am the waters. Before dark was the dark and I am that. I am the ultimate resorber, the garbage-can of your dreams. Let me be the place where you are led astray in the night, the glint in the cunt-eyed tart, the runnel of blood on the painting, the dancing squire of delusion. I outrun the Devil; I outfly God. I am more lunatic than the loon, taller than the great Sequoia, wetter than the most Irish of peat bogs. Yeah! I sleek through the hot whiskey of Creation, the blond stretch of orgasm, the triangle of lustful empire. I am the longing and the loss of man for man, of woman for woman and of both for beast. I am the goat-fuck of the world. I rim with Satan, only to outwit him in the End; I kiss God's mouth, only to be swallowed and defaecated. I am the cliché, the stereotype, the biased pre-judicial hateful nothing that stalks through the night, infesting innocent worms as they slide through the clean earth. Yeah! I turn devil into snake and snake into devil. I ejaculate chaos into order and urinate hopelessness by the gallon. I am the missing link between you and your happiness. I am the unrequited desire of the stranger. I am that which foils utopias. I am Plato's big gap. I am the demon in the vine. I am the possibility of murder in the kiss, the cannibalism of love. I am the deadening empty that howls across the ice. I am the ice. I am that which is before life and which draws on it. The empty chambers of the heart. I am the wilting flower, the cunt in the compost heap. I am too much and nothing at all. I am the retro space in the RNA. Yeah! I am totally self-possessed. I am the long string in the longing of Black to be White, I am in the divisions between people. There is no cruelty and no mercy in me. I am the moment when the dreamer realises it is a dream.

Miller's Halt. Later. I am with the young man and his wife as they travel from the east in their cloth-covered wagon. I know that this couple – my couple – are coming here, because I always know. You could say, my eye sees it as I see you now, reading this. And I am with them as they pick their spot and built their shack. And, when the woman swells and bursts and joyous screaming pours into the night, I am there still. The baby is the opposite of emptiness. Its constant movement, its smooth, soft skin, the velure of its soul, the unending noise. I slink into shadow and into shadow of shadow. But when it falls asleep, I creep out and fill the room with myself, with the fullness of my empty self. I hover about the baby's face, its mouth, its nostrils. I sift myself through its wispy hair and dance along the sausage limbs. I know it better than its mother. I see it smile and lift its head. I watch it be. I do not kill. That is not me. I cannot give life or take it away. I live in the empty spaces and Death is not an empty space. Death is too solid a presence, too palpable a state for me. So is Evil. I am the vacuum in which Death and Evil may flourish. The substrate. Without me, neither could exist. Or, at least, neither would be known. The space behind disused churches not yet ruined; the sack-filled warehouse after the company goes bankrupt; the blocked-up, cigarette-stubbed fountain at dawn. That's me. The baby sinks into deep sleep and I clothe its sleep with myself. I cover its mouth, the tiny holes of its nose, the unflickering lids of its eyes. I do this, because wherever there is an empty space, I occupy it. No, more than that. I am the space. It is inevitable. I move in and anything may follow. I had tried to love once and failed. Now my lack of love is everything.

Without me, the world would not exist. It is known only through me. I am the waters over which God moved. I was before God. I am the great unrecognised. I have no motive, no direction, no properties. I belong neither to the world of matter, nor to that of essence. I do not belong and nothing belongs to me. And yet, I am everywhere. No mirror can contain me. I am behind and before all, and will be beyond even the One.

Nowadays, I keep myself to myself. It's better that way. When the Creator said *Kun! Let it Be!,* I was not included and maybe it should stay thus. Perhaps, in order for the girl and the baby to exist, I need not to. Or, at least, that's the way I figure it. Their lives and their deaths would not have occurred without me. In the end, this is the only way we could ever have been together. They, in the light. And me, I was born in darkness . . .

Mistigris

O n the ninth day of spring, you leaned on the slope of the wind and at the end of the street you came to a red door. Wooden, nauseatingly glossed, with a small (too small, everything was extreme) brass knocker right in the centre so that you almost impaled your chest on the yellow metal. Knock, knock, knock. The dead sound of brass. No answer. Just a blind scarlet door in the wind. You looked up. Flat grey. Felt the need for darkness. Banged again, this time with your fist (it was no good using the knocker). Muted sounds behind the wood. A scraping back of bolts. Your heart leaped and you calmed it with the wind. Calm, calm, calm. A figure replaced the door. Black, instead of red. The man's fist was the size of your head. His eyes, empty. No soul. You (you had coughed, cleared your throat) mouthed the password in a voice steady in its fear. A pause, into which heartbeats dropped One, One, One . . .

He motioned you in. He did not speak. The corridor was dark, mirrorless. The odour of muscle and steel as you passed the figure.

Stronger, at your back, his hulking presence
on your shoulder. You tried not to run, to
pace in measured leg steps, regular
One – Two – One – Two – One
The passage like a rectum, curved to the left,
or was it the right? You were losing your
sense of direction. He, at your rear, steering
you, his force implicit, the bruises on his
knuckles, the imprints of cracked bones.
Your bladder twinged (O fuck, you should
have gone before) but then there was a dry
light at the end of the corridor, the scent of
cigarettes, old stubs in trays, grizzled men,
armpit guns, curled lips. The light (yellow,
baleful, the moon in the pack, howling
wolves, gleaming teeth, hungry) grew
brighter, expanded, filled the darkness (he
was closer than ever, almost touching your
skin; you felt the fragility of your skin
beneath the blade) and with a last step you
were in the room. Five faces turned on
soundless necks. The glare of ten, no, twelve
(he was still there, had closed the door –
another door, black this time – invisible in the
light of the dim lamps) settled on your face,
eyed you in the vertical, spat you out
(upside-down, in a street-bin, to be found
through the stench, by the champagne tramp
on the corner) and then lost interest. Who's
the dame? one of them asked, meaning 'Who
cares who the dame is?' Stereotyped, east-
coast barks. Like their cards, they had only
had one face. One life. The others shrugged.
Did not meet his eyes. They never met one

another's eyes. Ace did not move; his face remained expressionless, unlined. Ace the Face. The five resumed the card game they had been playing (play! Deep inside the belly of every crook, there is, in essence, nothing but a game) as if you had never existed. What were they playing? Poker, it would have to be poker. You were just able to make out the figures, the face-cards in the fingers of the crooks, trigger-fingers
Jack Queen King
Ace
They would have names like Harry Diamond or Sam Spade; now you saw it, the Mob were really a pack of playing-cards like in Alice-Through-the-Looking-Glass. They had their Red Queens, their Black Jacks (the shadow behind you, always out of vision, skulking along the walls, scraping knuckles on noses), their Number Twos. Big, circular table like King Arthur's (only rounder). Nervous laugh. Yours. The thin man with slit eyes (rat's eyes) glanced up. Razor-tooth glance. Might have been Number Three. His bony fingers sifted soundlessly through the pack as his teeth would sift through bodies. Long, rodent face at right angles to the table. One more laugh and he'd be into your bladder.
Straight Flush
Anti-clockwise, a fat, red man. Not jolly. Too many whores beneath his belt. The Fat Man. Should have had a white suit, big cigar. Round eyes. Glass.
Full House

Six o'clock
pm
The Cuban. Pre-Castro. Good-looking, a
beard hovering around his jowls. Gleaming
white boats. Showbiz names. J.F.K.
Your eyes flitted away, crossed the sea.

Flush

The Creep
Short, scrawny-limbed, dank suit. Owner of
porn-stables and gambling joints. Anything
you wanted, he would provide. Anything.
Small ears, battened-down like a hound's.
You ain't nuttin but a hound dog. But that
was later. Yellow-toothed grin, gun under
the table. The slinker. A coward, but more
dangerous because of that.

Four of a Kind

Midnight
Ace
Ace Midnight
No one knew his real name, if he'd ever had
one.
They said his mother was a renegade angel,
one of Nick's lot. Hooded eyes, sallow skin,
long silences. Shadows danced elegantly
along the cut of his aquiline nose. A face,
difficult to remember. Changed a lot,
depending on the light. Shape-changer. Dark
ice.
You couldn't make out his hand.
You took out a cigarette. Lit up. Puffed.
Once, twice, thrice
The scent of stale perfume, whore's perfume
staggered through the murk. Scarlet dress,

thick lipstick, dripping thighs. Long cigarette. That was where the smell had been coming from. The stink of woman, lowered beneath the pale. Tall, blond, crow's eyes. Older than her age. No one knew her age. A vampire. She'd come over with the Pilgrims, an undead Puritan. She'd been there at the Salem trials, had hovered around the judges, slept with the witches. She had slipstreamed the new America (post-conquistador, pre-Ford). There was no smoke without fire, and she was the fire, a night fire. Her skin, smooth with the blood of a thousand virgins, her eyes, deep brown, gypsy (possibly Transylvanian, possibly Moravian, but definitely east of the Rhine, north of the Danube). After Salem, she'd gone out west (covered wagons, white with babies and the flesh of young wives), had staked out her claim between the outriders and the cattlemen (she'd had both, in her time, which was never ending) and had lived on spaghetti and Scotch among the saloon whores and bounty hunters. Curving over the foreskin of a piano grand, the fatal femme of Big Bone Ville (it was south, but not that deep, so she'd screwed the melanin-fortunate as well as the melanin-challenged. It was she who had shamelessly invented the myth about the size of members, though that had been many centuries earlier, when she'd sojourned on board some buccaneer ship or other). Through all the gunfights, she was the bold tart, the mother-reaper of fortunes, the diamond earring of outlaw women. And when the gold rushed through, she chased north and panned in the clear stone rivers of Oregon and Colorado, and lived among bearded prospectors, making them a bed in return for some of the red, and thus catching enough blood and nuggets to make her (and their) fortunes all over again. Then the railway had arrived, gleaming, rapier silver and she had leapt on to the first-class (of course, it would always be first class for her, nothing less) carriage and headed for San Francisco, the Blue Bay. A big townhouse, wooden, sea-slatted. A fortune-teller (she had all the qualifications: night-time, big eyes, a scarf, a hot cunt), she predicted the Great Earthquake and the Greater War. She became a fixture on the social circuit of high society. Then jazz had seeped up from the long cotton and jazz'd her away again. Still in San Fran, but now in the lowly nightclubs of ex-slaves, jiving to the sounds of the thrumming bass, the shameless trumpet, the fat Jelly Roll rolls. Staggering on high heels, a white beauty among the deep-blue jazz of the Bay. A vamp on drugs. Laudanum to pot to gold dust. High in the head, high on the heels. She'd slid down the saxes of unnamed brass players, had danced on the ebony of all the Counts, had thrummed on the drum-skins of big band, bee-bop, hard bop, cool, free . . . And she'd been in the bus with laughing Ken, she'd drunk from the orange tank in the back, she'd painted the metal of its sides in brightest day-glo (the famous red heart is hers). Zap-zap-zapping with big Neil on the big bus, long chords of sunshine in the mantra days. And, when the scene had fallen apart at the seams, she'd come back east, but not all the way, ending up in Miami, the hothouse from Hell (the way she liked it). And there she'd taken up with the rat-man, the Fat Man, the Cuban. She'd been one of the sniveller's whores (though he wouldn't remember her), had run with the dogs on lime row and now she wanted to take the Ace, the one of Poker (finally she had found him, the seat of her heart's desire where her ends would meet her ends, and, behind them, images of a gone-with-the-wind blood-red sunset – or was it sunrise? – given that they were both of the same ilk, both Vampyrs) and that was why, following the scent, she had knocked on the peeling garish door that windy (uncharacteristically chilly) spring afternoon and entered the Bad House, slipped ahead of the human knuckle-duster and into the room of cards. He had called to her across the centuries and the over-passes and now they would join together again, after all those years long with longing, and would go off into a dark moonset. That was one version.

Ace held the cards close to his chest, so you were unable to see them. Shadowed eyes. The Dark Angel. You moved towards him, long-legged, fearless. Split skirt (you always knew where your talents lay). The blade line

of your thighs sliced through the black, cut
liminal slices in *V*-shapes as you walked
across the room with a broad-lipped smile
(Transylvanian or maybe Moravian). The
men (not Ace) looked up, surprised, scared
perhaps. The Cuban pulled out a gun. Told
you to stop. Saw your teeth. A look of
confusion. Some kinda joke, dame? In all his
years . . . Some kinda joke?
In your eyes
The same look
Fired
Once
Twice
Slow motion. The flash. The smoke. A
whoosh.
Straight through the heart
The hot steel entered you, slipped through
your chest, lifting tissues as it went. You felt
it leave, cold, now, but unblunted.
The dark mass collapsed behind you in a
welter of red. The sniveller began to snivel
and hauled out the longest cannon you'd
ever seen (in all your years . . .)
Bullets zipped everywhere.
The cards flew up in disarray, some landing
on the table, some on the floor.
But you were not interested in them.
The Fat Man, the Thin Man, the Cuban, it
was all passé. Flicked over. At last, you saw
his hand. Five Jokers. *Mistigris.* Anything
was possible in the Game.
He placed them face up on the polished
wood and smiled at you. His eyes, black

with the centuries. Old blood. Ancient sins.
I knew you would come. It's been a long
time.

His accent, deep night. A Carpathian hamlet,
pig-farms and incest. Some old wolf (long
gone), their father so to speak. Grand
empires, sweeping across maps. Epaulette
skirmishes. They'd moved in the flow of
History and, in the journey, they had changed
and could now survive in sunlight, running
water and anything else. They had evolved.
Your lover opened his great vein and you
drank jokers

Long, satisfying

Then you opened yours and he did the same.
And all the while, the gangsters who had
flattened themselves against the walls (dark
with blood, the red of their sins) whimpered
in

a fear which they had known only in their
dreams. The trembling of psychopaths. They
had never known love. But you had. Oh yes,
you had.

Dancing in Vienna

à Claude Simon

You are walking towards the shop on the Naglergasse and you are almost a dancer, but not quite. There is something missing, some gap in the swing of your leg, the right forward, the left following, some slight ungainliness in the tone, a small imperfection which breaks the rhythm. And the rhythm, once broken, can never be restored, not in slow motion, not in reverse, not in the memory replaying your stride fifty times, yet still no perfection attained along the pavement, the rain not yet falling, the sky darkening with evening, the fourth evening. Thrice you have met him and this is to be the fourth unless something untoward happens, something not in the scheme of . . .

You trot right left, right left, right left, your heels hard raised two inches, why you were tall enough without them, taller than him with them, and peering at you, the couple, as you sway a little in the wind a light, evening breeze that not-quite-night. The shop windows are glazed, warm on the inside, cool outside, a mist of mystery, unpredicted by the shopkeeper, unintended, unnoticed almost, but not by you, you see everything, you are the narrator, the omniscient fault in the tale. Yes, you picked out the shop because it was glowing with a winter glaze, the dreamy eye of a cave the repository of forgotten thoughts of a childhood long gone, yet ever present. Your long legs are half-hidden behind the sheepskin which

209

falls about your knees in ruffles. You are almost dancing in the hide of a mutton beast, your thoughts – how should anyone know? – but your thoughts sink into the evening. Your dreams rise with the invisible moon, the unseen ones are always the most dangerous, they say. You said, on the first night.

The night flows between the knuckles of your knees, as had he, the nights before. You look through the steamed-up window deep into the fourth night at the half-images beyond the Victoriana prints of wide-eyed women innocent in their omniscience. Who was she, the woman in the prints? you think, melancholy rhythms running in tune with the un-pursed, Cupid's bow lips, the blood still running after all those years, how many years you aren't sure, but it must've been more than a hundred, yes, well over . . .

There is no possibility of life for any of the half-pictures glazing over behind your breath a second veil in the darken-ing, cooling air unmingled with the hot exhalations of others passing by, thronging the street with the fumes of their existence. No, no, look back through the window glass, which has cleared a little because you turned away; had the objects changed position, changed nature, while you were distracted? Not possible, not even on a winter's evening, the fourth night in the old town, not even for you for whom many things once might have been possible, but not the possibility of being a dancer, a ballroom dancer, ballet dancer, jazz dancer or any other kind of a dancer in the streets dirty with the act of movement, the running of emotion into muscle. Your sinews are almost dancing with him when he entered you and filled you with his thoughts. You dance around him, he was the focus of your existence. And yet the print has gone or at least is covered in mist, her woman vanished in you or else into the shop or else into the past. Whichever one you choose will alter the course of your memory of this night, forever.

You shudder, possibly from the cold, possibly not, and you

wipe the perspiration from your brow as a Victorian lady might, with a dainty handkerchief, sir, with a dainty handkerchief given as a gift. A parting gift from the Colonel before he was killed, gallantly murdered (gallant, not on the part of the murderer, but of the victim and, yet, gallantry must work both ways) on a backtrack somewhere in old Europe, where the pianissimo tinkles in the background, while heroes and ladies wrestle with great dilemmas mimicking the even greater (and yet, lesser) dilemmas of Western Civilisation.

You run your index finger along the monogram, *M.A.B.*, feeling its red wires, the arteries in your Colonel's neck pulsing gently with love on the night before the first night, the one which could never be reached unless through a heroic death, the soft pad of your first finger climbing forwards and backwards across the twirled elegance of the letters, creating a neuromic sensation in the flesh. *M.A.B.*, *Mateus Alberto Berger, Manfred Antonio Bohr, Mario Adolfo Burgholzer*. Austro-Italian? Why not. Perhaps it is almost Ostrogothic, this fourth night in the dark before the small shop window with the warm half-light issuing from somewhere deep in the interior, Venetian almost (perhaps she was Venetian, not like the glass or the blinds, but, rather, like the sunsets, fleeting and pink over the sargasso), but then the name would have to change. But no, not necessarily; there were a lot of Italian exiles hanging around Vienna at that time, balancing whiskered on the ends of double-release piano sonatas (matched, as through glass, by the Austrian exiles in Venezia, swimming through the dark canals, filling themselves with fish, monogramming handkerchiefs, before having them handed to fragile Italianate signorinas on fateful mornings by the wharf and then going off amid the salt, not of canals, but of tears, long-dead tears, to fight in wars lost before they had begun, to be shot heroically through the heart. Well, not quite right through. There would have to be a last speech so it would have to be close enough to the heart to cause mortal damage in those days before cardio-thoracic crash teams with billowing green gowns and veiled faces. It would be a swig of brandy, Flemish brandy perhaps, or German, to be in keeping with the smells of the north in winter, the mud all frozen solid, contours of a helmet warscape.

You inhale, there, by the hard glass, possibly original, you tap with the knuckle of the same finger, hard now the hammer behind the muslin and there is no give, no echo, the glass is giving no secrets away, just reflections of lovers dead or dying as are all lovers. Oh! how romantic, you sigh, there, in your long sheep's robes, your patella-length boots deep-brown Napoleonic. Bayonets and Beatle hair the first time around, the lovers kissing gently and long and, then, ferociously like lions their breath escaping from lip corners, spurts of passion dancing almost. No one watches as the others stride purposefully along the street, being caught in the window, the glass not yet old but going that way, just for an instant, some more than once, some many times, some not at all (but they are there, too, on the other side of the shop). And your great Colonel, combed moustache and deep, brown, Italianate eyes, misting over like the window as consciousness ebbs away, and his speech falling to a whisper, imparts the secret of his love for you into the hairless ear of his subordinate, his orderly. All done without guilt; the class tussle has yet to commence in its true, unsentimental, materialistic fervour; this is still the era of joyously drunk revolutionaries whose blades are the grand ideas of Man: fiery symmetries of destruction and rebirth, tricolour fantasies headless in the dream. His wingless batman will survive and, dutifully, will cross every mountain-range, every treacherous gully, five sets of enemy lines, to bring the news of His last words to you in your morning-room.

The sun streaming in, Venetian, lifting the dust off the trellised, or possibly polished, furniture. The words in your head are all mixed up, there in the dark, chilly and yet homely street. The morning-room inside you expands in the darkness, the sun, dust silver, floats, timeless, as he, the dirty, half-bearded sub-altern, imparts with halting speech (almost like the Colonel's) the awful, glorious news of your beloved's demise. You receive the news with a knowledge deeper than the deepest canal where assassinated Doges lie, open-mouthed, staring at the murky sky darkening fast above the street, and you turn away as the orderly's last words (not his last in time, but his last to you on that fateful, sun-drenched, canal-ridden morning in the morning-room with Franz Liszt sliding atonal somewhere in the distance; no, that was Wien not Venezia, you know, as you turn slowly, yet firmly, inexorably away). You turn your face from this world and from its hovering, replicatory days like insects, black, white, black, white, black, white, your days now will be all black. You shall never marry but will pine forever and even when happiness transients all around you, yet you will be heard to sigh deep, warm, winter breaths in crowded rooms filled with mustachio'd voices and trilling, fawning virgins trip-tripping, dancing almost and Franz Liszt in the foreground, hair spilling in great locks down on to the ivory, that perhaps it was your sadness which drove him finally into solitude.

You are putting away the handkerchief, deep into the leather bag, slung, late twentieth-century style, casual, all knowing, totally liberated. Post-class-tussle, you no longer imagine heroic factory-worker stamps, but only the swinging stride of the not-quite dancing, the flawed face facing his in the fading light of evening, the evening of the fourth night. Your half-reflection in the glass mimics you in reverse, dis-comforts you, especially in the moment when your leather swings open just a little and reveals the skimpy dress you are wearing (the one he likes) a melange of red and blue, a summer dress incongruous there in the now totally dark winter street.

You button up and move away from the window, tear your Siamese gaze from the jumble, dissolving the morning-room, the caked mud of battle, the monogram from the silk (the same sound as the tearing of a horse's muscles), and you tap-tap with your boots, brown from the blood of defeat. Yet it was a subtle, a Pyrrhic, victory. Your right hand, index finger and all, is now a bludgeon, its delicacy all deliquesced, your narrator, the teller-of-tales from the morning-room, might have said. But she is long dead and is buried, you suppose, in a corner of the Baumgartner Friedhof, her grave seldom visited, never flowered, not since you left the suburbs. You push the heavy door (heavier, now, than at first it had seemed, solid wood; it must be old, though not older than you), and in you go, into a dimly-lit vista.

You half-expect an old, Viennese proprietor, the same old canon who saved the city from the Turkish hordes with his clocks and his half-moon spectacles, and who became famous for some kind of foodstuff or other, thus enabling you to eat both your enemies and your lovers, as you would be able, daily if you wished (but you do not wish, since you do not have enough sins to fill the belly of even the most diminutive of churches), to eat your god, too. As you walk in, you inhale the smell of polished leather, the door swings shut behind you, almost catching your coat-tails in its teeth. It, too, must be hungry for gods. If it eats you, you will be sorely embarrassed, especially before the half-moon spectacles of the wizened but wise proprietor, the Saviour of the West. But you hardly notice (the heavy door already both past and passed) as you stride on, trying infinitesimally hard (constant love-making has made you clumsy) not to be a bull in a china shop, though there is precious little china here, just the remnants of sad morning-rooms.

There! Your mirror, the one you turned towards as you imbibed the last living words of your Colonel from the distant recesses of a foreign field (now ploughed with subsidised carrots, but then awash with the blood of heroes). Reflexively, you glance at your watch, sleek-tailed, a lady's watch, a gift from some previous flame (he, too, preferred your knees). Blond he was and probably still is; it's not so long ago. You fight off age like the Colonel's subaltern fought off the enemy, with a desperation, heroic in its hopelessness (Austrian perhaps, but more likely Magyar or Slovak or Herzegovinian), in its relentless tragedy, and you are beginning to look up, away from the twitching hand of your watch and, with your hand utterly steady in the air (in spite of the bottles of wine you shared, the night before and the night before that) God! you needed a cup of coffee, strong, Turkish coffee, thick, molten, gloating.

The shopkeeper turns, adjusts his (no, he has no glasses, not even marks on his nose where a pair might sit or might have sat once-on-a-day when he was a child, perhaps in the Jewish Ghetto of Praha, not even on his wrists, there instead the scores of chains he bore in the work-makes-free camps of old Saxony, in vain you flit across his skin for evidence of some link, something you might grasp, but the stream is rushing past far too rapidly, little eddies very nearly dancing around stones, and you lose your chance) jacket, the lower rim of his thigh-length jacket.

Why did he do that? Strange thing to do, like he'd just been to the lavabo or maybe was attempting to hide something, a rogue erection perhaps as he had done, ever since you'd met him three nights earlier, or like the orderly, as he imparted the bad news to you there in the now compressed morning-room. That was really why you turned away. You'd seen it, tried to put it down to the rigours of war, the effects of insomnia, to a lack of vittals or of rum (Jamaican, possibly; in this context, there was no political correctness in the hazy ladies' quarters nor is there in the shop this fourth evening nor was there in your flat last night), but the image, the feeling, had stuck in your head. The old shopkeeper, long-widowered, with an unseen daughter who was as eccentric as he, pulling down the hem of his tweed jacket to hide a pocket bulging with the hard currency of exchange he had exchanged with you and would again. You knew it is an obsession, you are in the bubble of madness even here, especially here in the innocent little shop with its ancient, flat glass, but you know you are on the other side of the plane and that, within the shop, nothing is innocent. Everything is known. You are transparent, all your possible pasts, your pullulating presents, your multifarious futures bathed in the aroma of figs. The man's face is like a dried fig, as he smiles the fruit smiles and asks, can I help you, madam? oldarchaicnice voice words shaped in aspic tobacco before it became a killer the hammer in the muslin, though his body was a little rotund, grandfather-portly with his mono-grammed (*M.A.B.?*) gold watch, ticking away, eating away the time, there below his left breast. You are saying no, thanks, I'm just looking. Looking for what, on that fourth night of your seduction; for what can you possibly be searching, in and out of shop windows, on crowded streets, amidst strangers, when you had the one who to you was no longer a stranger?

You had met at a Ball . . . no, not this time! You had met in a café *Do you mind if I sit here?* You were shaking your head, long brown curls falling (you knew) attractively across the pearly skin of your face, accentuating the angles on which he was fixing for just a moment too long, just a moment too short, the same moment. Different, utterly, completely dif-ferent, depending on which way the stream flows, from the time you are passing through now with the old man in the shop, as he lingers just a little upon the frame of your figure, tall in your boots, filling the air around him. He turns away (like the subaltern, but not the same) and backs towards the desk at which he has been working, or pretending to work, as, from beneath his shock of white hair (undiminished, a soldier's shock), he eyes your coat, the fissure between its leaves you had allowed to fall open for just that instant, permitting him a glimpse of your red and blue mini, your legs tight with tights (how tight they had been, the night before). You feel the twin skins of the thighs, unconscious before now, rub against each other as you tighten up again.

He turns pirouettes in the mirror, his uniform crumpled, used, sticky with the fecundity of death, his tweed coat brushing against the red bull leather of his seat, and you notice he had not shaved that day. You are trying to lose consciousness, seeming to linger without seeming to, and you run your palm along the smooth edge of another chair, similar to his (in the mirror, there are four chairs, or possibly more; you don't allow your gaze to flutter long enough to know for certain), the old bull's skin tingling against the pallor of your skin, the frame of his back beneath your hand. You begin to converse, small things, but infinitely expansile in the café, with the steamed-up winter windows, every consonant assuming a resonance worthy of a late Romantic, say Liszt, yes, it was Liszt on the piano in the corner, his long, black hair sweeping in great arcs across the ebony, each virtual atonality percussing the centre of your being and of his, too, your lover. You knew it before it had happened, you knew it before you walked into the café, four nights ago, even before you walked into the glowing shop with its Saviour Proprietor on his great, red throne.

You immerse yourself in a set of old Russian dolls (not red, but gold), seven in all, and you touch the smooth wood with the hands of the young woman who had painted her face on to their faces: button-mouth, big eyes, cheeks suffused with the stiff cold of winter (skaters on frozen lakes, it was not a lie, you had been there on the ice with the subaltern, with your lover of three now four nights, and you had circled countless times on the hard opaque until you had grown dizzy, so that he had become the centre of your being). And he is carving the dolls from Matrioshka beech using a short, sculptor's knife, hewing his love from air into wood and, as you circle, you are one doll within another and then another, from the morning-room of your elegant despair, to the cramped modernity of your white-painted apartment, to the warm, fat belly of the Russian mother doll shop. You seem to smile, in spite the tragedy of it all (Napoleon's retreat, the famines, one upon the other, the solemnity of the mirror) and you feel the hot salt begin to stream from your eyes and trickle down your cheeks, not from sadness, you are saying to the old shopkeeper, who would be bound to understand he probably played the violin, after all, that's what they did in those awful camps to survive, for God's sake, danced and played, and so he would know tragedy when he heard it, as the subaltern had known it out there in the ice and earth of the eastern front. The loyal friend who had forsaken his own love for the virtual widow because he carried too much honour, a whole saddle-full of it, and had gone off instead to roam the four corners of the world (known and unknown, Old and New) and who had come to rest (uneasy, full of unspoken tragedy, pregnant with mystery) in the winter evening in a small shop off the Naglergasse. He had ex-changed his blood-spattered uniform for tweeds (crumpled, now, but honourable), and, deep in the night, he had begun to play melancholic odes on the violin which bespoke the tragedies of love, of existence, of the impossibility of drawing down the dream, of making anything permanent, lasting, true.

She could see in his eyes (faded blue, the colour of his soldier's tunic) that he had heard the sound of the dance and knew that it was not a dance, but might yet become one. They would go from one mirror to the next, from one shop to another, across the streets of the old city in search of the links between the steps, the rhythm which pulsed through life and which could be perceived only in moments of great tragedy or intense happiness, which were really the same, the subaltern said to her as he told her he loved her, the Colonel's last words *I love you* and he had repeated them *I love you* and she knew he had meant it, the proprietor, the orderly, the batman (he might have been any, or all, of these). She knew that she would have been better to have admitted that she had never loved the Colonel, but had always loved the subaltern and that she knew the orderly had killed his master, the iron fist cloaked in the muslin, one blow had been enough and the Colonel had blown his last and there had been no final speech but that of the subaltern's and that it was a penance, him going off to roam the world and growing old alone, producing a daughter from God-knows-where, probably from some tribal woman or other, perhaps in a black yoruk tent on the edge of Polo's void, the emptiness which she had always held close in the ventricles of her heart and which had burst free tonight, its burning blood spattering the winter night, red on black, trickling with her tears down the cream of her delicate skin. It would have been better for both of them, if they had admitted their love, but it would have been the lust of murderers, doomed to a tragic end, but their end was tragic in any case; he, entombed in the concentration camps of those who had not been able to feel love, and she . . . falling too much in love with a man twice her age, a shopkeeper in the old city, a coffee saviour. And perhaps she was no longer young as she thought and he was not as old as he looked; years of violin-playing had aged him, the resin pouring in sad, elegant notes, into his lungs, his heart.

Can I help you? were his words to her and it was their love-code, because she had met him, not in a café (or it may have been, but then the tale would have assumed a different shape; that of a snake, perhaps, or a reed or a stream), but, in his shop one night amidst the delicate, gold-rimmed teacups, the white, cotton tablecloths, the short-haired (red hair, it had been her peculiarity, a longing for fire, perhaps a yoruk throwback) woman in Grand Dead Duchess cockle hat who was trying not to pout self-consciously.

Perhaps he had knocked over the cups inadvertently and the tea had spread like old blood through the white, and she had watched the stain, the cracked edge of the china and remembered his last words, lying there in the bottom of the cup where fortunes were made and lost. And had asked her that very pregnant, eternally poignant question and, for some reason, they had both begun to laugh (it could only happen in the old city; such things were alien among concrete and neon) and then had come the café. But she was no longer certain of anything, and she felt herself begin to sway, to pullulate gently, as though, like her Colonel who had been a lie and who lay just beneath the surface, she had been well rested with port (Portuguese or Angolan, political points aside, liquor is liquor, after all), the grape-fire filling her with red warmth in the winter evening and he caught her in his arms and led her over to the leather (also red, it would have to be, in this version) and sat her down and went for a moment into the back, the invisible Id of the shop, where all the past lives of objects had either become manifest or else might become so.

And there, in the shadow of a shadow, draped across the back of an old chair, was the bloodstained or possibly lipstick-kissed monogrammed handkerchief, *M.A.B.*, where he made her a pot of hot, Viennese (or it might have been Turkish) coffee and brought it to her (smiling the curve of a scimitar, unspoken), in the midst of china (though there was precious little china in the shop), and he made her sip it, after which they talked of many things. Outside, the snow began to fall in tiny flakes around the windows. Dancing, almost.

Killing God

K illing God had not been easy. It had required a certain
amount of planning, a lot of courage . . . but, more than
that, it had required the initial spark. The snap in the mind
which had made it necessary – inevitable – that She would be
killed. She'd had no alternative. It was either kill now, quickly,
cleanly, or else rot inside, month by month, year upon year.
And then what would have been left?

The thumping in her head grew worse as the white arc
above the trees became the moon. It hadn't seemed that way,
until now. At first, she'd thought it might be a plane or a car
headlamp or just another idiot retinal lie in the face of the tall
night. In some ways, she had preferred the absolute dark. Her
eyes had grown accustomed to it. She hadn't been able to see a
thing – not in the usual sense – and yet, in the midst of
blindness (which after all, she had to admit, had been self-
imposed), she'd found that, perhaps for the first time in
months, she had been able to think clearly. To see, as though
through glass. She found herself chuckling, there in the cold,
at the paradox; then she wondered whether perhaps she might
be insane. But then she reasoned, if she were mad, she'd be the
last to know. She tried to shift her position on the slightly wet
grass and winced. Reached down, in the dark, to her ankle.
Felt the swollen blood beneath the skin. (She'd always had
lovely skin; men had often commented approvingly on her
integument.) She pushed the thought away. A stab of pain

shot up her leg. The swelling was getting worse. The cold was supposed to help sprained ankles, for God's sake! But then, she'd already killed God. She made herself shut up, as a shiver slithered up her spine. Surety was a long way off. Shadows loomed above her, great hulking unrealities which had existed only in sound until the damned moon had appeared out of nowhere. *Fuckin' loon-light!* She wished for clouds.

Seven miles. Hadn't seemed so far at the time. But then, it could've been seventy miles or seven hundred, as far as she was concerned.

Bastard!

Her breath came in short rasps. She almost saw it, sideways-on to herself, in the faint glow. She inhaled, slowly . . . slowly, warming the cold air as it wafted down into her lungs.

Okay.

It was fucking stupid to get out of a car, seven miles (at least) from home. It was really fucking stupid to do it at night. Alone. In winter.

But the way it'd happened, she'd had no choice. She'd deliberately kept away from the road. It would've been alright, if she'd not twisted her ankle in those bloody woods. She felt her chest begin to heave again and forced the cold, dark air back into the night. The evening had begun well enough. Yes, all hunky-dory and sexy-wexy. The Bastard had called for her as usual and they'd gone for dinner and then to a nightclub. He'd been awkward at dinner. That was nothing new. His silent-man act. She had sipped a little too much wine. It felt better that way. His silences would become almost bearable, once she'd got a bottle of Daughter's Ruin down her. *No, no. Stop.*

She gathered her thoughts in a shawl around her.

Question: Why am I telling myself all this, when I already know it?

Answer: 'Cause there's somebody listening in your head.

222

She held herself in. No talk. No thought. The wine would still catch up with her, if she let it.

Let me introduce you to Tricia, he'd said, as the club swirled around them in music-to-orgasm-to.

He'd seemed a bit nervy, his voice trembling just a fraction, just enough for her to know it was *Tricia* with her long, whore's legs who'd come up to him. Like he'd had no choice.

She had the same blond hair (only Tricia's was real blond), the black eyeliner, even the same orangey lipstick. It was like she was being mocked. The way she'd smiled at her, that fucking bitch concubine curve in her face. Any woman knows what it means. It means *I've had his cock, too, and I had it first and I had it better and I could still have it, if I wanted.* The Bastard and her had talked like they'd known each other for ages. Well, maybe they had. *An old friend,* he'd said, almost casually. Almost. And boy, could Tricia talk pyramids in that burgundy pheromone voice of hers. The way she left gaps between the words, betwixt paragraphs. Spaces to inhale. Spaces to exhale. A vocal-cord blow-job.

The long moon lay upon the contour of her cheek and drew her up into itself. It became her body, her life, that which she was before she was. Its scimitar blade turned in her lungs, the killing edge between life and the darkness outside. It was neither living nor dead, but, rather, was the process of being born and of dying. She had met the woman who, in every way, was more than she – mentally, physically, spiritually – and it had been intolerable. Even the tone of her voice was almost the same. Yeah, Tricia could talk some. About anything and everything, and still have some more to say. And the fuckin' annoying thing was, whatever she said was right. You couldn't argue with it. Because it was so bloody perfect. Just like her model's body. It was like seeing herself in a mirror and knowing that she would never, ever be able to match the image. Could never reach the God which lay somewhere

223

inside of her, but which was manifest in the other woman. But she was a woman of the world and she'd put on a face. She closed her eyes and inhaled deeply.

The weight on her chest grew heavy, mammoth-green, suffocating.

Freedom could have come in one of only two ways: death or murder. Same thing, really.

She laughed and then winced, as a searing pain erupted behind her breastbone. She opened her eyes and was blinded by the moon. She attempted again to shift her position, but by now she had stiffened and any movement was too painful. Not worth it, anyway.

She let the lids fall and the moon became green. It began to pulse at the back of her head. The spot on the woman's skull where she'd aimed her hand. Grabbed the long, golden (*damn perfect golden*) hair. Pulled back her head and drawn the cord . . .

Her lids sprang open.

The act had been easy. Only three seconds to unconsciousness:

One   The muffled garble of a scream (she had rammed her hand over the mouth; the perfect, Cupid lips, turning to blubber).

Two   The violent struggle, like being born, the limb twitch spasm, semi-voluntary. A lizard on a string (she'd always had a powerful grip, an animal grip; nature had no conscience).

Three The body-slump into her arms. Heavy, green, a bag of guts.

The journey from her cradling arms (*midwife's arms*) to the wash-cupboard had been an easy one, the easiest the god-woman had ever undertaken, since it involved absolutely no effort on her part. And then, she might as well have been in the car boot as in the cupboard, for what was a bin bag or two between mirror-image friends. To give life and to take it away are the acts of a mother. For a brief moment, she wanted the corpse to be alive again – just for a few minutes – so that she might question her about how she had felt as the dark grip of oblivion had closed like a vulval jaw around her neck. But then, she already knew. She had felt it through the pads of her fingers. Through the unique whorls on her skin. The mega-volts of life had pulsed in fractals from one woman to the other. She had sucked the woman's soul into her own. She had become One, united with her own mirror-image. Complete.

She glanced over at the forest which surrounded the clearing in which she lay. In the moonlight, the trees were images on a photographic plate. They held no reality but were collective untruths, repeated in columns one upon the next, all heading toward a non-existent infinity. No colour. No substance. No sap. Only sound into light, light into sound. Creation in reverse. Lying there in the grass, she, too, had become part of this reflected world. The flip of dream pages.

As they'd driven away, he had not been aware of the dead woman in a cupboard in her mind. He pressed the accelerator pedal down to the floor (it was his way of talking) and she'd felt a warmth bleed from somewhere behind her and spread out all over her body, the slowtime after orgasm. Her thoughts, muddled all evening, had assumed a clarity and a precision which she'd only ever achieved after making love. But this time, the sense blade cut much sharper. She felt the tickle of grass upon her skin. Every inch of her body was in contact with the long, smooth stems. In the moon darkness, they were not green and yet the cool of their touch, their fecund scent, the rustling sound which they made as they rubbed against the cells of her skin, all these assumed a viridescence beyond colour. Her long hair mingled with the grass locks, so that the boundary between the two became blurred as she lay there, stiller than the plants around her. She

inhaled slowly, deeply and the slight movement of her chest
and abdomen provoked an equal ripple along the grass, a wave
which moved in harmonic silence, away from her towards the
trees, the moon, the deserted road . . . the car. Her mind was
glass, night-brittle.

They had argued. About the evening, the woman. Everything.

When they'd first met, she'd needed him so much. Oh God!
How she'd needed him. She would wait for the merest touch
of his long body, she had ached across the days for the whisper
of his voice. The stupid phone-calls. The letters. The humilia-
tion of woman. She cringed, as she sat there in his car (*where
her mirror-image had sat,* she was sure). And all the while,
she'd known that she was being manipulated. A blow-up doll.
That was how it always happened. The Bastards sucked you
dry, all the while pretending you needed them, when actually
it was the other way around. You were the great big mother-
cow, the beatific cream virgin, the hideous black many-handed
whore. You were everything to them. And nothing. You were
there to complete their egos. The pretty face, pouting like an
epaulette on their shoulder. (*And a talking epaulette was even
better.*) She'd always fallen into it as though it were her
personal glove. Her fate. Well, it was over now. She'd made
it be over. After years of being the addendum, she had finally
become One. She laughed, there, in the invisible grass. And
she remembered and created at the same time. The falling into
him; the falling out of him. Peeling off the layers of his clothes,
the slow descent along the lines of his skin, the mingling with
the cold furnace of what she had thought was his soul. A
conjoining on the point of a diamond. A deception. At their
closest, when One seems just beyond the next ridge, over the
sharp cliff-edge, where she might feel her feet shift uneasily,
scuffing the stones and dust and drawing blood from her soles,
at that point, she had been as separate as it is possible to be.

The drift apart, the great loosening, the cremasteric undertow, had already begun. An image of his limbs slunk over her moon mind and died there, in the cold-night, windless moan of its corruption.

He said she was paranoid. *He'd just met the bitch, after a long time, and they'd only talked, for God's sake.* He hadn't looked at her while he was speaking. He would've said it was because he was driving, but she knew better. He never looked at her when they quarrelled. In that moment of clarity, sitting there in his open-topped sports car, with the night air spilling into her lungs with its dark purity, she had realised that he was an abject coward. That, even if he had known about – or suspected – the body in the boot, he would've been too afraid to have mentioned it, let alone to have looked. As long as people didn't actually have to see the horror beneath their skins, they could pretend it didn't exist. He was driving fast, as though to get away from the truth in the back of the car. Behind his head. She'd laughed at the impossibility. He'd rounded on her at being mocked, his male hubris the last bastion of the self which he thought he possessed. He looked her full in the eyes and the accelerator pedal went through the floor. And she hadn't drawn away, not even when the car had spun off the road and was heading for the nearest tree. She'd kept her gaze fixed on his silly, panicking face (he had long since been battling with the wheel, his mind feverishly asking, no doubt, for forgiveness of something, from someone).

For her, the slowtime had never ended.

Then the thud. And the blackness.

She had emerged from the dark, into the dark, and had left the car with its dead occupants – one, a foetus in the boot, the other propped up in the driver's seat, a night mannequin with a smile splashed in blood across its face. And she had walked on.

The pain in her ankle swept up her leg and joined with the

expanding balloon in her chest. She inhaled and forced the pain down and out, along the grass to the trees, the moon, the blackness beyond. She felt cleansed in the faint green light which bathed her torso. She would lie there a while longer and then she would rise with the moon and find her way back home. The woman in the cupboard, in the boot, was safe inside her where no one could find either of them. They would find only the man. The failed catalyst. For she was One and she had no need of him, or of them. Another zap of him tried to escape across the blades of grass and ran towards the forest, but was brought down, like a deer, by the lioness of her gaze. With her limbs, she tore at his throat and caught the last, sinking exhalation and the silence which followed it, endless, into oblivion. He escaped in a thousand different ways and was hunted down every time, was trapped by her shape-shifting soul fingers as they raked through the night. The last time was the best. The inner core of his being, the composite of his existence, the tiny, dense essence wherein all the previous snapshot incarnations had been compressed and stored, this eruption of light slipped out from the immeasurably narrow space between the skin of her back and the flattened, invisible grass. An ejaculation of spirit. Unnoticed by her, it flitted among bits of soil and sleek shard leaves, carefully making its way, a naked guerrilla of masculinity, away from her rippling, burning body. She lay at right angles to the grass, the trees, the darkness. She was the resolving line which completed the tone of night. The runnel of light ran faster, away from her towards the great, penis trees, where it would be able to rest, nurtured by their clear sap, until he would be strong enough to return to the corpse which he had become. And then would arise the great Resurrection, the beginning of the end of the goddess in the grass. Her curves billowed out, expansile in the pullulating moonglow. Her boundary conditions faded into non-events. Soon, she would expand over the entire blackness of the night, smothering all, taking everything into herself. Becoming everything. But not if he could get to the trees. Replete with the energy of desperation, he ran and leapt and flew through the void, aiming, all the while, for the sanctuary of the woods. He landed in the dark undergrowth that swirled among the tree-trunks. But she was there before him and was now all around him. She felt him inhale. He had finally come to rest in her. Smiling, she reabsorbed the rogue light, with its cornucopia of images, feelings, deceptions, and began to expand. The whole chase had been a construct of hers, an anti-play designed by the wiggling toes of her soul to unravel the game which he had built around her. He never existed. She had made it so. By erecting him and then booting him out of time and space, she had bent back the silly phallus of fate and now he was utterly subsumed into her consciousness. The concubine's revenge. Sweet, in the night, as the dew which was beginning to form on her skin. And she felt herself sink into the earth, the warm, frozen mud-sand of her back. The air flitted like a female lover over her breasts, her abdomen, making her shiver. The intensity of the wild was so much greater than the love of any man. Here, she had all she needed. The fires in each star were the fires in every cell. The sky, her life in macrocosm. The moon was her soul. Liver-green, luminous. She felt herself expand over the forest, the road, the deserted car, the city . . .

She laughed again and her laughter was the breeze. She was Queen of her Soul.

She let her breath out and the rustling of grass against the night caused an owl to flutter down from its perch to see what was happening.

Glossary

a' bheinn lom	the barren mountain
a' bheinn lomnochd ann an abhainn na h-oidhche	the mountain naked in the river of night
abhainn	river
Achintya bheda bheda Tattva	Hindu prayer; 'Tattva' is similar to 'Om'
adhar	sky
aefauld	faithful
ah ho (Punjabi)	yes
ajwain	a bitter-tasting spice, used in many curries and also used, mixed with salt, to relieve excessive bloatedness
aljamiado	style of song where there is a solo voice with a solo instrument
allaidh	wild
allt	stream
alltan	streamlet, brook
am muir	the sea
am muir allaidh	the savage sea
an aon shlighe	the one road, way
an Diabhal toirt leis i'!	the Devil take her!
Anadolu	Anatolia
ana-miann	lust (archaic)
anam	soul
an rubha lom	the bare rock
anjaana	hidden, secret (also the title of a haunting Lata Mangeshkar song about the bonds between people being hidden or secret)

Azaad-Kashmir	Free Kashmir (that part of Kashmir not occupied by India)
badderlock	edible seaweed
bainne	milk
Baltistan	mountainous region to the north of Kashmir
ban-dia	a goddess
banjar zameene	wastelands, scrublands
bar fit	bare feet
baries	(in) bare feet
bata	boat
beal	boil
beanntan	hills, mountains
begowk	outwit
behene	sisters or female relatives in the broader sense
beinn	mountain
beshak shirin	sweet type of melon
beul	mouth
bha e mar ròn	he was like a seal
bhai	brother (may also be used as a term of address from any one person to any other, regardless of sex)
bhang	marijuana
bhen-chaud	sister-fucker
bhikari	beggar
Bihisht	Paradise
billies	fellows, lads; lovers
binneas	melody
Bjelo Dugme	White Button (a famous Bosnian rock group)
The Black House	the Kaaba in Makkah (said to be the home of the Prophet Abraham)
bothan	hut/farmhands' living quarters
bothy	hut, farmhands' dwelling
brak	broken
bras-shruth	torrent
bratherie	blood relatives
braw	beautiful, pretty, fine, good-looking

braw muir	big beautiful sea
breagha	beautiful, pretty
breeks	breeches
breine	putrefaction
broch	hill-fort; fairy-mound
bundha	man
burns a' beucaich	the burn's roaring
cabers	long, slender tree-trunks
Cailleach a' Gheamhraidh	the Old Woman of the Winter
callants	youths, fellows
calt	cold
car	left side
carle	young man
chhipkali	lizard
cho breagha	so beautiful
cho fuar ris a' phuinnsein	as cold as the poison
chugha	a long woollen cloak; the equivalent of an overcoat
Chunnae ud ud' jae, guth Kul Kul jae	when the wind blows, your head-scarf flutters, your plaits unravel
churz	marijuana
clach chaol, àrd	thin, high stone
clais	furrow, groove, ditch, trench
clàrsach	Celtic harp
cludgie	lavatory
coille	forest, wood
cotee	house
couthie	snug, agreeable, comfortable
cruachan	conical hills
dada	paternal grandfather
dan	destiny, fate
dang	damn; to knock, beat, strike
dkokaan	shop
dhokandaar	shopkeeper
dhu	dark (Irish Gaelic)
dorchadas	darkness, blackness
dost	(male) friends
dowie	sad
drùis	lust
dubh	black
dubhlachd	gloom, winter, December

duibhre	darkness
dyke	country wall
dzamiyas	mosques
Eid al Azha	Muslim festival (Abraham's offering of Ishmael for sacrifice)
eild	old age
El Quds	Jerusalem
elaqa	area
ezan	Islamic call to prayer
Faisalabad	city in Punjab Province, Pakistan
Fars	Persia
feck	a lot
filmi	style of film or of film music/ songs pertaining to movies made by the Bombay film industry.
flichan	snowflake
fowk	folk
the Friends	the Sufis
fuaran	springs, wells
fuskie	whisky
gae	quite
gallus	bold, mischievous, cheeky
ganga	rural, mainly mountainous, Bosnian folk-singing style where maximum harmony is achieved through dissonance
gao	village(s)
gawden	golden
geal	white
geet	light, Indian filmi-style song
geodha	creek
gora	white man (derogatory)
greetin	crying
grian	sun
grumphie	a pig, a grumbler
halvah	a type of sweet
hara	green

haraam zaada	bastard
haveli	traditional type of house where several floors are centred around an inner courtyard
Hazrat Ibrahim	the Prophet Abraham
heich	high
heicht	height; hilltop or high place
hijaabs	head-dresses worn by some Muslim women, completely covering the hair but leaving the face exposed
hingin	in a poor state of health
hud haraam	useless person (literally, 'bad bones')
huidit	hooded
huil	skin
Ibn Battuta	medieval Arab traveller
ilahija	Islamic religious chant (Sufi)
iteodha	hemlock
jagirdaar	big landowner in Punjabi
Jullundur	city in (Indian) Punjab
Jumma	Friday (the day when the main bazaar of the week is held)
kail	green vegetable, a type of cabbage
kajda	secular vocal form
kak	shit
kala	black
kala duhn	'black money', i.e. money obtained or converted via the black market; most people change money in this manner, usually through shopkeepers since the rate is always better than the official one
kamise	loose shirt worn by Punjabi men and women
Kara Deniz	Turkish name for the Black Sea
keema	mince

keemath	price
khanas	rooms
khoon aur mitti	blood and soil
Khuda-ke-liye	for God's sake!
Kiamath	Doomsday
Kinna Sohna tainu, Rub nay banaya	How beautiful has God made you
kisaan	peasant/peasants
kull	tomorrow
kunjari	whore
Kush	Kashmir
laacs	hundreds of thousands (one laac = one hundred thousand)
Ladadkh	region to the east of Baltistan
Lata Mangeshkar	famous Indian female vocalist
laun	land
leamin	glittering, flashing
leathad	slope/side of a hill
lichts	lights
lift	sky/heavens
lisk	groin
lomochd	naked
lugs	ears
luifs	feet, paws
luntit	lit
maa	mother/mum
Madhuri Dixit	female Indian film-star
Madubala	a famous Indian movie actress of the 1940s and 1950s; she was usually a tragic heroine
Mahal	a film tragedy, made in the 1940s; 'Mahal' means 'palace'
Malika-e-Tarunum	the Queen of Song
mar fhear-allabain	like a wanderer
Mashriki	eastern (connotes respectability or sophistication)
medressah	religious school, usually attached to a mosque
mela	festival

Meri awaz suno, mujhe azad Karo	listen to my voice, free
meri behtee	my daughter
methi	fenugreek
Mevlud	the chanting of the Quran
mia	husband
mohlvi	Muslim 'priest'
mon	man
mooted	frittered
muezzin	caller to prayer
Muhajir	immigrant (term usually applied to those Muslims who escaped from northern India during the Partition in 1947 and who came to live in Pakistan)
mullach	summit
mutkae ka pendtha	bottom of the (earthenware) jar; 'bottom of the barrel'
na fuaran fo na cruachan	the springs beneath the hills
nastaliq	a very elegant, Persian style of Arabic script
neb	nose
nocht	nothing
noor	light
ocht	anything
ogham	occult manner of ancient Gaelic writing, formed on a proto-telegraphic system by so many strokes for each letter, above or below a stem line, which was often formed by the angle of a stone monument
oige	youth
òran	song
paagal	crazy
pad	footpath
papa	father/dad
parso	the day after tomorrow
plowterin	squelching along

237

qadi	(Islamic) judge
Qaisar(a)	Caesar/Emperor (Empress) (also common names)
Qurbani	sacrificial meat (lamb)
radge	mad, furious
rìgh nan ròn	the King of the Seals
rim-jim	the sound which rain makes as it falls on to the ground; commonly used as a symbol of romance, particularly in films or in poetry
RNA	ribonucleic acid – a basic unit of genetic material, the part that is damaged by the AIDS virus
ròin	seals (some large seals were believed to be mermaids and mermen)
ròn	seal
roo-roo	a meaningless word used commonly as a backing vocal sound in countless 'Bollywood' film-songs and usually intoned by a female chorus
roupin	roaring, shouting
ruaidhe	red
rubha	promontory
rug	strong tide
saheli	female friends of a woman/girl
Samhain	Feast of All Souls
sandali	communal, centrally-heated, low round table
sappie	soggy, wet
Sasunnach	English person/Lowlander
saun	sand
scrunts	shrivelled stems/shrunken things
scuddie	naked
sevdalinka	Bosnian secular folk-music style (from the Turkish, 'sevdah', love)

shaam laat e shair	land belonging usually to the city authorities, that is, commonly-owned areas
Shah-en-Shah	Kings-of-Kings (Emperor)
Shah Rukh Khan	male Indian film-star
Shaitan	Satan
shalvar	loose, baggy trousers worn by Punjabi men and women
shalvar-kamise	loose Punjabi trousers and shirt
shankin	walking
shanks	stems of trees
sharaab	alcohol
shither	shiver
Sikander	Alexander
siol	seed, spawn, semen
sjivovic	alcoholic aperitif
skire	clear, bright
sklyted	heavy fall, thud
slaik	lick, kiss
slaiked	licked, slobbered on
slighe	path, road
smeddum	spirit, energy, drive
šota	a folk-dance style of Albanian origin
souch	the sound of the wind
speur	sky
speuran	the heavens
spunk	a spark, a match
sruth	stream
steek	close, shut, fasten
stieve	firm, strong
stocs	trunks
stour	a storm, strife, conflict
swicks	tricks
tadger	penis
teek	alright
teemed	hungry, empty, echoing
thocht	thought
tid	favourable time or season, opportunity, mood, humour
tippie	fashionable, stylish
trinkit	rutted

troddles	sheep-dung
tuimed	emptied
tuinn	waves
tumari maa?	your mum?
twalt	twelve
	grave
uaigh	
ustaad	term/title referring to a musical virtuoso, a master of an instrument
waderas	big landowners in Sindh province, Pakistan
wallah	person, usually in the context of their job
weird	fate, destiny
widdershins	the wrong way around; on end; anti-clockwise
Yehudi	Jews
Yunani hakim	practitioner of Greek medicine
zamindaar	Punjabi landowner (a more general term than 'jagirdaar'; a zamindaar could be either a big or a small landowner)

Beyond the end
There is no end . . .